"I've never touched a woman in anger before."

Neal's voice was flat, as if he'd tried and condemned himself. "It won't happen again."

Remorse was one thing, sackcloth and ashes another. In the interests of fairness, Karen noted, "I was angry, too."

He frowned. "Hell, I damn near threw you on the ground and ripped your clothes off! And I kissed you!"

"I kissed you back."

His frown had turned into a glower. "Damn it, woman! Do you have to argue about everything?"

"I don't want you to walk out of here determined never to kiss me again." There. She'd been honest. The look she saw on his face—incredulity and desire and something else—made her heart skip a beat. She took a step forward.

"I'm not used to a woman like you."

And then she was in his arms and he was kissing her again.

ABOUT THE AUTHOR

Janice Kay Johnson is the bestselling author of over twenty books, and her deeply emotional and involving stories have enthralled readers around the world. It will come as no surprise to her many fans that Janice is an enthusiastic gardener and quilt-maker, or that she's an experienced "soccer mom." She lives in Washington State with her two daughters, two dogs and five cats.

Praise for *Her Sister's Baby*, Janice's last Superromance novel: "Janice Kay Johnson is at her best as she creates characters struggling with heart-rending dilemmas and invents solutions that work for all." —*Romantic Times*

Janice Kay Johnson
In the Dark of the Night

Harlequin Books

TORONTO • NEW YORK • LONDON
AMSTERDAM • PARIS • SYDNEY • HAMBURG
STOCKHOLM • ATHENS • TOKYO • MILAN
MADRID • WARSAW • BUDAPEST • AUCKLAND

ISBN 0-373-70648-0

IN THE DARK OF THE NIGHT

This edition published by arrangement with Harlequin Enterprises B.V.

Printed in U.S.A.

In the Dark of the Night

PROLOGUE

CHELSEA CAHILL flopped back on her bed, arms flung wide, and stared at the ceiling. What a day. Amanda had jumped from tabletop to tabletop like an orangutan in the zoo. Peter cried all day because his dog had just died and the other kindergarten boys teased him. In the lunchroom Chelsea had briefly turned away to speak to another teacher. When she turned back around, a slug had mysteriously appeared on her tray, right next to the chicken nuggets. A check for slimy hands had produced no suspects. And in the teachers' lounge there'd been talk of a strike. To cap it off, dinner at her parents' house had been fraught with the usual tension. All in all, today had been a real winner.

With sudden decision she sat up and kicked off her shoes. Music was what she needed. Something elegant, timeless, soul-stirring. In the small living room of her old house she mulled over her collection of CDs, at last choosing one to pop in the player.

A moment later the haunting first notes of the "Blue Danube Waltz" slipped magically out of the speakers. Chelsea swayed to the melody, then dipped a curtsy to an imaginary partner. In her mind she no longer wore tight jeans and a sweatshirt; bare toes no longer curled in the carpet. She could feel the satin that clung to her breasts and fell in elegant folds to her matching slippers. Diamonds shimmered around her throat and soft dark tendrils curled artfully about her face. Her living room had become transformed by sparkling chandeliers and the rich scent of flowers. Laying one gloved hand delicately on her partner's shoulder, her eyes half closing, she began to dance.

Lilting, compelling, the waltz gained power and Chelsea swept about the room, twirling, smiling, dreaming. As though it sensed her mood, the music became softer, more romantic, part of the dream. Only at the very end did it climb to a crescendo, and Chelsea's partner swung her in a dizzying circle. In the sudden resonant silence, she smiled and opened her eyes.

Reflected against the night dark glass in the French doors that led to a broad front porch, she saw herself. For an instant she couldn't see beyond that gilded reflection. In the next second, her smile faded and the hair prickled on the back of her neck as her heart took a sickening leap.

The darkness outside had taken on a shape. Tall and bulky and faceless, still the nightmare figure had eyes that watched her through the glass. And a hand that reached for the knob.

In another fraction of a second she knew that the shape was no figment of her imagination, but a man dressed in dark clothes, wearing a ski mask and gloves. Panic clutched at her throat, turning her scream to a whimper, as Chelsea backed toward the arch that led to the kitchen. In a mocking counterpoint to her fear, the music began again. The "Emperor Waltz." But there was no more satin, no more diamonds.

Were the French doors locked? Dear God, had she even bothered to check them when she came home? The soft click of the latch, the whisper of the door swinging in, were her answer.

On a sob she turned to run. In her terror she was clumsy, stumbling, striking her hip painfully against the sharp edge of the kitchen counter. She fell against the back door just as the hand closed on her arm from behind.

Fighting like a wildcat, Chelsea wrenched her arm from his grip. But her bare toes made no impression on his jean-clad shins, and her slashing fingernails snagged in the knit ski mask. The back of his hand connected with her cheek, knocking her against the door that should have been her escape. Tasting blood, she screamed, but her cries were swept away by the powerful waltz cascading out of her stereo system.

He dragged her, still fighting, back into the living room. Another blow flung her to the floor where she lay, whimpering.

The masked man who looked down at her said in a muffled voice, "I won't hurt you again if you do what I say."

Chelsea's head bobbed with an eagerness she despised.

"Take your clothes off."

Hating herself even more, but too terrified to defy him, she did as he asked, until she stood naked and vulnerable before him.

"Dance."

When she hesitated, hearing the music only as a meaningless blur, his hand lashed out again. She lurched, held herself upright, and felt with shame the hot tears slipping down her cheeks, stinging where her face swelled.

"Dance," he said again in that raw whisper.

This time Chelsea obeyed. Just as she was to obey every other command he gave her that night.

CHAPTER ONE

KAREN LINDBERG fumbled out of darkness, unsure for an instant what had awakened her. When the telephone shrilled from her nightstand, she groped for it, mumbling under her breath. The brightly lit clock-radio informed her that it was twelve-thirty. She'd only been asleep for an hour and a half. If the caller was one of her daughter Abby's friends, Karen was going to kill. It wasn't the first time she'd been awakened by a cheerful teenage voice.

"Yes?" she snapped into the receiver. Nobody answered, though she could hear the sound of breathing—or was it whimpering? Karen came abruptly awake. "Who is it?"

"Karen?" The soft voice trembled. "It's... it's Chelsea."

Karen sat up in bed. "Chelsea, what's wrong?"

"Could... could you come over? I... I'm afraid."

"Afraid of what? God, Chelsea, what's happened?"

"He..." A sob was swallowed. "He said not to call the police. But, Karen, I'm scared by myself! I need somebody, and I didn't know who..."

"I'll be right there." The receiver tucked against her shoulder, Karen had already flicked on the lamp and was reaching for the jeans she'd draped on a chair.

Sounding ashamed, her friend said, "I didn't think about Abby. You shouldn't leave her. I . . . I'm sorry. I'll . . ."

"Don't be silly," Karen said robustly. "Abby is fifteen, for heaven's sake. I'll leave her a note in case she wakes up." Which was highly unlikely. Karen's daughter would sleep through an earthquake.

Wriggling into her jeans, reaching at random for a shirt hanging in the closet, she said, "I'll be there in five minutes. But, Chelsea, if you're scared I can call the police for you."

"No!" The voice hovered on the edge of hysteria. "No! Don't do that. Promise!"

"All right, all right." Damn. Why was she fiddling with buttons? "Chelsea, can you tell me what happened?"

"He might be out there listening."

A chill crept up Karen's spine. "I'm on my way right now. I'll be there in about two minutes," she promised, and promptly dropped the phone. "Oh, hell." Snatching up the receiver, she slammed it into the cradle, then shoved her feet into tennis shoes and reached for a sweatshirt from her drawer.

In the kitchen she found a pad of Post-Its and scrawled, "Emergency. Gone to Chelsea's," then stuck the paper on the inside of Abby's bedroom door. The dark lump that was her daughter breathed peacefully, not even shifting as the light fell across her face.

In the carport Karen threw herself into her car and gunned the engine as she backed out of the drive. Her mind raced as she envisioned one frightening scene after another. What could have happened to Chelsea? Who was "he"?

She covered the route that usually took five minutes in less than three. The tree-lined streets of the small town were quiet, the houses dark. It was all so peaceful, so normal.

In contrast, Chelsea's 1920s-era bungalow with the wide porch and dormers blazed with light from every window. In the driveway Karen climbed out of her car, eyeing the darkness beyond the detached garage, the shadows under the low hedge that separated yard from street. Chelsea had been afraid that he was still out there. It was true that there were too many hiding places. *He* could easily be lurking, shielded by the night as he stared up at those windows.

Karen shivered and hurried up onto the tiny enclosed back porch, which was the entryway Chelsea and her friends always used. She knocked hard and called, "Chelsea, it's me! Karen."

Silence. Karen looked apprehensively over her shoulder. Finally through the door came the same tremulous voice that sounded as though it belonged to a frightened child. "Karen?"

"It's me, Chelsea. Can you unlock the door?"

Leaving the chain on, her friend peered through the crack. A moment later she'd released the chain to swing open the door. Karen was scarcely inside before, with trembling hands, Chelsea locked and double locked the door behind her.

When she turned around, Karen gaped.

"Oh, my God, Chelsea! What happened?"

The kindergarten teacher who had become one of Karen's best friends was vibrant and very close to beautiful. Tall and thin, she had a face that made you look twice, with high cheekbones and smiling dark eyes. Now only fear looked out of eyes that were nearly swollen shut, and one side of her face was grotesquely distorted, already turning purple. Tremors shook her and she hunched inside a bathrobe, though the house was comfortably warm.

She flinched at Karen's question and her mouth worked, but nothing came out.

Karen felt a burst of pure rage as she understood with shock that the nightmare scenarios she'd imagined during the drive were true. "Who was it, Chelsea? Did he rape you?"

Teeth closed so hard on her friend's lower lip that Karen saw a droplet of blood. Chelsea nodded jerkily and stared at the floor.

"We have to call the police."

Instant alarm. "No! He said—"

"I don't care what he said," Karen interrupted. "He's long gone. You can't let him get away with this."

Chelsea's eyes at last met Karen's and suddenly she was crying, at first silently, then with huge gasping sobs as Karen reached out for her.

When at last her friend quieted in her arms, Karen held her away. "Chelsea, was it someone you know?"

Slowly, painfully, Chelsea shook her head. Her voice was husky, tear-thickened. "No. At least I don't think so. He wore..." She stopped, swallowed. "He wore a mask. I couldn't see..."

"Okay." Karen gave her a warm hug. "I'll call the police right now."

She put water on to boil before she reached for the phone. Chelsea needed something hot to warm her from the inside. The kettle rumbled softly as Karen dialed 911.

The man on the other end of the line took the information calmly. After she hung up, Karen turned off the whistling kettle and poured water over a teabag, steeping it only a minimal time before handing the sweetened brew to her friend, huddled in a chair at the kitchen table. As they waited, it seemed to Karen that Chelsea was withdrawing further, shivering inside the blanket Karen had found to wrap around her. Karen began to wonder if she shouldn't have asked for an ambulance, as well. But surely the police would be here soon. They would know what to do.

Worried as she was, it felt like an eternity before they heard the crunch of gravel of a car pulling into the driveway.

Reading the panic on Chelsea's face, Karen went to the window and peeked through a crack between the curtains. "It's okay," she said quickly. "It's a patrol car."

A second had pulled in behind the first by the time footsteps sounded on the porch.

A firm knock was followed by a muffled masculine voice. "Police."

"Just a minute." Karen undid the separate bolts and chain and cautiously opened the door. The dark-haired man who stood under the porch light was reassuringly large and solid in his blue uniform, with the gun resting against his hip. When he held out a leather folder with identification for her glance, she stood back. "Come in."

Once inside, he instantly dominated the small kitchen. His dark assessing gaze moved swiftly from Karen to Chelsea, who shrank back in her chair and watched him with the wide frightened eyes of a hunted animal.

His voice was gravelly but gentle as he inclined his head. "Miss Cahill. Miss . . . ?"

"I'm Karen Lindberg."

"Chief Rowland. Can you tell me how long ago the attack took place?"

When Chelsea didn't respond, Karen said, "She called me about fifteen minutes ago. She was afraid then that he was still out there."

"If you'll excuse me just a minute?" He disappeared onto the porch where she heard the low rumble of voices. When he returned he stopped just inside the back door. Nodding at Chelsea, he said, "Your friend needs to go to the hospital. I've called an ambulance. Do you know whether she's been unconscious?"

Karen shook her head. "I don't know. Let me try asking her."

Crouching in front of her friend, Karen took her hands. "Chelsea. Chelsea, listen to me."

Chelsea's terrified gaze stayed fixed on the policeman and she didn't answer. At last, biting her lip, Karen sank back on her heels, then rose and crossed the small kitchen to where the police chief watched in thoughtful silence.

"She wasn't like this a few minutes ago."

He kept his voice low. "Some sedation might calm her so she can tell us her story more comfortably."

"I want to go with her," Karen said, half expecting an argument, but he only nodded.

CHELSEA SEEMED to relax the moment they reached the hospital, as though she felt safe there. Nevertheless, she clutched at Karen's hand when Karen rose to step out of the curtain-walled cubicle where they'd placed her. "Don't leave me. Please!"

The doctor, mercifully a woman, stood waiting at the foot of the bed. "Ms. Cahill, your friend can wait right outside. We need to take an X ray, and then I'll do a brief examination. It'll only take a few minutes."

"Oh, God." Chelsea's eyes closed and tears squeezed out. Slowly she released Karen's hand. "Just...can you be here when that policeman comes in? Please?"

"Of course I can." Close to tears herself, Karen slipped out of the cubicle. At the reception desk, she said, "Is there a phone I can use?"

"Certainly."

It took ten rings to wake up her neighbor, who sounded as grumpy as Karen had felt an hour ago.

But Karen had gotten only as far as explaining that she'd gone with a friend to emergency when the older woman said, "Do you want me to check on Abby? Why don't I take an afghan and just curl up on your couch so you don't need to worry?"

"Thanks, Joan."

When she turned away from the desk, the policeman stood waiting only a few feet away. His dark eyes were steady, his face expressionless. "Can you give me a few minutes, Miss Lindberg?"

Karen was suddenly very tired. "Yes, all right. And by the way, it's Ms., not Miss."

Petty, she thought. But somewhere inside she was angry. Maybe that was her way of expressing it.

Crossing the lobby, she stumbled, and his large hand reached out to grip her arm. She was unnervingly conscious of his strength, and understood in a way she hadn't before why Chelsea had felt frightened by him. He wasn't the kind of man who faded into the uniform, letting you see him only as a disembodied representative of the law. He was too big, too powerfully built, his face too hard.

If he'd been twenty years younger, Abby would have called him a hunk. He looked too much like a marine to do anything for Karen. Short brown hair, square jaw, bullish face. Great, she thought. Just what Chelsea needed, Neanderthal man with a rifle rack in the back of his pickup. Karen met his level gaze as she sank onto a hard plastic seat.

He pulled a chair out from the wall and sat so that he was facing her, his knees only a few inches away from hers. "I'm the new chief of police, Ms. Lindberg. I don't think we've met. I'm Neal Rowland."

Had there been the slightest emphasis on the "Ms."? Was he mocking her? She was too tired to care.

"No," she agreed. "We haven't. I own the Cottage Garden Nursery, down by the bridge."

"I've seen it." There was silence for a moment as he studied her.

Karen became instantly and acutely conscious of her uncombed blond hair, probably sticking out in all directions like a wild woman's, of the shirt collar poking crookedly above the sweatshirt, of the grubby jeans and lack of socks. Her face didn't even bear thinking about.

Fortunately his uniform was no great shakes, either. The blue shirt was wrinkled, the cuffs unbuttoned and rolled up to expose strong brown forearms. His dark hair was just long enough to be disheveled, and a shadow of a beard emphasized the hollows beneath his cheekbones. For the first time it occurred to her that he, too, might have been roused from a pleasant night's sleep. Either that or he'd had a long day that this call had made longer.

When he propped his elbows on his knees and leaned forward, Karen could see the dark lashes that framed those intense brown eyes.

"Tell me what happened, Ms. Lindberg. From the minute your friend called you."

Remembering Chelsea's shaky voice and battered face, Karen felt a wave of fury. Things like this weren't supposed to happen in Pilchuck. Rural innocence still existed here, neighbors watched out for each other, and merchants trusted their customers. Maybe teenagers shot up mailboxes and PCP had found its way to the high school, but residents didn't brutally rape each other.

She watched Rowland's reaction carefully as she told her story.

He listened without comment, apparently without emotion. Only when she finished did he lean back in the chair and close his eyes for an instant, moving his shoulders as though to relax tense muscles. Weariness made every one of his forty or so years show. When he opened his eyes, they revealed the lingering ghost of some powerful emotion that he'd tried to hide. Anger to match her own? she wondered.

"Tell me," he said slowly, "did the man make your friend do anything besides the obvious? Anything...unusual? Do you know?"

Nonplussed, Karen stared at him. "What do you mean?"

His eyes searched hers, and then he sighed. "Never mind. It was just a thought. Most of the time rape is simple and brutal. Once in a while you get a rapist who shows a pattern. Likes something bizarre. Or maybe just enjoys leaving a signature.''

Where had Neal Rowland come from, she wondered, that rape was so commonplace? But she understood what he was reaching for. "You want to know if he's done it before.''

"That's the idea,'' he agreed. They sat in silence for a moment, until the doctor emerged. The policeman pushed his chair back and went over to her. After a low-voiced conversation, he gestured to Karen.

"I'm going to talk to your friend now. Apparently she insists on you being with her.''

"I think she's afraid.''

One dark brow lifted. "Of me? Well, I wish we had a woman on the force, but unfortunately we don't.''

"Maybe you should remedy that.''

His laugh was short and humorless as he gestured for her to go ahead of him. "Politicking?''

"Why not?'' she said. "Or don't you think a woman could do the job?''

Glancing over her shoulder, she caught his sardonic expression.

"As it happens, I have nothing against women cops. I had one as a partner for a couple of years.''

"What happened to her?''

This time there was faint amusement in his voice. "She got pregnant.''

Karen bristled. "Not every woman—''

"She came back after maternity leave. By that time I'd been reassigned.''

"Oh.'' Karen stopped outside the curtained enclosure. She took a deep breath before she pushed the curtain aside, very conscious of the man who entered quietly behind her. The sight of her friend's swollen discolored face shocked Karen afresh.

"How are you, Chelsea?"

She didn't answer, but a thin hand crept from beneath the blanket to clutch Karen's. Through puffy eyes, Chelsea watched Neal Rowland with a fear that trembled on the edge of hysteria.

He stopped at the foot of the bed. "Miss Cahill," he said with surprising gentleness, "we'll make this as short as possible. I need you to tell me what happened. I'm especially interested in a description of the suspect, what he wore, whether he had on gloves. Anything you can think of might help."

"Will he . . . will he know I called you?"

"It's unlikely," he said.

Her voice rose in panic. "I don't want him to find out!"

"We'll do what we can," the chief said. "But you won't have to worry about him at all once he's in jail."

Chelsea rolled her head away and Karen saw the tears that streaked her cheeks. During the long moment of silence, Karen ached for her friend, who would never feel a sense of security again. Would she even be able to describe the horror, or had she hidden somewhere inside?

"I was . . . I was dancing." Chelsea's voice, just above a whisper, cracked on the last word. She didn't look at either the policeman or Karen. As though they weren't there, the story came out in small painful rushes.

"He never took off the mask. I can't tell you what he looked like."

"What color were his eyes?"

"I don't . . ." She bit her lip. "I don't want to think about him."

"I understand." The face that had earlier been so impassive now showed compassion. "But we can't stop him from hurting someone else like he hurt you unless we can identify him."

Chelsea shuddered and didn't answer, her head still turned away. Karen saw Neal Rowland's frustration.

Squeezing her friend's hand, she said, "Chelsea. You're safe now. We're here with you. I know it's hard, but you have to be brave and close your eyes and remember, just for a minute. Can you do that?"

A sob shook Chelsea. Karen's eyes stung as she stroked the dark hair back from her friend's battered face. When Chelsea spoke, she was barely audible. "Brown. His eyes were brown. Like yours."

Neal Rowland only nodded. "Was he tall? Short? How was he built?"

Chelsea looked as though she were staring at death, and again there was a painful pause before she answered uncertainly, "I think he was tall. And... and muscular. But he didn't take his shirt off, and... and he turned off the lights before..." The words quavered and died.

The police chief was relentless. "What about his voice?"

She shuddered again. "He didn't talk very much. He... he whispered."

In the momentary silence, Karen couldn't look away from the horror in Chelsea's eyes. She tried to imagine how it would feel to be hurt like this, but somehow she couldn't relate it to herself. When a picture of her daughter flickered in her mind, though, she felt a sickening wave of fear mixed with anger. If somebody had done this to Abby, she'd want to kill him.

But Abby was forgotten when Neal said slowly, "Miss Cahill, I want you to think very carefully. Was there anything familiar about this man? Did you at any moment have the sense that you knew him or even that you'd seen him before?"

"I don't know," she said in a choked voice. "I keep seeing him over and over. I'm never going to be able to forget him. And I just don't know."

He nodded. "Thank you, Miss Cahill. You've been very helpful. When we catch him, when he's punished for doing this, you'll find it easier to put tonight behind you."

She turned her face away again and her hand disentangled from Karen's. There was a note of finality in her low voice. "I don't care what happens to him, just so he never hurts anyone again."

"We'll do our best." His eyes met Karen's. "Ms. Lindberg, can I speak to you outside for a minute?"

Karen touched her friend's arm. "I'll be back, Chelsea." She followed the police chief through the curtains.

He stopped in the empty hall near the reception desk. Whatever gentleness she'd sensed in him earlier was gone now. His mouth was compressed in a hard line and his dark eyes were bleak.

"I need a promise from you."

"A promise?" she repeated, puzzled.

"This has to be kept quiet. You don't tell anyone."

"I don't understand."

The muscles in his jaw tightened. "I'm going to tell you something in confidence. Can I trust you to keep it that way?"

Karen held his gaze. "That depends what it is."

"I'm asking this for your friend's sake."

She felt a jolt of anger. "I don't like making blind promises."

"All I'm asking for is your cooperation," he said. "Or don't you give a damn about your friend in there?"

Karen's hands curled into fists. "You know I do. That's the only reason I'm still standing here."

There was a flicker of answering anger in his narrowed eyes. "Tell me, *Ms.* Lindberg, do you dislike police in general? Or is this personal?"

"Maybe it's neither," she said. "Do *you* always take it personally when somebody doesn't leap to 'cooperate'?"

They glared at each other. "Ms. Lindberg," he said with exaggerated patience, "it's very late. I might conceivably not have been as diplomatic as I could have been . . ."

It was almost funny. Could he possibly not realize how autocratic he sounded? Or was it she who'd overreacted? In all fairness, she had to admit that he'd been kind to Chelsea, and as much as she could tell thus far in the investigation, thorough. Would she have been as antagonistic if he'd been five foot eight and homely?

She cleared her throat. "Uh, listen, maybe we could start over. You're right. It's late, and I'm not at my best in the middle of the night."

His frown cleared slowly. "You're not alone."

"You've done better than I have," Karen admitted. "*Can* we start over?"

"Why not?"

Looking tired again, he propped his shoulder against the bare wall and reached up with one big hand to rub the back of his neck. Karen's gaze followed his long blunt fingers working at tight muscles, and her stomach knotted. Feeling light-headed, she glanced down the empty hall toward Chelsea's cubicle. That beige curtain was a reality check, a reminder of why she was here.

Maybe he'd reminded himself of the same thing, because he sighed and straightened, letting his hand drop to his side. "Ms. Lindberg, I need your help. Your friend is the second woman raped in a little over a week. I don't have any doubt that it was the same man."

Shocked, Karen stared at him. "The second? But why wasn't there something in the newspaper? Nobody has even been talking about it! This is a small town. A kid can't steal a bike without everyone knowing! Why...?"

He held her gaze with sudden intensity. "The first victim didn't come to us until the next day, and then made it clear she wouldn't testify against him. We agreed to keep it quiet. She's a very frightened woman. The rapist made some ugly threats." He nodded toward the cubicle. "Your friend in there is just as scared. The lack of publicity isn't going to influence whether we can catch him or not. In fact, it might help. Because both women called us, we can see his pattern. He'll change that pattern if he knows we're waiting. That's why I want you to keep this to yourself. As you say, this is a small town. If you tell anyone at all, by tomorrow evening everybody in town will be talking."

"What about Chelsea? What's she supposed to do? Lie? Tell everybody she fell down the stairs?"

He grunted impatiently. "I'm only talking about a matter of days. The bastard is on a high now. He's going to go after somebody else. If we're lucky, and smart, we'll be waiting for him. He's got to be watching each victim for days ahead of time. He knows her routine. He knows when she's alone. But he can't lurk out there in the dark all those hours without someone eventually noticing, not in a town like this. We've stepped up foot patrols at night. We'll get him. But we might not if he lies low."

"If women could be warned—"

His interruption was brusque. "Are you married, Ms. Lindberg?"

She blinked. "What does that have to do with anything?"

"Are you?"

"No!"

"Okay, you're warned. There's a rapist running loose in this town. How are you going to protect yourself?"

"I can at least be more careful about locking my doors!"

His hard mouth curled derisively. "Do you seriously think a locked door would have saved your friend tonight? How long do you think it takes to shatter a pane of glass? One second? Two?"

"She might have been able to get to a telephone. Scream. Something."

"Sure," he agreed. "And she also might have gotten hurt worse than she did. Face it, Ms. Lindberg. We have to catch him. All I'm asking is a chance to do that."

"What if you don't?" Karen asked quietly. "What if another woman gets raped?"

His face stayed impassive, though his voice sounded rougher. "Are you asking whether I'll feel guilty?

Yeah, I'll lose sleep over it. But I'm not infallible. I can't promise you that I am. All I can do is try to make the best call. Do you expect more than that?''

Karen stood silent for a moment, unwillingly impressed by his speech. At last she made a helpless gesture. "No. No, I don't expect more than that. I'll do as you ask. I just hope..."

When she didn't finish, he only nodded. "I hope so, too."

CHAPTER TWO

THE WEEK WAS HELLISH. Karen dragged herself through the next day at work only because she didn't have a choice. Her fledgling business wasn't successful enough yet to allow her to hire the kind of help she really needed. When she collapsed gratefully into bed Tuesday night, she was desperate for a good ten hours of sleep.

The first noise she heard was the refrigerator turning itself on. She stiffened, then made herself relax when she realized what the clunk and hum were. She almost missed the first creak in the hall, because she was punching her pillow into shape. Her fingers still curled into a fist, Karen froze. Had she imagined it?

Another creak, farther away. The dining room? Her eyes strained against the darkness as she stared at the doorway that led into the hall. A muffled thump brought her bolt upright in bed. Her heart was pounding even while she told herself it was the cat, it had to be. By this time Karen had so much adrenaline pumping through her body that she knew she had to look. Just so she could relax once and for all.

She padded silently across the bare floor of her dark bedroom, then stood in the doorway listening for a long moment before she snapped on the hall light. No flurry of movement followed. Karen edged down the hall to Abby's room, feeling ridiculously exposed in her nightgown. Of course her daughter was sound asleep. Maggie, the long-haired tortoiseshell cat who ruled their lives, lay languidly stretched out at the foot of Abby's bed. Her eyes were slits as she gazed at Karen, uninterested in the possibility of a prowler.

Of course there wasn't a prowler. Disgusted with herself, Karen still searched every closet in the house, peered under beds, checked locks on doors and windows.

How long had the cop said it would take to shatter a windowpane? Not very long. Maybe she should think about getting a dog.

Back in bed, wide awake, she listened to a tap on the window. Through the thin curtains she could see the swaying black silhouette of two arching stems of the Constance Spry rose that framed her window so romantically. She had too many foundation plantings, she thought. Too many old shrubs. Deep shadows behind the two huge lilacs could hide an army of intruders. The roses, some still blooming even now in September, screened the wide front porch. The clematis-draped arbor, the yew hedge beside the driveway, the . . .

Hell. She rolled over and shoved her pillow angrily. What was she supposed to do? Strip her overgrown, fragrant cottage garden until it was as bare as one of those Japanese meditation courts that had nothing but gravel raked into swirls around an exposed boulder or two?

Karen fell asleep eventually, into an obscure but disturbing dream. She was dancing with a faceless partner. The music was country-and-western, a long-drawn-out whine, and her partner's boots clicked on the floor as he spun her.

The music alone was enough of a nightmare, she decided tiredly the next morning. If she had to pattern a dream so obviously on Chelsea's rape, why couldn't she at least be waltzing, instead?

She searched the house again the next night and the night after that. Houses were noisy, she discovered. Nothing to wake the dead, just creaks, scratches, whispers, clicks. Enough to keep her eyes burning and her muscles rigid. And when she did sleep, she dreamed of the faceless man twirling her, the music always the same, a wide ruffled skirt of the sort square dancers wear rustling around her legs, the click-click of those damn boots.

When her alarm went off Friday morning, Karen whimpered. She tried to bury her head in the pillow, then realized how silent the house was. Now it was quiet when it shouldn't be.

"Abby!" she called. "School bus in—" blearily she grappled with the addition "—twenty minutes."

Silence, then a muffled, "Shit!"

"Abby!"

Her daughter's bare feet thumped on the floorboards. "I can't get ready that fast," she wailed. "Will you drive me?"

Karen buried her head again. A minute later Abby stood over her. "Mom, didn't you hear me? Will you give me a ride?"

"Oh, hell," Karen muttered.

Half an hour later she locked the front door behind her. She had bags under her eyes, jeans that were wrinkled because she'd forgotten to take them out of the dryer yesterday and hair that was still damp, which meant that by noon it'd be as limp as a thirsty black-eyed Susan. Besides which, she was starved. There was only so much you could do in half an hour.

Naturally, Abby was perky. Flawless makeup made her blue eyes look huge, her short blond hair was deliberately spiked, and she wore a baggy cotton sweater with a lace neckline over tight black jeans that had little zippers up the ankles. She bounced into the car.

Just looking at her made Karen feel even more tired. She also had one of those weird flashes in which she wondered how Abby could possibly be hers. A child of the sixties, Karen had tried to raise her daughter to have a social conscience. The best that could be said for it so far was that Abby hadn't yet joined the cheerleading squad. Probably because she was too busy hanging out at the mall.

"Can I go to the dance tonight after the game, Mom? Shelley says Brian wants to dance with me." She wriggled happily. "He's really cool."

"I thought what's-his-name was cool."

"Don't you ever *listen* to me? He wanted me to hop into *bed* with him. Well, not really bed. It's, hey, do you want to dance, and then let's go out behind the gym and do it. Really romantic. I mean—"

"Do it?" Karen slammed to a stop at a red light and turned her head to stare incredulously at her daughter. "Of course I listen to you! I'd have heard that."

Abby flounced in her seat. "Well, I'm sure I told you. I mean, what a jerk. His eyes are too close together, anyway. Brian's better-looking. He scored two touchdowns last Friday, not that I care. I haven't even figured out what a down is yet. Do you understand football?"

"Once, long ago, I understood it," Karen said. "I don't have time to watch anymore."

"Come on, it hasn't been *that* long."

"No?" Karen said hopefully.

She got what she deserved. Abby studied her. "Do you feel okay today, Mom? Your hair looks kind of weird. And that sweatshirt..." Her lip curled.

"It's advertising." Karen liked the shirt, which had a frowsy-looking woman surrounded by fat roses and a tipsy hollyhock and said Flowerwoman. "That's what I am, remember? Besides, it keeps people from taking a close look at my face."

"That's probably a good idea," Abby said, and jumped out of the car in front of the high school. "Thanks. See ya."

Depressed, Karen stopped at the bakery. A couple of women she knew were just coming out. One of them apologized for the odd way she talked.

"An abscess," Marta Peters mumbled. "And of course the dentist doesn't open until ten. *He's* probably sleeping in."

Karen offered her sympathy, then chatted with the teenager who took her money and gave her the boxed doughnuts. All the time she couldn't help wondering. What if your jaw was swollen and you didn't want to tell people why? An abscessed tooth would make a damned good excuse. Who was going to ask the dentist?

The trouble was, Karen had spent the week studying every woman she stood in line behind at the grocery store, every woman who wandered through the nursery, every woman who dropped her kid off at the high school. Was one of them the first rape victim? Would the experience *show*, if Karen looked closely enough?

She looked at the men, too. Brown eyes were less common than blue or gray around here, since the American Northwest had been settled by Scandinavians. But there were plenty of men who might fit the profile. Reasonably tall, brown eyes, nothing really obvious that would distinguish them. If the rapist was a local, as Chief Rowland had seemed to imply, chances were Karen knew him, at least slightly. How could a man be that warped and nobody have guessed?

She was getting paranoid. Thursday night she'd closed the nursery early, because she was alone. What if a brown-eyed man walked in? Should she scream? Hide? Ask if she could interest him in a fifty-dollar tree peony?

This morning, Karen parked in her spot behind one of the greenhouses and let herself into the only building. She turned on a pot of water for tea before she started devouring her doughnuts and the weekly paper. A few minutes later she stuffed the last bite of doughnut into her mouth and slapped the newspaper shut. Nothing. No rapes, no rumors, no hysteria. She was going to go crazy soon, she thought, staring unseeingly at some dried flower wreaths. She never had been good at waiting, at not taking action. This time, there wasn't a damn thing she could do, however, except be as good a friend as possible for Chelsea.

The tea and doughnuts gave her the strength to turn the sign on the front gate from Closed to Open and to call Chelsea, who was staying with her parents.

"How am I doing? Lousy," her friend said. "My face hurts, so I can't even eat. And my mother is driving me up the wall. God. I'm ready to face a horde of five-year-olds, if somebody'll just let me out of here."

Karen leaned against the doorjamb, so she could watch for customers. "You must be feeling better."

"Only when I don't think about it."

"Do you want to come down and have lunch with me?" Karen asked. "I could call for a pizza— Oh, shoot. You can't eat it."

"No, but I could inhale the smell." There was silence for a moment. "Do you think people know about what happened?

"No."

Another silence, then, "Half of me wishes everybody did know. Even . . . him."

"Yeah." Karen forced a smile for a woman who'd leapt out of her car and was headed straight for the perennials. When she was out of earshot, Karen added, "I think lying about it stinks."

Chelsea's voice changed, became duller. "It makes me feel . . . dirty."

Karen kept her anger out of her voice. "Chief Rowland said it wouldn't be for long."

"I told my mother, anyway. What was I supposed to say? That I fell going down the stairs and now I'm afraid to be by myself?"

"I don't think your own mother counts."

"She's driving me crazy," Chelsea said gloomily. Even over the telephone, Karen heard her long shaky breath. "Oh, heck, my jaw's starting to hurt. I'd better skip seeing you. Maybe tomorrow."

"Okay," Karen said, and after a moment hung up. Wandering outside, she called to her one and only customer, "Let me know if I can help you find anything."

"Just looking."

It did stink. Sure, Chelsea and the other victim had begged for silence. But coming out and talking about the rape was supposed to be therapeutic, wasn't it? Going into hiding must make them both feel ashamed. Had Chief Rowland thought about what was best for the two women in the long run? Did he care?

Karen wished she knew how Chelsea was really doing. She was trying hard to sound flip, depressed only on the surface. But Karen couldn't forget Chelsea's face. Not the bruising or swelling, but the pain and fear. Something inside her had been damaged and might never heal. Would she ever want to dance again? Live alone? Would she ever be able to enjoy a sexual relationship?

If only they'd catch the bastard. Until that happened, Chelsea wouldn't just look at every man and wonder. She would look and be terrified.

Somehow, after the way the week had gone, Karen wasn't surprised when a pickup truck pulled in a few minutes later, rifle rack and all, and Chief Rowland himself climbed out. Since he'd never darkened her gate before, she didn't deceive herself that he was here in search of a handsome shrub.

He nodded. "Morning."

She nodded in return and rang up the two small columbines the customer had chosen. The grand total was eight dollars and thirty-two cents. Her day was off to a bang-up start. She'd covered the price of the doughnuts.

Chief Rowland stood in front of the register, thumbs hooked in his pants pockets, pretending to study her selection of pruning shears and grass clippers. No uniform today. He wore jeans and a cream-colored cowboy shirt with pearl snaps under a denim jacket. Karen leaned forward slightly so she could see over the counter. Cowboy boots.

"Can I help you find something?" she asked.

His eyes met hers squarely. "Just thought I'd see what you have here."

She came out from behind the counter. "Do you garden?"

The image was ludicrous. She couldn't see him crawling around on his hands and knees digging in the dirt. Smelling the roses, putting together a nice floral arrangement for the dining-room table. Except, maybe he had a wife who did that.

"Never have before," he admitted. "I bought an old place with some flower beds, though. I'm going to have to do something about them. Some big bushes are covering the windows."

Karen moved in for the kill. No reason he shouldn't pay a price for checking up on her. "Well, let's take a look at some low-maintenance shrubs that won't be so tall," she announced, and briskly headed out the door. He didn't have any choice but to follow.

Her nursery was modest. Four small greenhouses, potted perennials laid out on tables and a pretty good selection of flowering shrubs, roses and fruit trees. In the one small building, painted gray with white trim, she sold dried flowers, terra-cotta pots and books on gardening, as well as fertilizer, sprays, seeds and tools. Business wasn't booming, but she'd only been here two years. She was building up a decent mailing list and had realized this year that she needed to specialize if she wanted to draw customers from out of town. She'd settled on her first love: old roses. Now all she had to do was scrape up the money to *do* something with that mailing list.

"How high are your windows from the ground?" she asked over her shoulder.

"I'm not sure I really—"

"Fall's the best time to plant. Why lose a year?"

She heard him swear softly and looked back to see his fancy boots squelching loose from a patch of mud. She wore rubber boots.

"What color's your house?"

"Uh...white."

"I'm fond of the lace-cap hydrangeas." Karen stopped in front of a raised bed of sawdust set with potted shrubs. The large-flowered hydrangeas were voluptuously in bloom, the frilly blue and purple flowers of the lace-caps making a fine foil for deep red geum and spikes of blue veronica. "And of course there are plenty of rhododendrons that are compact enough. They're glorious in the spring. Where are you from?"

"L.A." He barely glanced at the shrubs. "I really didn't come here to buy anything."

She looked him straight in the eye. "Then what are you here for?"

He planted a booted foot on the two-by-ten that framed the bed, and Karen realized for the first time that he wore a shoulder holster under the denim jacket. At his belt hung a pager. "Just...curious," he said.

"About whether I've kept my mouth shut?"

"Maybe."

"I keep promises," she said. "But I don't think it's good for Chelsea, and I don't like knowing something my neighbors don't. How much longer is this going to go on?"

"Until we catch the SOB."

"Or someone else gets raped?"

His heavy brows drew together. "No one else has, if that's what you're asking."

At that moment, she disliked him intensely. Was he as indifferent as he sounded? What was this—some macho game? Did he enjoy the hunt?

She said abruptly, "I'd better get back to work. If you're not interested in the plants—"

"Pick out half a dozen for me."

For once, she was taken by surprise. "Me? Don't you know what you like?"

His gaze dropped from her face to her baggy sweatshirt and faded jeans, then traveled back up. "Yeah," he said, and the corners of his mouth twitched. "I know what I like. Something that flowers and smells nice. Nothing I have to baby, though I don't mind if it looks delicate."

She didn't appreciate his double meaning or the way her body had responded to that once-over. "I'll think about it," she said. "Why don't you stop by next week?"

"Okay." He looked around. "You have a nice place here."

"Thank you," she said, trying not to sound too grudging, and started back for the building. The mud squished around her rubber boots, and she took pleasure in knowing what it was doing to his hand-tooled boots. Had he worn them the other night with his uniform? She couldn't remember noticing, but it made sense. Maybe tonight in her dreams her dance partner would have a face. And maybe his boots would be too muddy to click on the hard floor. There was probably something Freudian about those dreams, but she didn't know what, beyond the obvious.

At the front gate she stopped. He was right behind her. Looking at the high-powered rifle that hung in the rack on the back window of his pickup, she asked, "Do you hunt?"

"Only bad guys. Killing isn't my idea of a good time."

She nodded at the truck. "So why the rifle?"

His dark-browed face was as impassive as ever. "There's one kind of killing that might be my job."

Karen thought again of her daughter. If Abby was threatened, Karen would kill, too. "Sorry," she said. "Whether you hunt or not isn't any of my business."

She might be imagining the glint of humor in his eyes. "You weren't just making conversation?"

"I don't like guns," she admitted.

"Or me?" When she didn't answer, the hint of a smile disappeared and he said, "I don't much like 'em, either. If 'Nam didn't cure me, L.A. would have."

"You fought in Vietnam?"

He nodded.

"My brother was killed there," Karen said.

"Mine, too."

For a moment they stood in silence, unintentionally united. Karen doubted that would last long if he knew she'd started joining antiwar demonstrations when she was thirteen years old. By that time, he was probably already a soldier, wading through rice paddies or running around in the jungle, watching friends die.

The phone shrilled, saving her from their awkward conversation. "Will you let me know?" she asked.

Their eyes met and she saw that he understood her. "One way or the other? If I can," he agreed.

By the time Karen had assured the caller that the nursery was indeed open, the police chief was gone.

THE SKY WAS MOONLESS Friday night, as dark as his worst nightmares. Neal eased the car forward slowly, headlights off, as he studied the black-on-black scene, only faintly illuminated by a streetlight almost a block away. A hedge—why the hell did everybody in this town have hedges?—the bulk of a detached garage, the slope of a back porch. He'd seen movement, something black slipping into the deeper shadows. His pulse had picked up and familiar tension sharpened his awareness of everything from the murmur of the car engine to the flick of a porch light coming on down the street.

There was an opening in the hedge and a driveway that looked more like two wheel tracks with grass in between. He gunned the engine as he swung in, flicking on his high beams. He could see a glassed-in back porch, two garbage cans with a stuffed bag sitting on top, a bike lying on its side on the lawn.

And a dog. A big black Lab who shot out from behind the garbage cans and vanished under the hedge.

"Damn." Neal dimmed his headlights and backed out as quickly as he could, hoping he hadn't scared the shit out of someone inside. A dog. That was the way his night was going. The way his day had gone.

Why the hell had he told Ms. Karen Lindberg, the Flowerwoman—he'd liked her shirt—to pick out shrubs for him? He didn't have time to plant them. The fence around the pasture already needed replacing. He didn't like barbed wire. That was asking for a horse to be hurt.

Krista and Michael needed his attention, too. He'd put them through the misery of a move partly so he would have more time for them. Instead, his days were fourteen, sixteen hours long.

He couldn't seem to let it go, even though at best the heightened police presence would only put off the next rape, not stop it. He shouldn't even be out here. His job wasn't patrolling the town, it was finding the rapist. To do that he'd interviewed the two victims over and over again. Checked up on every man whose name appeared on both their lists of acquaintances. Visited every business they both frequented. He'd taken the two women through the past few weeks, again and again and again. Where they'd gone, who they'd talked to.

They *knew* the rapist. Nothing else made sense. Both women were single, young, attractive—and alone the nights they were attacked, less than a week apart. They couldn't have been randomly chosen. The bastard *had* to know them. But how?

Neal had always become easily obsessed; Jenny had hated it when he got this way. But now it was his town, his responsibility. As long as he was out here, maybe no one else would get hurt.

He'd only covered another block when the radio crackled. "Yeah?" he said into the handset.

"Something going on at the high school. Dance tonight, you know. One of the chaperons called. Just a fight, but she couldn't break it up."

"Okay, I'll check it out," he said. Fortunately he wasn't a quarter of a mile from the high school. On the way he considered the possibility that their local rapist had a CB radio and listened in on the police band. And Neal had just announced to the world that he would be occupied for a while.

He was getting paranoid. Rogers and Erickson were out there somewhere. DeSalsa was walking a beat. They'd catch him. Sooner or later, they'd catch him.

It was the "later" that scared Neal.

The high school's acres of asphalt and grass were lit by yellow sodium lamps. Finding the fight was no problem. A crowd was cheering it on, as usual. These same kids would have a hell of a good time watching a cowboy get trampled by a steer at the rodeo or a car hit the wall at Indianapolis. Neal had less patience with them than he did with the combatants. He shoved a few aside, a little rougher than he had to be, then grabbed collars and wrenched the two boys who were rolling on the asphalt basketball court to their feet. Their first instinct was to struggle, until they saw his uniform and then his face.

One boy had a bloody nose and an eye already swollen shut. The other was spitting blood.

"Out of here," Neal snapped to the eager audience. "Now."

He waited until he was reluctantly obeyed. The woman who'd been hovering on the fringes made flapping motions and herded them toward the gym.

"Okay, what's this about?" Neal said to the boys.

He felt the muscles become rock hard under his hand.

"He told a bunch of people he screwed my girlfriend. I don't have to take that shit."

Neal sighed. If there was one thing most men learned when they grew up, it was that it didn't matter who she'd had before you. Some men learned to keep their mouths shut about who *they'd* had, too. Unfortunately some didn't.

"So you thought she'd appreciate having her honor defended."

A head shorter than Neal, the kid smeared blood across his face with the back of his hand. "She doesn't want garbage like him talkin' about her."

Neal gave them both a good shake. "You ever think she might be embarrassed by this?"

The boy who'd started the trouble with his big mouth had already shrunk a little. He hung inside his coat like it didn't fit.

"You ever think how she's going to feel when her parents find out you two've been fighting about who's been in her pants?"

The boyfriend began to shrink, too. "I'm a juvenile. Even if you arrest me, the newspaper can't print my name."

"What difference does that make in a town like this?"

The kid started to open his mouth, then shut it, looking sullen.

"I have a teenage daughter myself," Neal said, his voice almost gentle. "If that was my daughter you were fighting about, getting arrested would be the least of your troubles." He gave them another shake. "You understand me?"

The bigmouthed one gave a hurried nod. After a moment the boyfriend nodded more reluctantly. Neal let go of them. "Then get the hell out of here. And don't let me see your faces again. Got it?"

Neal watched them bolt toward the crowd clustered around the gym doors. The lights on the top of his cruiser flashed rhythmically. He turned them off, then joined the cars slowly circling in the single lane used for picking up and dropping off. Stop and start. It was like being stuck in the relentless one-way flow at the airport.

Even through the closed windows of the cruiser he could hear the music slamming out of the gym, see the blur of a strobe light snapping frozen vignettes. A boy laughing, his cigarette dangling from his mouth. A couple who didn't look any older than Krista making out. The hapless chaperon, flapping her hands again.

Thank God Krista hadn't asked to come tonight. Like any parent, Neal had mixed feelings. He wanted his daughter to make friends. He was just hoping they'd all be members of the chess club whose favorite music was Mozart.

He didn't want to wonder what Krista was doing out behind the gym or think she might get in a car with some teenage hotshot whose brains were below his belt. He didn't want her to grow up.

The car ahead of him was a small blue Civic. When it stopped in front of the gym, a girl separated herself from the pack and hurried toward it, her hips swinging. She wore all black and had spiked blond hair, but there was still something puppylike about her. Neal's fingers drummed impatiently on the steering wheel as he waited while she opened the passenger door of the Civic and bent to duck in. The woman behind the wheel turned her head just then. With the interior light on, her profile was instantly recognizable.

The Flowerwoman herself. With a daughter near Krista's age, if he had to guess. So he had more in common with Ms. Lindberg than their dead brothers and the way they felt about guns.

She was single, too, he thought, with an unpleasant jolt. Single and pretty. He hoped like hell that one man hadn't noticed that.

CHAPTER THREE

THE GYMNASIUM was packed and hot. Karen didn't remember the Parent Group meeting ever being so well attended. The bleachers had been pulled out and a couple of rows of metal folding chairs set up facing them with a microphone in front.

Karen half expected cheerleaders to bounce out with their pompoms to lead a rousing cheer. Maybe it was the creaking of the bleachers and the clatter when someone climbed them, or the smell, a combination of floor polish and sweat. Karen never felt quite grown-up here. She suspected she wasn't the only one. A woman near her kept tugging at her hem, her knees awkwardly turned to one side. The man in front of Karen fiddled with his baseball cap, putting it on, taking it off, putting it on, adjusting it, twisting it in his hands. Karen wanted to snatch it away from him.

At last the president of the Parent Group advanced to the microphone. Vicky Thomas was one of Karen's least favorite human beings. She liked nothing better than organizing a bake sale. Or a car wash. She loved car washes. Vicky's oldest daughter was a senior; Karen was pretty sure Vicky had been room mother for all thirteen years. If the school district had had a hall of fame, Vicky Thomas would have been retired to it. Karén had learned to run the other way when she saw her coming. She hated baking.

Unfortunately Vicky loved to garden, if planting rows of flaming orange begonias and bright yellow marigolds could be called gardening. Karen had learned to smile, keep her mouth shut and take Vicky's money. She'd also learned to listen to Vicky's pep talks with a pleasant smile fixed on her face.

"I'm so delighted to see this kind of attendance," Vicky gushed into the microphone. "Now, if you'd all volunteer for our next Fun Run, think what a success we could make it!"

The woman who'd been tugging her skirt hem muttered, "I'd rather write a check."

"I know many of you are here because you've heard talk about the new system of rewards the teachers and administrators are using. Since Mr. Bradley, the high-school principal, has been good enough to agree to field your questions, I'll turn the microphone over to him without further ado."

Carl Bradley looked less than delighted with the opportunity he'd been given, but Karen felt no sympathy. In her opinion, he was an idiot. Finally, thanks to this issue, other people were beginning to notice.

He cleared his throat and smiled blandly. "Let me explain first what we're up to. For too long, schools have punished bad behavior or failure, without adequately rewarding good behavior or success. At the elementary level, gold stars work, but when you're dealing with teenagers, you need to come up with something a little more age appropriate. So we asked ourselves—what do teenagers like?" He chuckled. "The answer—music, clothes, members of the opposite sex and movies. We figured movies would be cheaper than new wardrobes."

Not a single parent laughed. Not even Vicky Thomas. Bradley was in big trouble.

He cleared his throat again, pushed his glasses up his nose and assumed a serious mien. "Now, I'll be the first to admit that it's possible some bad judgment was used in selecting which movies students would earn the right to see. But obviously teenagers aren't going to be motivated by *The Little Mermaid.*"

The father near Karen slapped his cap back on his head and stood up. He said loudly, "Some of these movies are R-rated. Our kids can't see them in the theater without parental permission. Showing them to freshmen in high school is more than bad judgment, I'd say."

The meeting, Karen was glad to see, deteriorated thereafter. Several teachers rose to explain why they needed to bribe their students with *Halloween III* or *Hot Spot.* A few parents ventured the opinion that the teachers should figure out why they were failing to motivate their students in the first place.

Marta Peters, who'd presumably had root-canal work done in the last week, rose to ask what had happened to the excitement of learning for its own sake. The visit to the dentist didn't seem to have improved her mood. She added tartly, "Praise from a good teacher should be enough to motivate any student." Her pointed emphasis on "good" didn't seem to find favor with Bradley.

Another mother stood up. "The newspapers are full of statistics about falling SAT scores and how much better education kids in Japan and Germany are getting. Our kids are in school few enough hours a week now. Why waste any of that time?"

Bradley had to wait until the applause died down before he said, "A reward that motivates students to work harder the rest of the week can't be considered wasted time—"

Karen stood up. "I think many of us *do* consider it a waste of time. If nothing else, you're suggesting to students that the task of learning is so unpleasant it has to be sugarcoated. What kind of message is that to give to our kids? The school should be exciting them, challenging them, making them think. They should be gaining the ability to analyze problems and find reasonable solutions. They should be discovering the wonderful literature out there, learning to argue persuasively. Maybe they should even be facing the fact that sometimes they need to finish a project that isn't exciting, consider a point of view that isn't theirs, wait patiently when they're bored." She looked around. "They're not far away from having to face the real world, and I don't know a single employer out there who's going to reward a couple of hours' good work with *Terminator II*."

More applause. Karen sat down to the accompaniment of it. The gym was hot and faces were flushed. She spotted friends in the audience and a few teachers who had stayed conspicuously silent when Bradley had lined up the troops in his defense. Peter Merck, a chemistry teacher who came often to the nursery, gave her a wink. And there was Frank Morris, Abby's algebra teacher. Karen couldn't imagine him standing up to speak, no matter what side of the issue he was on. And Joe Gardner, a PE teacher and coach. Good God, did the jocks win the right to spend Friday afternoon at the movies by dunking the basketball?

The bleachers were nearly full and more parents stood down at the end. Leaning against the bleacher support was the police chief, in another Western shirt with pearl snaps. What was he doing here?

Watching her, for starters. When her eyes met his, he gave her a half smile and a thumbs-up. She'd wondered whether he was married, but it hadn't occurred to her that he might have kids. Or was he here on business? Maybe just acquainting himself with the community?

If so, he was getting an earful.

More parents spoke, only two in favor of Bradley's system. At last Vicky Thomas stood up and took over the microphone again. She beamed. "We've certainly heard an interesting mix of opinions, lots for Mr. Bradley to think about. Why don't we give him a big hand in appreciation for him coming tonight?"

Bradley flashed a sickly smile. The applause was desultory. Fortunately Vicky Thomas had the brains to finish the rest of the minor business quickly, before she lost her audience. The bleachers groaned and clattered as the crowd filtered down onto the gym floor, where the parents collected in small vociferous groups. Karen began to circulate.

She'd gussied up tonight for this exact purpose. Alien though it was to her nature, she was running for political office. Years of being the gadfly didn't seem to have done the trick. This year, she intended to be *on* the school board, not provoking it from the floor. Unfortunately winning elections required smiles, handshakes and conciliation. It required thinking twice before she opened her mouth. Tonight, it had also required wearing a dress and panty hose.

"Certainly we want our teachers to think creatively," Karen agreed with a father. "But surely they can also use common sense."

A sugary voice spoke from her elbow. "I'm surprised to find you on our side tonight."

Karen immediately amended an earlier thought: no, Vicky Thomas was not her least favorite human being; Lareina Parsons was. Lareina had home-schooled her children to protect them from the corrupt humanist values the public schools endorsed. Apparently, however, she'd conceded that her own high-school education didn't equip her to teach her son and daughter algebra, biology or advanced English composition. They now attended the high school, to the dismay of the administrators and teachers, who had to deal with their mother.

"I think we were nearly all in agreement tonight," Karen said tactfully. "Our tax dollars should be supporting education, not questionable entertainment."

"I am so grateful that my children reported to me what was going on." Lareina clasped her hands to her bosom as though to suppress palpitations. The gesture might have looked more natural if she'd worn ruffles, instead of a T-shirt that said Soccer Mom in large letters. Karen knew from grim experience that soccer mothers had to be competent to deal with blood, sweat and tears; palpitations didn't cut it. Still striking a pose, Lareina said, "I try to raise my children with real values, and to think what they might have been exposed to!"

"Exposed is right," muttered a father. "I don't want my daughter seeing Don Johnson's butt."

At another time or place, Karen might have said flippantly, "No, but I wouldn't mind." Tonight she merely shook her head in apparent dismay.

Lareina said, "To think, our children can't pray in the classroom, but they can watch filthy movies!"

Figuring she'd reached the limit of her tact, Karen eased away. She turned, ony to find herself face-to-face with Neal Rowland. He inclined his head. "Good going, Ms. Flowerwoman."

Genuine praise, or was he baiting her? She side-stepped that one and said, "What a pleasant surprise to see you at our Parent Group meeting. Do you have children, Chief Rowland?"

"As a matter of fact, I do," he said in that gravelly voice. "Two. Michael is ten and Krista is fourteen."

"Krista? Oh, my daughter's mentioned a new girl. I think she's in a couple of classes with Abby."

"I saw you picking her up at the school dance the other night. Cute girl."

"Thank you." Karen was seized by an almost irre-sistible urge to chatter. But what the hell, he was a voter, wasn't he? "So," she challenged, "what did you think of tonight's doings?"

"Exactly what you thought." Rowland crossed his arms. "It was a damned stupid move on the part of the administration. Makes you wonder how they earned master's degrees."

"I didn't hear you speaking out."

"You spoke for me." They both retreated a step when the group near them swelled. "Besides, I figure I'm in a sensitive position. I try to stay out of poli-tics."

"Surely you vote."

"I vote." He lifted dark brows. "Who are you campaigning for?"

"Myself. I'm running for the school board."

His gaze moved over her in another of those sweeping assessments that could be taken two ways. "I like what I saw tonight," he said.

"And what was that?" she asked.

"A smart woman with spirit."

Something dry in his voice made her wonder if he really liked women with spirit. Or smart ones. But maybe that was her prejudice speaking, which still thought the rifle rack and cowboy boots could tell her all she wanted to know about this man.

"Then I'll hope for your vote," she said. "Would you excuse me? I see somebody I need to talk to."

As she circulated, Karen remained conscious of him off to the side, watching her. Or was it her he watched? A chill went down her spine. Maybe he was more interested in tall men with brown eyes. Maybe he was looking at all the women, just as she'd been doing, wondering who the rapist would choose next.

Karen chatted with several more groups of parents, though a part of her remained detached. Was the first rape victim here tonight? Was the rapist here?

Just ahead, a woman making her way toward the exit caught Karen's eye. Abby idolized her English teacher. Lisa Pyne was an adult version—barely—of Abby: petite, perky and blond. Looking at her depressed Karen, who had to wonder if this was the kind of woman Abby really wished she had for a mother. Karen wanted to dislike Lisa, but the woman seemed to deserve her students' adoration; she was genuinely sweet.

Abby had spent the week bemoaning Lisa's absence. The substitute was using class time to have the students silently read *Great Expectations*. Dickens had been published in serial form in his day, a sort of "NYPD Blues" that had presumably kept his readers in suspense. By the standards of modern television, however—and what other standards did teenagers have?—Dickens's novels moved at a pace slower than the high-school cross-country team. In other words, to quote Abby, who cared?

Karen felt sure that Lisa would have made her students care. Lisa's was one class that didn't require Arnold Schwarzenegger at his goriest as motivation.

"Lisa," she called, and the small woman stopped.

She seemed to hesitate before she turned. "Oh, Karen. How nice to see you."

With sudden dread, Karen saw the black eye and dark bruise that disfigured a face usually animated enough to seem pretty. The discoloration wasn't fresh; around the edges of the bruise that ran down one cheekbone, the blue had faded to a pasty yellow.

Karen calculated even as she exclaimed, "Good Lord, what on earth happened to you?" Surely she was wrong. The first victim had been raped almost three weeks ago now. This bruise wasn't a week old.

Lisa smiled, too quickly and too brightly. The smile was gone almost before it had dawned. "I look awful, don't I? But I'm fine, truly. I stayed home this week just so I wouldn't scare the kids. They might think Halloween was early."

"But how...?"

Her hands fluttered. "Oh, I fell from a horse. I said whoa and he stopped. I didn't. This—" she touched her cheek "—isn't the only bruise. I should have hidden out for a couple more days, but I wanted to come tonight. I don't think our principal got quite the reaction he'd hoped for, do you?''

Trying to hide her disquiet, Karen went along with the change of subject. ''Heaven knows what he expected. I don't suppose he had any choice but to come tonight. Although he could have offered up a sacrificial goat...''

''Who? He'd have had to catch somebody first.'' For an instant, Lisa sounded like herself. Then her gaze drifted away. ''Well, say hi to Abby for me. I'd better get on home.''

''Lisa—'' her own voice had changed ''—are you sure...?''

Alarm flared in the young teacher's blue eyes, before she managed a smile as brittle as the first. ''Sure? Sure about what?''

''That you fell off a horse,'' Karen said quietly.

The change in Lisa was remarkable. She seemed to fold in on herself, her shoulders hunching as though to ward off a heavy weight. Or a blow. ''Don't be ridiculous.'' Her voice was shrill. ''Of course I did. What in God's name are you suggesting? No, never mind. I don't want to know. Listen, I really need to stop in the washroom on my way out. I'll see you... well, I'll see Abby, anyway.''

Karen stood flat-footed, watching Lisa hurry away. Her instinct was right. It had to be right. Only Lisa wasn't the first rape victim. She was the third.

''That son of a bitch,'' Karen muttered. ''No wonder he's here.''

NEAL SCANNED the crowd, mildly bemused. Feelings ran hot here tonight, and he had the impression this issue had led to some peculiar alliances. Half the parents were incensed about the waste of time; Neal was in that camp. The other half objected to the choice of movies. Those were divided, too. Some didn't mind a little violence; it was the sex they objected to. The others figured Don Johnson's butt was okay, but they didn't want their kids seeing heads getting blown off.

He thought grimly that they ought to see what happens when sex and violence are combined. Unfortunately some of the women here tonight had a damn good chance of seeing just that.

Like Ms. Flowerwoman, who'd surprised him. So, she could be affable when she felt inclined. He'd listened to her working the crowd, as smooth as any politician he'd ever met. Of course if she'd let off too many fireworks in the past, it might be a little late to fool the voters now. He'd be willing to bet, for example, that the man he'd overheard talking about getting back to the three R's and not coddling the damned kids wouldn't be casting his ballot for Ms. Lindberg.

Hardly aware he was looking for her, Neal turned his head until he found her near one of the exits. She wasn't twenty feet away, talking to a pretty blonde Neal recognized as his daughter's English teacher. The conversation wasn't a light one. Even though neither woman had raised her voice, tension emanated from them in waves.

Neal straightened, frowning. Hadn't Krista said something about a substitute this week? The teacher hugged herself and took a couple of steps back from Ms. Lindberg. When she turned and hurried out of the gym, he saw her face. Damn!

A few strides took him to Ms. Lindberg's side. She was staring after the teacher.

"Did she say how that happened?"

The Flowerwoman gave a start at the sound of his voice. Unfortunately surprise didn't keep her down for long. Her eyes glittered with anger. "What? Did you coach her to tell a certain story?"

"I've only met the woman once," Neal said evenly. "When I took my daughter to her first day of school."

She searched his face. Then a long sigh seemed to deflate her. "Oh, God. She said she was going to the washroom before she left. I'm going to push a little harder."

"I'll be waiting outside," Neal said, matching her strides. "Yell if you want me."

"Yeah." Ms. Lindberg sounded wry. "If."

Lined with brown-painted lockers, the wide hall was deserted. The linoleum had a dull gleam that showed special care had been taken for tonight. Just outside the girls' washroom, Neal grabbed her arm. "What was the teacher's story?"

"She fell off a horse."

"You know, we might be jumping to conclusions."

"I don't think so."

"Is she married?"

Ms. Lindberg shook her head. "Was the first one?"

"No."

"Oh, God," she said again, and pulled away from him. When the washroom door swung shut behind her, Neal leaned against the wall and waited.

THE WASHROOM HAD a double entrance/exit that jogged into the large room with its row of stalls, a long sink and mirror, and graffiti decorating every wall. A feeble summer effort to start afresh had needed a second coat. Dark lettering could still be seen through the pale wash of yellow paint. Screw You. Different handwriting said No, Screw Jon.

How imaginative. With one part of her mind, Karen tried to remember whether she'd ever written on a washroom wall. If she had, it had probably been a peace sign, a symbol far from the thoughts of her daughter's generation.

For a moment she thought the washroom was empty. Then she heard a rasp of breath. One stall door, down at the end, was closed. Another harsh breath, then a hiccup she recognized as a sob.

"Lisa?" Her voice echoed.

"Leave me alone."

"Aren't you scared alone?"

Silence. Another deeper sob. Karen said bluntly, "Two women here in town have been raped in the past month. The police are keeping it quiet."

"Oh, Lord."

"Will you come out, Lisa?"

A long moment later, the stall door swung open. In the too-bright light, the young teacher's face was ravaged. Smudged mascara gave the effect of two black eyes. Her complexion was waxen, her lids puffy and red, her eyes haunted.

"Two women?" she said.

Karen nodded.

"How do you know?"

"One of them was Chelsea Cahill. We're friends."

Lisa closed her eyes and swayed. "I thought it was just me. I thought he must be watching me, that he'd come back. He *was* watching me, he said so!"

Her own eyes wet with tears, Karen reached out to pull Lisa, who looked far too much like Abby, into her arms. "Yes, I know. But he's not watching you all the time. He can't be. Because you're not the only woman he's attacked."

"I've been so afraid." Lisa's voice shattered into tears. Karen held her as she cried and talked in fragments. "I never saw him, just this mask. It was like a skeleton with empty eyes. Only...only there *were* eyes. They watched me. The whole time. The whole time I..." She shuddered. "I'll never do it again."

"Do what?"

It came out with a rush. "Dance. I'll never dance again."

Karen closed her eyes and held on tight. When she opened them, she saw Neal's reflection in the mirror; he was standing just inside the washroom. The fury she felt toward the rapist was all mixed up with her anger at Neal, who'd let this happen. With an effort she shoved her emotions out of sight.

"Lisa," she said softly, "you have to talk to the police."

"No!" The young woman stiffened and pushed away. "I won't! He said—" She saw Neal and swung to face him. A foot away from her, Karen could still feel her trembling. "Who are you?"

Karen touched her arm. "Lisa, this is Neal Rowland, our new police chief. He...he saw your face tonight."

"I fell off a horse! You can't prove I didn't!"

"You'll never feel safe until the bastard is behind bars," Neal said. His voice was hard. "If you don't fight back, you won't be able to live with yourself."

Lisa's teeth were chattering. "He'll kill me!"

"No. He's done everything he meant to do. He's scared you so badly you won't stand up for yourself."

It was all Karen could do to listen to this crap, to look at Rowland's unyielding face, the contemptuous twist of his mouth. But she wasn't sure he was wrong. She didn't know how else to reach Lisa. So she said nothing, though she despised herself for it.

"Talk to me," Neal said. "Fight back."

"How can I?"

"Tell me everything that happened, everything you saw."

Her mouth trembled, but Lisa said defiantly, "Why? You haven't caught him yet."

"I will."

"And...and why didn't I know there was a rapist on the loose?" Her voice shook. "Why?"

His gaze met Karen's. She stripped her own voice of emotion. "That's a good question. Why don't you answer it, Chief Rowland?"

Anger flickered in his eyes before he looked at the teacher. He responded flatly. "The other women were as scared as you are. They didn't want him to know they'd called the cops."

Lisa was just dazed enough to buy it. Karen wasn't. She didn't believe women were helpless to protect themselves. If Chelsea had known, her door would have been locked; she would have had that extra few seconds to grab a weapon or escape to a neighbor's. Plenty of women in this town had guns. They could be taken off closet shelves and kept handy. Karen wouldn't have a gun in her house, but she'd slept a little better since she'd started keeping the fireplace poker beside her bed.

Chelsea was a good friend, but Karen still didn't think her fears should come before the safety of all the other women in town. The odds were against the rapist taking the risk of punishing a victim who'd talked. On the other hand, it was a safe bet he would rape again. And soon, if the last month was any indication.

"Well?" the police chief asked. "Are you going to talk to me?"

Lisa nodded, suddenly docile. She looked pale and spent, past arguing. Perhaps she was relieved to have been found out, to have the illusion of police protection.

"I'll need to take you to the hospital. We can document..." Even he had the grace to stop that thought. "For your own safety," he finished lamely.

The small blond woman nodded again, the response so mechanical Karen was reminded unwillingly of Chelsea's retreat from reality that night. Was this the only way a woman could cope with male brutality?

When Chief Rowland steered Lisa toward the door, Karen went, too. Hurt and biddable, Lisa reminded Karen even more of Abby. There was no way Karen would desert Lisa now. Rowland glanced at her when she marched right beside Lisa out to his dark patrol car, but he made no comment.

Once in the car, he didn't reach for the ignition. Instead, he began his questions. And Lisa talked, seeming to take comfort from the dark anonymity. The parking lot emptied around them as Karen heard the same story again, but more detailed and less emotional, thanks to Rowland's crisply worded questions.

"Height?"

Lisa's small hand curled like a tightly coiled wire in Karen's reassuring clasp. "I don't know. It was mostly dark and shadowy and he never really stood in front of me."

Rowland sounded surprisingly gentle in contrast to his earlier challenge. "Miss Pyne, I won't ask how much sexual experience you've had. But keeping it in mind, when the man was...actually raping you, did you have any sense of his height or how big his frame was?"

There was a long silence. Lisa had begun to shake. "He...he crushed me. I felt smothered, like I'd never escape. There wasn't any point in fighting. I was too small next to him."

Her dry sob ripped at Karen's heart. Rowland only nodded, as though she'd confirmed a calculation.

"He never turned on the light?"

"Only...only when I danced."

"Did he request any special music?"

Her fragile voice regained some composure. "There was a tape playing. Dire Straits. I didn't really know how to dance to it."

A nod, seemingly noncommittal.

"Did he make the others dance?" Lisa asked.

"Yes."

Karen had sat silent, unwilling to give Rowland an excuse to throw her out. Now curiosity pushed her to ask, "What about the first woman? What kind of music did she play?"

His gaze moved to her face, though she couldn't read his expression. "Country-and-western. Garth Brooks. Again, it was chance. The tape was lying on top of the player."

"So he doesn't care about the music."

"Only that the women dance."

Karen wondered if Lisa had even heard them. Her eyes had closed and her head was bowed. Rowland had to touch her shoulder and repeat his next question.

No, the rapist had never taken off the ski mask. She had no idea what color his hair was. The eyes were brown. Yes, she was sure. She would never forget his eyes.

She remembered nothing else that was useful. The rapist had been careful. Like the other women, she hadn't seen his hair or his features. The assaults had all taken place at night, and he had turned the lights out before removing any of his clothing. He'd never raised his voice above a whisper. Chelsea and the first victim had fought back, but neither thought they'd left a mark. Lisa had apparently been terrified into obedience without a struggle.

"I should have tried harder to get away," she whispered miserably. "Maybe—"

"Maybe you'd have been hurt worse," Rowland interrupted, his voice harsh. "You're a small woman. You wouldn't have escaped."

Lisa subsided with a tiny nod, but Karen had the feeling she wasn't convinced, that acknowledged or not, the belief that she was at fault for not struggling would remain like an ulcer to erode her confidence.

Their arrival at the hospital was an anticlimax. Just before Lisa was whisked away, Karen asked her, "When you're done here, do you have someplace to go where you won't be alone?"

Lisa nodded. "I'm staying with a friend. You know, Gretchen Williams. She's a counselor here at the high school. I told her what happened."

"Then I'd better say goodbye." Karen squeezed her hand. "Abby'll wonder why I'm so late. I'll phone you tomorrow. You're going to be okay."

Lisa looked at her with desperate eyes. "Do you think somebody else will be raped because I didn't call the police sooner?"

Karen didn't want to tell the young teacher how little good her recitation of events had done. She hadn't added anything to Chelsea's story. The rapist was tall with brown eyes. He had a thing about dancing. He was a cautious man who planned ahead. He had to live in Pilchuck, or he wouldn't have known all three women were single and lived alone. He could not have stalked them as efficiently if he hadn't already known something about them.

For the first time Karen was afraid. But she managed a wry smile and said, "No. Your story will help, but I don't think the difference of a few days matters."

"Thank you," Lisa whispered.

Guiltily Karen knew that she hadn't been thinking of Lisa tonight, only the crime. She pressed her lips together and nodded. "I hope I did the right thing."

And then Lisa was gone, efficiently swept into the pristine white embrace of the hospital. Behind Karen, Rowland said, "I'll drive you back to your car."

"I can walk."

"Don't be ridiculous."

She turned to face him. "You don't need to wait?"

"I'll come back."

"All right."

They walked silently out to the patrol car. Karen was conscious of how dark the parking lot was despite the streetlights. She was glad she wasn't alone and angry that she had to feel dependent.

The drive back to the high school was just as silent. Her Civic sat in the midst of a now completely empty lot. Except for the sodium lamps, the school was dark. Chief Rowland turned the patrol car into the slot right next to hers. He surprised her, then, by shutting off the engine.

In the sudden quiet she heard the breath he let out before he laid his left arm on the steering wheel and faced her. His tone was impassive. "Okay. What are you mad about?"

"Mad?" she repeated. "What, you think I'm a nine-year-old who's sulking?"

"No, but I know damn well there's something you've been wanting to say all evening."

He was smarter than she'd given him credit for. "All right," she said for the second time tonight. "I think this rape didn't have to happen. Just like Chelsea's didn't, if you'd warned the community. What rape victim isn't afraid the rapist will come back? That never stops the police from going public. I think you're playing games. You figure women are helpless creatures, anyway, so you have to hide the brutal truth from us. You think a hunt in the dark is fun, when your enemy can't see you coming. The women involved are just pawns. Isn't that right?"

His mouth was a hard line, his face no longer impassive. "You don't know what the hell you're talking about."

"Maybe not," she said, "but these women are my friends. What happened to them can happen just as easily to me or to my daughter."

"I have a daughter, too."

Karen opened her door. "I gave you a chance, even though I thought you were wrong. I'm not making any more promises."

"Did I ask you to?"

"I figured it was just a matter of time."

The police chief's voice was tight, contained. "Tell me, Ms. Lindberg, are you ever wrong?"

"Frequently, but my mistakes haven't been this deadly." Karen relieved some of her anger by slamming the patrol car door, shutting off whatever he intended to say. Conscious of him watching, she stumbled on the damned high heels she'd earlier deemed so important to make an impression. High heels, she thought, that would make it impossible for her to run. She opened her car door, glancing behind the seats when the small dome light came on. Safely in, she locked her door again and started the engine. The patrol car hovered until she put her own in gear and cut diagonally across the parking lot toward the exit. Then it passed her, leaving her to find her own way home.

Karen felt very alone.

Tell me, Ms. Lindberg, are you ever wrong?

She couldn't let herself think about the times she had been. She had to follow her conscience. It was the only way she could live.

CHAPTER FOUR

KAREN STOOD in the doorway of her daughter's bedroom and watched her sleep. In the light from the hall, Abby looked so young, too young to be propositioned by some high-school jock. Her face cleaned of makeup, she was a child.

A child on the brink of becoming a woman, Karen reminded herself grimly. On bare feet, she crossed the room and checked the window lock. Which would stop the rapist for a few seconds. Longer, she told herself, because this window was high above the ground. High, and protected by a particularly thorny rugosa rose, Therese Bugnet. Sleeping Beauty was protected by brambles. Karen touched her daughter's cheek, felt the warm stir of her breath. Safe.

But how safe was she really? How safe was Karen, with a serial rapist on the loose in the midst of their small community? How many young single women were there? If he ran out, if he couldn't find one alone, would he look to the high-school girls?

Karen saw again Lisa's pale face, the fading bruise, the shame. Remembering, she was gripped by anger. If Lisa had known she wasn't the only victim, that she was no weaker than any other woman, the self-doubt might never have insinuated its way into her soul. Even if foreknowledge hadn't prevented the rape, Lisa shouldn't have had to suffer the belief that she alone had been chosen, had submitted. Damn it, she should have been warned that the bastard was hunting women!

At last Karen went to bed, only to lie awake again. She *had* promised silence. *Before* Lisa had been raped. She'd promised to give the chief a chance. Well, he'd had his chance and failed. Silence hadn't delivered up the rapist. Women deserved a warning.

She didn't let herself hesitate the next morning, have second thoughts. She watched out the front window until Abby actually got onto the school bus, just as she had when her daughter was eight and determined to be independent. God forbid that Abby should look back and see her.

Karen took a little longer than usual with her makeup and hair, a modern woman's armor against the world. Then she drove straight to the newspaper office.

The *Pilchuck Times* was a weekly with a circulation that depended on folks looking for school news and garage-sale ads. A police-beat column summed up the town's crime: a male juvenile arrested on suspicion of malicious mischief when he reportedly threw a stone at a passing car, breaking the side window; some occasional domestic violence and a petty theft here and there. The circulation clerk kept a box of lost-and-found items under the counter. She called people by name when they walked in the door.

Like today. "Karen!" Graying and cherubic, Dottie Webster smiled. "Samantha tells me you lit a fire at the Parent Group meeting."

Karen smiled back. "That fire was already burning. And as I recall, Sam had a few things to say herself."

Dottie shook her head. "She always does."

"Pete in?"

"You kidding?" Dottie lowered her voice. "He does the *Herald's* crossword puzzle every morning. Don't tell him I told you."

Karen smiled again and found her way into Pete Eksted's office. Pete and Dottie both were too old to have kids in school and neither of them were gardeners, but Karen knew them reasonably well since she advertised in the *Times* on a regular basis, and her habit of annoying officials meant she'd been quoted on the front page often enough.

A gaunt rangy man with a receding hairline, Pete didn't try to hide the folded newspaper with the crossword puzzle half-completed. "Karen. What can I do for you?"

The fire of her anger had burned out sometime during the night, but the coals were still warm. She sat down in the old wooden office chair facing the desk, her back straight, and said baldly, "There've been three rapes in town in the past few weeks."

His eyes narrowed; his chair squeaked as he leaned forward. "The police?"

"Asked the victims and their families to keep quiet."

Pete's gaze bored into hers. "God, Karen, not you..."

"No. A friend of mine. I'd rather not say who."

He gave his head a shake. "You know I wouldn't print the women's names, anyway." Pete was silent for a moment, contemplative. "Damn," he said. "We're not talking some transient here, are we?"

"No."

He grabbed a yellow lined pad and a sharpened pencil. "Details?"

She gave him a few, told him he could get the rest from Chief Rowland. "In all fairness," Karen said, "I think his investigation has been thorough. But once a third woman was raped, I just couldn't sit back. People should be warned."

"Damn right they should be." Pete reached for the phone and Karen beat a retreat. As she was wishing Dottie a good day, Karen heard Pete's voice. "Chief Rowland? I have a source who tells me..."

It was kind of Pete to try to protect her, but Karen was pretty sure Rowland would guess the source. Any guilt she felt was singed clean away by her next thought: the source *had* to be her, because the three women who'd been raped were too traumatized right now, too ashamed to come forward. And, by God, Chief Neal Rowland had to shoulder a share of that responsibility.

Karen went straight to work, skipping the doughnuts. At the nursery a sea of mud greeted her. No rain for four days, but her teenage helper had left a hose on. Stepping gingerly into the slippery morass—her rubber boots were inside—Karen followed the hose to the faucet and turned it off.

"What do teenagers do with their brains?" she asked the ranks of rhododendrons. They chose not to answer, maybe because they didn't have a clue, either.

Shaking her head, Karen opened up shop, put on the coffee and her boots, spread a few shavings to soak up the worst of the water and answered the ringing phone.

"Most of the bulbs won't be in for a few weeks. Normally about the middle of October. Yes, we buy ours from Skagit Valley growers, except for a few of the more unusual ones. We do have conifers on sale this week, thirty percent off."

In the next hour, two browsers wandered through. Karen kept an eye on them from the greenhouse where she was starting cuttings from old roses. She was still buying grafted hybrid teas and floribundas to sell in the nursery, but as a gardener she preferred own-root shrub roses, and starting this spring, she'd offered them to buyers. They looked puny compared to the fat thriving grafted roses, but she'd been able to persuade a fair number of customers into giving the tiny sticks with a few leaves a chance. Those that hadn't sold, she would repot into half-gallon containers, and by next year they would look more impressive.

It took Chief Rowland exactly two hours to deal with the repercussions of the "leak." Two hours and five minutes after she walked out of the newspaper office, a squad car barreled into the nursery parking lot. The uniformed chief slammed his car door and stalked past several customers without a glance. Karen continued methodically dipping rose stems in rooting hormone.

Despite her outward confidence and her inner simmer, she couldn't help noticing as he approached that he was a very large man. The blue uniform and heavy black belt and holster were designed to intimidate. She had a flash of remembrance: herself at thirteen or fourteen, part of a march protesting the Vietnam War; the sound of firecrackers, a cop on a big bay horse with great iron-shod feet, riding inexorably into the crowd, driving them. She saw again the cop's stony face. Not angry, for he hadn't cared about them, he was just doing his job.

But the remembrance was mistimed; the cop who stood with his black hand-tooled boots about six inches from her knees *was* angry. His eyes glittered under heavy brows as he glowered down at her.

His voice was harsh. "Do you know what kind of damage you just did?"

Karen cocked her head and kept her response cool. "Damage? I'm hoping to prevent some."

Neal said something obscene and half swung away from her in a gesture of suppressed violence, turning back to say from between clenched teeth, "I intended to go to Eksted this morning. But you had to jump the goddamn gun, so now we won't be going public in a plea for assistance from Pilchuck's law-abiding citizens. No, the front page of the *Times* will offer an exposé, which the *Herald* will no doubt pick up, making the police department look like a bunch of incompetent good old boys. I'll spend the next two weeks defending myself, instead of hunting a rapist."

"You weren't getting anywhere hunting the rapist, anyway, were you?"

She actually shrank back from the expression on his face. His voice became very soft. "How would you know?"

"Lisa—"

"Got raped. We haven't found him yet. That doesn't mean we weren't closing in. Tell me, Ms. Lindberg, were you a policewoman in a previous life? Maybe taught criminology?"

"No." For the first time, Karen stood to face him. She unobtrusively backed up a step so that they weren't nose to nose.

His tone still dangerously soft, he asked, "Did you think we've been sitting around the police station all this time playing poker?"

She didn't like feeling defensive, but couldn't help it. "I told Pete Eksted I thought the investigation had been thorough."

Neal leaned toward her. "And how the hell would you know that, either?"

Her mouth was dry. "I was trying to—"

"Soften the blow?"

She matched him glare for glare. "Give the devil his due."

But he surprised her again. Frustration and tiredness deepened the lines in his face. "I'm not the one you've hurt here. It's all those innocent folks out there who've just had their confidence in the police department eroded. The ones who might hesitate to call now. The school kids who are going to hear their parents talking. In five minutes you've undercut the respect we've won with years of visits to the schools and the DARE program." He shook his head. "You could have discussed this with me first."

"You could have told me what you intended."

"And why should I have?" Neal's brown eyes were opaque now. It was as though he'd dismissed her. "Who decided you had the authority to make the moral decisions around here?"

"We all have the obligation to do what we believe is right." It was her creed, her touchstone; she offered it automatically.

Neal shook his head. "Your problem, Ms. Lindberg, is that you always think you're right and everyone else is wrong. Did you ever give a thought this time to all the other people involved?"

He didn't let her answer, assuming she'd known what to say. He walked off, not once glancing down at his boots squelching in the soggy sawdust. He went straight to his squad car, got in, slammed the door and drove away.

Karen stared after him, shaken by more self-doubt than she'd felt in a long time. Was he right about her being one of those people who were infuriatingly certain of their own opinions? Did she make a habit of righteously marching into business that didn't concern her, sure she could manage better than anyone else?

Only slowly did her surroundings soothe her: the buzz of fat bees humming among the asters and Japanese anemone on the tables of perennials, the strong sweet fragrance of Rose de Rescht's flush of small quartered blooms and the wondering rise of a child's voice. "Mommy, look at the butterfly."

A garden always had the power to calm her, to put her problems in proportion.

Damn it, she couldn't stand aside if she could make a change for the better! Too many people, decent well-meaning people, swallowed their doubts and stayed silent. Karen had always believed that the Vietnam War would never have been fought and lost on the scale it was if Americans had raised their voices sooner. Her brother had died two months before the evacuation from Saigon. His death had been pointless, wasted.

All she was trying to do was the right thing. Maybe this time she'd gone wrong in the way she went about it. And maybe not; maybe forcing the police chief's hand hadn't been a bad move. She could only follow her instincts.

But in her heart she knew that Neal Rowland, too, had believed *he* was doing the right thing. And she had sabotaged him.

"MOM! YOU DON'T HAVE to go talk to my teacher like I'm just a little kid or something."

Karen kept walking briskly across the high-school campus toward the new wing that housed the science and math classes. Her daughter scurried along beside her. Abby's shoulders were hunched and her head was down, probably in a futile effort to avoid recognition. What might it do to her reputation to be seen with her mother? Even if said mother had gone to great lengths to dress and apply makeup in a way that wouldn't embarrass her daughter.

Patiently Karen said, "Abby, my speaking to your teacher does not belittle you, believe it or not. I just want to find out if Mr. Morris thinks you need some extra help. God knows I don't remember my algebra well enough to be useful."

Her daughter mumbled sulkily, "So why do we have to learn it if we never use it again?"

Good question. Karen tried to sound more positive than she felt. "Because the concepts are important to understand, even if the specifics eventually escape you. Besides, there *are* professions where you use math more complicated than fifth-grade division."

They had arrived. In the pristine halls the smell of cleansers battled with something more pungent. Formaldehyde? Karen remembered queasily the days of dissecting frogs.

"Why don't you just write him a note or something?"

"Because I'm here now," Karen pointed out reasonably. "Besides, I made an appointment."

In black leggings and a sweater that kept slipping off one shoulder, Abby looked fragile and feminine. The disgruntled sound she made didn't go with the wide blue eyes and delicate features. "Mo-om."

Karen smiled. "If you want a ride, stick around."

The door to room 109 stood half-open. Karen knew Frank Morris, the algebra teacher, by sight, but had never actually spoken to him before. He was sitting at his desk, head bent, but he glanced up and then stood when Karen knocked and came into the room.

"Ms. Lindberg?"

"Yes, I'm Abby's mother." Karen held out her hand and was surprised when he hesitated before taking it. His palm was slightly damp. Thank God he wasn't the biology teacher, she thought, remembering again the formaldehyde and frogs. Even so, she wiped her hand surreptitiously on her jeans.

"Ah . . . please sit down."

She took one of the student desks just in front of his. Instead of speaking immediately, he fumbled in a drawer. Craning her neck, Karen saw him shake some miniature mints into his hand and then pop them in his mouth.

Karen took the opportunity to study him. Brown hair, brown eyes, medium height, ordinary face. Not one of the teachers who excited students to intellectual heights, but decent. At least he had standards.

Which Abby wasn't meeting. Hence this conference.

"As I told you on the phone," Karen began, "I'm concerned about the low scores I'm seeing on Abby's homework and quizzes. I guess what I need to know is whether she doesn't understand the work or whether she's just being lazy and not studying."

He didn't quite meet her eyes. "Probably a combination. She didn't get it right away, and instead of working harder, she, ah..."

"Slacked off," Karen finished for him. "I can easily imagine Abby deciding it wasn't worth the effort if she was going to get lousy grades, anyway."

The teacher nodded, his expression earnest. "Kids this age don't like to ask for help, or admit they're falling behind."

Karen kept her thoughts on that to herself. She and Abby would be having a little talk. "The question is," Karen said, "what should we do now?"

He tapped a pencil nervously. "Actually Abby has done a bit better this last week or so. See—" he pulled out some papers and Karen stood to look "—eighty percent and eighty-four percent. I think another girl has been helping her. The new one."

New? Karen searched her memory and was struck by a horrifying possibility. "Not the Rowland girl? Uh, Carol, Kari, Crystal—something like that."

"Krista. That's her. The new police chief's daughter."

Oh, Lord. Karen thought wistfully of the comfortable relationship she had with most of the parents of her daughter's friends. They traded chauffeuring duties, sleepovers and worries. She couldn't quite imagine discussing menstrual cramps or the mores of teenage dating with Neal. Maybe she'd get lucky and this friendship would die, stillborn.

That is, once Abby had pulled her algebra grade up to a B.

"I haven't met her yet," Karen admitted. She sighed. "I take it you're recommending I leave well enough alone right now. Will you call me if these improved grades don't continue, or if you think she needs some extra help?"

"Yes, of course." He stood with such haste that he knocked a book off the desk. When it clattered against the metal wastebasket he flushed, leaning down awkwardly to get it.

Well, she'd heard what she'd come for. Karen said quickly, to his back, "Thank you. I won't keep you any longer. It looks as though you have papers to grade."

A little flushed, he straightened. "No, I'm... that is, I do have papers, but if there's anything else... ?"

Karen assured him that there wasn't, and departed to look for Abby in the hall. She found her outside in the quad, with another girl and the PE teacher/football coach. From what Abby had said, half the girls in school had a crush on Joe Gardner. His dark blond hair was sun-streaked, and his brown eyes—why, all of a sudden, did every man she encountered have brown eyes?—were velvety and warm. He was also six foot two, muscle-bound and given to wearing tight T-shirts that showed off his pecs. Furthermore, his dimples were cute, which might be why Abby and the other girl had pink cheeks and were giggling.

Upon spotting Karen, her daughter said, "Oh, cool. Mom, this is Krista. Remember I told you about her? Can we give her a ride home?"

"Sure." Karen managed to find a smile for the girl, who, after all, couldn't help who her father was. She was tall, willowy and pretty in a modest way. She had his dark hair and eyes as blue as Abby's.

Then Karen turned to Joe Gardner. "You aren't out there cracking the whip. Did the team earn a day off?"

He threw up his hands. "You kidding? After the way they played Friday? Nah, I just came up to the gym to grab something. But I've been meaning to call you, and Abby said you'd be out in a minute."

Karen braced herself. "That sounds ominous."

Vicky Thomas had a more convincing smile when she moved in for the kill. But Joe was young. "Hey, the kids are great. And I know I can always count on you."

"Let me guess. You need a chaperon for one of the dances." A worse possibility occurred to her. "Tell me it's just for one."

"October twenty-first," he said promptly.

Abby was just catching on. She looked aghast. "You want my *mom* to chaperon?"

"It could be worse," Karen said flippantly. "How about Krista's dad?"

The football coach had no sense of humor whatsoever. "Yeah, that's a good idea. I'll call him."

"But I never even go to the dances," Krista said in a meek voice.

Karen was beginning to enjoy herself. "But your dad probably does. I hear he's broken up a few fights."

"They're good kids," Joe said again. "We only had the one fight. I tell you, chaperoning is a breeze."

Karen wondered if his fingers were crossed behind his back.

He glanced at his watch. "Gotta go. I'll put you down on my calendar. See you, girls." He headed for the field at a trot, leaving them to go to the car.

Abby had apparently been containing herself until he'd left, because now she grabbed Krista's arm. "You'll be disgraced! You can't let your *father* chaperon!"

Karen rolled her eyes at her daughter. "Come on. Krista has absolutely nothing to be ashamed of. Or at least, no more than you do."

Abby gave her mother a pleading look. "Can't you get sick or something?"

"Do you want the dance canceled?"

"They wouldn't do that."

Karen opened the door to her Civic. "Darn right they would, if they didn't have enough chaperons."

Abby flung herself into the car and uttered a deep sigh as she buckled her belt. "Well...pretend you don't know me, okay?"

Karen started the car. "Fair enough, as long as you don't embarrass *me*." She glanced in the rearview mirror. "Krista, you'll have to give me directions."

Only a few minutes later, she drove down the long lane leading up to an old white farmhouse. It was dwarfed by two enormous yews planted on either side of the front porch. Whoever had done the planting had had no conception of what they would grow to be. Now, massive dark columns blocked the front windows and overwhelmed the graceful lines of the old house.

Karen eased the car to a stop. She saw no other vehicles. With luck, she wouldn't have to face Krista's father. She laid her arm on the back of Abby's seat and said brightly, "Well, Krista, it was nice to meet you. Welcome to Pilchuck."

The girl picked up her book bag and reached for the door handle. "Um...thank you."

Abby was already opening her car door. "Wait a minute. Mom, hold on a second. Krista, remember that assignment you were going to tell me about?"

"Abby—" Karen began.

The car door slammed. Already Krista had dug a notebook out of her book bag and was opening it on the hood. Tempted to grab her daughter by the scruff of her neck and toss her into the car, Karen sneaked a glance toward the house. Damn. The front door was opening.

Naturally who should appear but Mr. Pearl-Snap Cowboy himself, the police chief.

Karen rolled down her window. "Abby!"

Her daughter flapped a hand at her. "Just a minute, okay?"

Karen closed her eyes for a moment to compose herself, then climbed out of the car. She might as well set a good example for Abby by displaying a little maturity.

Neal was sauntering toward her, thumbs hooked in the pockets of his well-worn jeans. "Ms. Flower-woman."

Over the roof of her car, she nodded back. "Chief Rowland."

His imperturbable gaze left her to linger on Abby, who had turned with Krista to face him. "You must be Abby," he said. "How do you do?"

Her tone uncertain, Abby said, "Okay, I guess." In a motherly assessment, Karen figured her daughter could have done worse. It was lucky she hadn't had a bad day at school. She might have told him all about it. Sometimes Karen could swear Abby had been born talking and hadn't quit since.

"This is my dad," the other girl said unnecessarily.

"Krista, why don't you take your friend to see the horses," he suggested. His unsmiling gaze was back on Karen's face.

She said hastily, "We really should be going—"

Too late. Abby's face had lit up. "You have your own horses?"

"Yeah, they're Arabians. Dad, can I saddle up Fancy?"

"You bet."

Karen opened her mouth again, but the two girls were off. Talk about playing dirty. She leaned against the Civic, crossed her arms and asked, "Are you just being friendly, or did you have something you wanted to add to yesterday's diatribe?"

"I thought some of the inner-city kids had chips on their shoulders. I hadn't met you yet."

There was enough justice in his comment to bring a flush to her cheeks. Maturity, she reminded herself. "You're right," she admitted. "I'm sorry. I'm not usually so combative."

"No? Bradley might not agree." Neal's hand lifted to rub the back of his neck. "Forget I said that. Our worthy principal deserves whatever he has coming." Uncharacteristically he hesitated. "Actually I, uh, wanted to apologize. You were just doing what you thought was right. If more citizens did that, instead of looking the other way, we'd have a hell of a lot less crime."

His generosity made Karen even more ashamed. "No, I'm the one who ought to apologize. I should have warned you at least. Going off on my own like that was unfair. I'm sorry."

He contemplated her for a long thoughtful moment. Finally he drawled, "I don't know about you, but all this humble pie doesn't sit well with me." He jerked his head toward the barn. "What do you say, shall we go see if your daughter has been tossed yet?"

Karen found herself smiling. Too bad she and Neal Rowland were such poles apart in political persuasion and general attitudes toward their fellow humans. She could get to like the man.

"Why not?" she agreed, falling into step beside him. "But Abby's not a bad rider. She coaxed lessons out of me when she was younger."

"She looks like she could coax blood out of a turnip, as the saying goes. Or damn near anything out of your average sixteen-year-old boy."

"Better than the other way around."

He grunted. "Twenty years ago, I wouldn't have agreed with you. Having a daughter myself, I have to admit those mouthy jocks with their Corvettes scare me to death. Aside from everything else, where the hell do they get the money?"

Karen shook her head. "You know, I keep hearing about kids who got cars from their parents on their sixteenth birthday. New ones sometimes. *I* couldn't afford half the cars in the high-school parking lot."

"Do you think there's more drug dealing than meets the eye?"

Karen really thought about that one as they both rested their forearms on the paddock fence and watched Abby swing her leg over the back of a pretty bay mare.

"No," she finally said. "I won't say drugs aren't here, but alcohol is still a bigger problem."

Krista appeared out of the barn leading a dapple-gray gelding with a gorgeous arch to his neck and a wicked eye. "What a couple of beauties," Karen said. "Abby will be Krista's friend for life."

"I grew up riding, even did the rodeo circuit for a while. First thing I bought after the house were those horses. They're Krista's dream. My son's less interested so far."

Karen stole a glance at the man beside her. He'd propped one booted foot on the lower rail. Considering how dark he was, his forearms were only lightly dusted with hair. His hands were big and blunt-fingered, but looked far from clumsy. The lines of his face were forceful, with strong bones and an unexpectedly sensual mouth. Jutting brows with a few creases between shadowed his eyes and disguised his intelligence. She probably hadn't underestimated his potential for violence, but her first assessment of him as Neanderthal had grossly underestimated the man.

Uncomfortable at admitting that to herself, Karen watched Abby post at a trot, then persuade Fancy into a smooth canter. Krista urged her gelding beside the small bay. Abby turned her head, laughing, and Karen's heart contracted.

"Are you…" She had to clear her throat. "Are you even getting close?"

He understood her, as she'd somehow known he would. "I can't tell." After a pause he said, "You know what scares the hell out of me?"

His gaze followed his daughter, who had spurred her horse ahead of Abby's. Smiling, shaking her dark hair, Krista was more than pretty at this moment; she was a chrysalis, unformed but on the verge of spreading glorious wings.

Karen said softly, "That he'll go after a girl, instead of a woman. Maybe even one Abby and Krista's age."

Neal bowed his head and she saw that his eyes were squeezed shut. Roughly he said, "I keep telling myself he has a pattern. Why would he change it? His...needs are obviously real specific, and maybe a teenage girl wouldn't fill them. I hope to God not."

"Amen." Almost despite herself, Karen touched his arm. "He'll make a mistake. Or...if you're right and he knows all the women, surely Lisa's eliminated some suspects."

"Yeah." He drew an audible breath and lifted his head to look at her with all the force of those dark shadowed eyes. "She also added a few."

"There must be *something* those three have in common."

"What? Damn it, tell me what!" A muscle in his cheek throbbed and for a fleeting instant she saw the savage beneath the laconic cowboy.

She even felt some of the same ferocity. If Abby had been raped...

"Two of the women are teachers..."

"The third one's not. She has a son at the high school, that's all." He growled, "You know what they have in common?"

"What?"

"They all shop at the same damn places. They go to the same medical clinic and the same dentist and the same nursery. Yours. In a town this size, there's hardly a business they don't all frequent. And half of the businesses employ at least one tall man with brown eyes."

"Yes—" Karen let out a breath "—I've noticed."

Tension radiated from him as he gazed frowningly at the two girls. After a moment, his mouth twisted. "Let's forget it right now. Come on." He nodded toward the girls. "Your turn."

"My tur—?" Karen began shaking her head. "Oh, no. Horses aren't for me."

"They're an acquired taste."

"I'm too old to acquire a new one."

"Come on." His grin was devastating, intoxicating. "You're a gutsy lady. I haven't seen you back down from anything yet."

She didn't budge. "Well, now you have."

Both the girls had pulled up beside the fence. "Come on, Mom," Abby said. "It's fun. Maybe you'll like riding so much we can get a horse."

In a soft voice, Krista contributed, "Fancy's really sweet. She wouldn't do anything you don't want her to."

Karen opened her mouth to tell them she wasn't getting on the horse's back even if Fancy was nominated for sainthood when she had a sudden picture of Abby at eight or nine years old. Abby had desperately wanted to take gymnastics, but when the coach had the girls start working on the balance beam, Abby had balked. In the end she'd quit because she was scared. Karen remembered her own irritation, her lack of understanding. She'd hidden her feelings, thank God, but still...

"Oh, fine," she said ungraciously.

Abby slid off the bay mare, making it look easy. Karen went around through the gate and stopped at the horse's side. Objectively she knew Fancy was a small horse with dainty feet. But from this perspective, the horse looked enormous.

Standing close behind Karen, Neal said, "Okay, left foot in the stirrup."

Hopping on her right foot, feeling as graceful as a floppy centifolia rose, she complied.

Hands closed around her hips and she started to turn, but he hoisted her and with a squeak Karen flung herself over the horse.

Naturally it had to be one of those useless little English saddles. "What do I hold on to?" she asked.

The wretched man was grinning as he lengthened the stirrups, placing an intimate hand on her calves to set her feet where he wanted them. "Her mane, if you need something. But at a walk, you can just sit there."

She'd watched Abby's lessons long enough to know that squeezed heels meant go, pulled reins stop. So with an appearance of dignity, Karen turned the pretty mare away from the fence and tightened her legs until Fancy got the idea and walked.

After a couple of circuits of the paddock, Karen decided this wasn't half-bad. "Can I trot?" she called, as she passed Neal and Abby, who sat on the fence with her toes hooked around a lower rail. Krista on the gray swept past at an elegant canter.

"You bet." Neal's mouth had an amused quirk. She didn't suppose he'd done something tame like calf-roping in his rodeo days. Heck, no, he'd probably ridden Brahman bulls or broncos at the very least. "Just give her a boot," he told her. "And relax."

Karen gave an experimental tap. Fancy strolled a little faster. Karen tapped harder. The walk became jerky. This time she kicked her. Firmly. With a jolt they were trotting. Or galloping. All Karen knew was that she was going too fast and that she was bouncing up and down with all the security of a basketball in the hands of the junior varsity center who was growing so fast he tripped over his own feet. And the ball.

She clutched for something, and came up with a handful of coarse black mane. Her teeth were rattling, her butt was rising six inches and then smacking down on the saddle with every step. She wanted to pull on the reins, but to do that she would have to let go of the mane, which was the only thing keeping her on the horse.

"That's good!" Neal called, and through watering eyes she realized she was passing him. "Sit up straighter, let yourself relax, go with her."

Go with her? Damn right she'd go with her, until somebody pried her fingers off the mane. "Whoa!" she tried, but Fancy kept right on trotting, jarring her up and down.

Another circuit, and Karen realized she hadn't fallen off yet. In fact, she was bouncing pretty much straight up and down. Uncomfortable, but not dangerous. Maybe she could let go with one hand, anyway, and lift her head. If she relaxed her lower back, it seemed as though she was going up and down more with the horse, instead of in opposition.

Krista came up beside her. "You okay?"

"I think so," Karen said, half-surprised. The next time she saw Neal and Abby ahead, she let go of the mane and pulled back on the reins. Fancy dropped into a walk so suddenly Karen's teeth snapped shut. The horse ambled over to Karen's daughter and shoved her nose against Abby's stomach.

"Satisfied?" Karen asked them both.

"You don't have to get off," Neal said with a straight face.

"I think I'm black and blue," she admitted. "Fancy won't walk away while I'm getting down, will she?"

That smile dawned again, making him likable and sexy. Karen wished he was neither. He came around to the left side of the horse and held up his hands. "Just slide down," he said, his voice low and rough.

Karen couldn't remember the last time a man had held out his arms to her. Maybe that was why such a simple gesture struck her so hard her breath caught in her throat and she hesitated. Something must have shown on her face, because his smile faded, though his dark eyes held hers. As if in slow motion, she swung her leg over Fancy's back and let herself fall into the police chief's arms. He gripped her around the waist and lowered her, letting her slide down the length of his body. She braced her hands on his shoulders. When her feet touched ground, neither of them took their hands back.

He was looking down at her, his gaze deep and lingering, and she could have sworn his eyes moved briefly to her mouth. Then her daughter's voice intruded.

"We don't have to go, do we, Mom? Can I ride some more?"

Neal's eyes narrowed for a heartbeat, and then he seemed to shake himself before he released her and stepped back. Feeling strangely dizzy, Karen blinked. "No, I..." Was that her speaking in that vague, die-away voice? She recollected herself and said firmly, "No. We do need to go."

"But, Mom—"

"You can come another day." *Without me.*

Neal had added an extra layer of gravel to his voice. "I have an idea." He cleared his throat. "Krista's going to be in the high-school play this weekend. Michael and I are going, and we'll be eating out first. Any chance you ladies would join us?''

There he went again, being courtly to disguise the fact that he was taking advantage of her daughter's eagerness. Abby, of course, was already delightedly accepting. It would have been rude for Karen to refuse now, even though part of her wanted to. Apology or no apology, she couldn't easily forget his harsh accusations.

But she was too honest with herself to deny the electricity between them. What could it hurt to date him once or twice, if that was what he had in mind?

So she smiled pleasantly and said, ''Why not? We'd planned to go, anyway.''

Her disquiet she kept to herself.

CHAPTER FIVE

"I'M SURE I see him out behind my mock orange! There's a man just standing there, looking up at my windows." A gasp. "He must see me phoning! Please hurry," the woman begged.

"Yes, ma'am," said Neal, shaking his head but noting her address and phone number, then dispatching one of his officers.

In theory, this was the kind of call they were hoping for. Unfortunately this particular woman didn't even come within nodding distance of the profile of the victims. She was sixty if she was a day and had a husband—though God knows where he was while she was peering out between curtains. She'd also called the last three nights in a row.

But, hell, maybe the bastard *was* standing out there, watching a neighbor's house if not hers. Maybe he'd slipped away the previous two nights before the patrolman arrived. They had to check. This was why they'd set up the hotline: so citizens would feel free to call, without overwhelming the 911 operators.

Neal let the dispatcher know he was leaving for the night and headed for the coffee shop on the corner to grab a hamburger before going home. Mrs. Feeney, the neighbor who watched the kids, would long since have fed Michael and Krista. The coffee shop was crowded, and heads turned as he entered. During the momentary lull in the talk, he took an empty stool, answering greetings with a nod. By the time he ordered, voices were rising again. As he waited for his food, he stirred cream into his coffee and listened to the conversations around him.

"Damn right I've got my gun out!" a man said from behind him. "Son of a bitch steps foot in my house and he's dead."

A chorus of others agreed with him. Another man said, "I took the wife and daughter for some target practice. The kid's got one hell of a shot. She could drill that bastard right between the eyes."

More talk of guns, everything from a Remington kept for deer hunting to a Colt .38 Special and even an assault rifle. It was enough to send a chill down the spine of any law-enforcement officer. If this went on long enough, somebody innocent was going to get killed. It could be a toddler finding a gun in the drawer of a bedside stand or a teenage boy sneaking back into his bedroom through the window late at night, mistaken for an intruder. Or an argument in front of a tavern turning violent because the disputants were armed. The possibilities were endless, and frightening.

If the rapist had any self-control at all, he'd be lying low right now. The townsfolk were engaging in collective hysteria. Electric bills were going to be an unpleasant surprise next month, considering that every porch and floodlight in town was on all night. A run on the gun shops had stripped their cases of anything that would kill.

"Shit," Neal said under his breath.

"Excuse me?" The waitress, looking startled, stood in front of him with his plate of food.

"Talking to myself. Sorry." When she retreated, he grimaced and took a bite of the hamburger. He wondered what Ms. Flowerwoman thought of all the talk about guns. Or did she keep a .32 Smith & Wesson under her pillow at night?

He ought to have been able to picture it. She was a fighter, the kind of woman who, 150 years ago, would have defended the family homestead with guts, determination and a rifle. But unless he missed his guess, Karen Lindberg was a liberal who probably considered the National Rifle Association the root of all evil. Well, these next few weeks might prove educational to her. She might discover she'd loosed her own brand of evil when she had "warned" the good citizenry of the monster in their midst.

Neal poked a french fry in the catsup and popped it into his mouth. What in hell had inspired him to invite her out on a date? Just thinking about her gave him a headache. He was lucky to be able to talk to her for ten minutes without raising her ire. Or her raising his. If he'd ever met a natural-born troublemaker, Karen Lindberg was it.

Her nature was an especial irony considering that he'd come to Pilchuck in search of peace. He'd felt himself getting hardened to the suffering he saw day in and day out in L.A., suffering that was echoed in his own home, where his wife was dying of cancer. After she was buried and enough time had passed for him to be sure what he wanted, Neal had looked for the smallest town that would hire him, the kind of place where domestic violence was a scandal, instead of an everyday occurrence, the kind where his kids could walk home from school and play tag in a vacant lot on summer evenings. The kind where they didn't have to worry that Dad might die today when he walked out the door in the morning.

He pushed his plate aside and stood. Hell, maybe he was a jinx. Pilchuck probably hadn't had anything approaching a big-city crime in ten years. Now they had a serial rapist.

And he'd invited a woman who rejoiced in battles out to dinner and a play.

Shit.

"I'M NOT TRYING to pin anything on you," Neal said patiently. "I'm talking to lots of people. But your name came up because of that incident last year."

The teenage boy, all six feet plus of steroid-built muscles, leapt out of the chair and kicked it away. "That bitch lied! She wanted it bad from me! Then she got scared her daddy would find out and started yelling rape. Well, it was bullshit!"

That wasn't the way Neal had heard it. Half a dozen people had brought up the boy's name. At seventeen Mark Griggs looked like a man and had a reputation for belligerence and knocking his girlfriends around. What had interested Neal was that one of the girlfriends had claimed he hit her when she tried to deny him sex. No charges had been filed, but the officer who told Neal about it expressed his regret.

"That's rape in my book," he'd said, shaking his head. "But hell, that's probably what he sees at home. His old man has been picked up after brawls down at the Blue Moon Tavern a few times. What chance does a kid like that have?"

Neal didn't buy that excuse. Everybody made choices. But right now, he didn't care what choices

Mark had made, as long as they didn't include raping three women.

He leaned back in his chair and watched the boy's angry pacing. In an attempt to cool him down, Neal asked conversationally, "Do you play football?"

The kid's chin thrust out. "Yeah, I play football. Is that a crime?"

"What position?"

Mark's jaw worked before he answered. "Center," he finally said grudgingly.

"College recruiters talking to you?"

His eyes narrowed. "You threatening me?"

Neal looked at him thoughtfully. "No, but I can do that if it would make you feel better. Those recruiters won't touch you with a ten-foot pole if the word 'rapist' clouds your name. Not even the community college would touch you. So if you want to keep playing football, it might be in your interest to help me eliminate you as a potential suspect. Am I getting through?"

"How do I know you're not trying to frame me?"

Neal rubbed a tired hand over his face. "Why would I want to do that?"

For the first time, the boy sounded a little tentative. "Because you look bad if you don't arrest someone."

"I'd look worse if I arrested the wrong man and some other woman is raped next week."

"Uh, yeah, I guess so."

"Sit down. Let's try this again," Neal suggested.

The kid glowered for another minute, then grabbed the chair and straddled it backward, facing Neal. His tone was still bellicose. "So, what do you want to know?"

"We have three rapes, three different nights. Let's see if you can remember where you were and what you were doing."

Half an hour later, Neal left the high school. He'd deluded himself that the average high-school kid could easily produce a witness who knew he was home on one of three given nights. Weren't parents supposed to know where their kids were?

Not this one's, and not the parents of the other two boys Neal had talked to. They all claimed they didn't have to tell their parents where they were going or when they'd be home. The rapes had taken place on different nights of the week: the first on a Saturday, the second on a Tuesday, the third on a Sunday. Not one of the boys had been home all evening on those days.

Didn't they have homework anymore? Neal wondered. Or was doing homework as childish as letting your parents know where you were?

Unfortunately Neal didn't have reason to suspect any of the boys enough to take this investigation to the next step: asking for a blood sample. Hell, truth be told, he had better suspects.

Like the ophthalmologist, Dr. Henry Lyons, whose name had come up repeatedly. He was especially interesting because he had dated two of the victims.

The moment his receptionist told him Chief Rowland was in the waiting room, he came out in his white lab coat. Shoes told a good deal about character, and Neal automatically noted the expensive Italian loafers.

"Chief, what can I do for you?" Dr. Lyons asked.

A handsome man in his late thirties, he had art-fully styled his hair to disguise how thin it was get-ting. He also topped six feet and had brown eyes.

"Any chance you could give me a few minutes?" Neal asked.

"You bet." Dr. Lyons offered an ingratiating smile that might even have been genuine. "Come on back."

In his office, elegant enough to impress patients, he settled behind the modern teak desk and waved Neal to a chair. Then he waited.

Neal began, "I'm sure you've read about the rapes here in town." He listened to the usual expressions of shock and dismay. "I understand that you know at least a couple of the women."

The doctor's expression became wary. "The news-paper didn't print their names."

"The grapevine hasn't been working?"

"I understand that one of them was Lisa Pyne. That was a shock. We were . . . friends at one time."

"Friends?"

"Dated."

Neal lifted a brow. "Recently?"

"Depends on what you mean by recently."

A blunt man himself, Neal despised word games. But he kept his expression bland. "Could you be more precise?"

The man frowned and pursed his lips. "Oh, let me see. Six months ago maybe?"

"Was this a couple of casual dates or a serious re-lationship?"

"Casual," he said promptly. Too promptly? "I liked her, and as far as I know she liked me. But I had the impression she was looking for something more serious." He shrugged. "I wasn't."

Neal made a noncommittal noise. "And Chelsea Cahill?"

The doctor leaned forward, his hands flat on the desk. *"Chelsea?"* With a seemingly deliberate effort he sat back and, after a moment, said in a troubled voice, "I didn't know."

Neal made a pretense of glancing at his open notebook. "Was your relationship with her casual, too?"

"Yes!" he snapped. "We only dated once or twice. The woman is a kindergarten teacher, for God's sake. She wants home and hearth. But..." He shoved his fingers into his hair. Disarranged, the wispy strands stuck out every which way. "Oh, hell!" he burst out. "Of all people! She's nice. God. That sounds saccharine. But you know what I mean."

"Yes, I do," Neal said levelly. "Miss Pyne strikes me as equally nice."

"Yeah." The doctor gave himself a shake, and one hand reached up to smooth down his hair. Composure regained. His voice unruffled again, he asked, "And the third woman?"

"Kathleen Madsen." Seeing Dr. Lyons's expression, Neal said, "I take it you know her, too."

"She has an astigmatism. But I don't suppose you care about her eyesight."

"She's a patient, then."

"Yes." Dr. Lyons had clamped down tight on any spontaneous remarks.

With careful lack of emotion, Neal asked, "Do you consider it odd that you know all three women?"

Far from appearing threatened, the doctor laughed. "In this town? I know everybody. If they're not my patients, they're members of the Rotary Club or the Garden Club or—"

"Garden Club?" Neal interrupted.

With dignity, Dr. Lyons said, "I grow prize-winning dahlias."

"Ah." Damn, another angle. "I suppose you're acquainted with Karen Lindberg."

A ripple of some emotion—dislike?—crossed Dr. Lyons's face. "Yes, of course. Although she doesn't know dahlias." His tone implied that he was revealing a serious character flaw.

Neal was tempted to pursue the subject, but for personal rather than professional reasons. Instead, he asked, "Are Lisa Pyne or Chelsea Cahill gardeners?"

"I don't recall either expressing an interest."

No wonder they'd been dropped. They hadn't aahed with sufficient enthusiasm over his dinner-plate-size blooms. Neal made a mental note to ask Karen about this guy. And about the psychological traits that went with passions for particular flowers. Did the meek vent their buried hunger for attention by their choice of gaudy flowers? Did confident people grow more subtly beautiful plants?

Or was the whole notion of deep psychological motivations for plant choices garbage?

"Is Kathleen Madsen a gardener?" Neal asked.

"I believe she's commented on working outside on nice days. She may grow tomatoes or something." When Neal didn't immediately ask another question, Dr. Lyons said stiffly, "I suppose you want to know where I was on the three nights in question."

Neal let his eyebrows rise. "I have no reason at this point to ask you, but if you'd like to tell me I won't argue. It would be helpful if you could establish your whereabouts on one of the three evenings."

"But of course I'm not a suspect," Dr. Lyons said ironically. He reached for a leather-bound calendar. "Dates?"

Neal gave them, although with little hope that the doctor would prove to have been out of town one of the days in question. The results were about what he expected: Dr. Lyons had a date on the Saturday Kathleen Madsen was attacked, although he'd parted from the lady by eleven. On the Tuesday evening Chelsea Cahill was raped, he'd attended a meeting of the Puget Sound Dahlia Association, going directly home afterwards. His large house on a bluff above the river was in a neighborhood of five-acre estates, which meant no neighbor could have seen him. He assumed he'd been home—alone—on the third evening in question. In other words, he had no witnesses to his whereabouts for any of the pertinent times.

Neal closed his notebook and rose to his feet. "Thank you for your cooperation, Dr. Lyons. I apologize for having to bother you."

The doctor was gracious, considering. As were most of the other men whom Neal interviewed that week. Only a few refused to talk to him at all once they realized the reason for his visit.

He was able to eliminate most of the married men as potential suspects, which helped. One divorced father, the manager of the local Safeway store, had his kids on alternate weekends, including the Saturday in question. He'd grinned ruefully. "Took 'em to see *Lassie* at the Everett Nine. Then we stopped at the Dairy Queen. We were home, oh, around midnight. And then I had to give my youngest a bath, because she'd dropped her chocolate-dipped cone in her lap. Believe me, that evening is lodged in my memory."

One phone call to the Dairy Queen, and bingo. An alibi. "Then I won't even ask you about the other dates," Neal had said with relief.

Too bad there weren't more devoted single fathers. The rest had all claimed to be home, sans kids, on those particular nights.

Neal made charts that he kept posted on the wall above his desk where he could stare at them in idle moments. Lines bisected where the women had factors in common: people they knew, businesses where they shopped, employers. The fact that two of the three were teachers kept prodding at him, but he couldn't make it mean anything. Unlike most people in this town, Lisa Pyne and Chelsea Cahill hadn't even known each other. One worked at the high school, the other at the elementary school on the outskirts of Pilchuck. And the third victim had nothing to do with the schools except that her son attended the high school. She didn't even volunteer, hadn't in years, not since her son had left second grade.

"I do coach a girls' soccer team," she'd told Neal.

Grasping for straws, he'd asked if they practiced on a school field. No, they used the soccer field over by the river.

Thanks to Dr. Lyons, Neal had now added a chart on hobbies. He'd spent another hour with each of the three women pursuing their interests. The only real gardener among the lot was Kathleen Madsen, who maintained an enormous vegetable garden. Neal remembered the faint sneer in the ophthalmologist's voice: *She may grow tomatoes or something*.

Hell, he thought, studying his chart. This wasn't a murder case where a dahlia grower was killing off his competition. The only hobby this bastard had was violent sexual satisfaction.

Too bad he hadn't insisted on a particular kind of music. That would have given the investigation a place to start. But clearly he didn't give a damn what music was playing, as long as the woman danced. Even the dancing in and of itself probably wasn't what mattered; it was the control, the humiliation. Maybe a woman dancing was erotic to him. Maybe he'd experienced a childhood trauma when he'd been forced to dance himself, or had seen his mother forced, or...

Neal shook his head. That wasn't the way to approach this. Motivation rarely was. Who the hell could understand why some sicko did what he did? It was details that counted: times, places, fingerprints, footprints. They were like a mathematical equation; they always added up. Sooner or later the perp would make a mistake, if he hadn't already. Neal's job was to understand the mistake when he saw it.

"GOL, MOM. Shouldn't you dress up a little more?" Abby studied her doubtfully.

"I'm trying to get into the spirit of the thing," Karen told her daughter. She glanced down at her snug denim skirt and gleaming black cowboy boots. She actually thought her choice of outfit was clever, considering the man who was taking her out. Besides, she hadn't looked too bad when she scrutinized herself in the mirror on the back of her bedroom door.

But her daughter asked, "Spirit of what thing? We're going to see *Charlotte's Web*."

"Never mind," Karen said airily. "You wouldn't understand."

When the doorbell rang, she found Neal standing on her front porch in clean jeans, a cream-colored Western shirt with pearl snaps and his usual boots. His gleaming belt buckle, depicting a bald eagle with spread wings, was heavy enough to make a lesser man stoop. Maybe he'd won it in a rodeo. Or maybe he wore it to stop bullets.

His gaze moved over her and one corner of his mouth lifted. "You dressed up special for me."

"Sure." She spun in a circle. "What do you think?"

He hooked his thumbs in his jeans' pockets and drawled, "I always wanted me a little country gal. Why don't we go line dancin' next weekend?"

"I'd stomp all over your toes. Besides—" Karen made a face "—dancing doesn't appeal to me a whole lot right now."

A muscle in one cheek jerked. "Sorry. I didn't mean to remind you."

Abby made her usual bouncy entrance, well-timed for once. "Hi, Mr. Rowland. I think it's radical that Krista's in the play. Especially being Charlotte. It was really brave of her to try out, don't you think?"

A trace of amusement returned to his eyes. "I do think. Shall we go?"

In the car he introduced his ten-year-old son. Michael looked extraordinarily like his father probably had before life marked him. Karen looked at the deep lines that furrowed the police chief's brow and wondered why he'd chosen a kind of work that scarred a man's soul the way his did.

He glanced at her as he backed the car out. "I hope you weren't expecting to be wined and dined with style. I promised Michael we wouldn't go anywhere with 'gross' food."

"I didn't expect style," Karen assured him. "Not with two kids along."

From the back seat Abby said indignantly, "You don't have to talk about me like I'm some little baby or something."

"I'm not a baby, either!" Michael declared.

"Well, great," Karen said. She smiled brightly over her shoulder at the kids. "How about that new Thai restaurant in Everett? Do you think we have time to make it there, Neal? Something really spicy would hit the spot."

Abby rolled her eyes. "Mo-om."

"Dad!"

It was the first time Karen had heard Neal laugh. His chuckle was deep and rich, momentarily lighting his shadowed eyes with amusement. "Can't you tell when someone's giving you a hard time?" he asked the boy.

Too quickly Michael said, "Yeah, sure I can."

Neal's glance at Karen was disarmingly intimate. "The café okay?"

"You bet." Why did it feel so natural to smile back at him?

The kids set the tone of the conversation over dinner, but Karen had a good time, anyway. She enjoyed Abby's company, and Michael was obviously a nice kid, even though he still seemed to be at the stage where he thought the height of humor was a loud belch.

Abby was friendlier to him and more tolerant than she might have been if she'd had a brother of her own. They went off happily together when Neal gave them a handful of quarters to use on the video games in back.

Karen became immediately self-conscious. She didn't date often, and the police chief wasn't the kind of man she'd have chosen, anyway. She leaned toward intellectuals, wiry, intense types who wanted to talk until two in the morning, not the kind of man who made her think of sweat and powerful muscles and primal urges. Her body was definitely interested, but the thinking side of her was wondering what they would talk about. Vietnam? Motorcycle races?

The kids had no sooner vanished into the back when Neal said, "I've been meaning to ask you something. You know gardeners, right?"

"Uh, is this a trick question?"

"No, I'm serious." He laid an arm along the back of the booth behind her. "Can you tell anything about people by the kind of garden they have? Or the kind of plants they like?"

She ignored his arm. "You mean, could you look at a garden and predict the owner's character? Like someone who has perfectly spaced marigolds is uptight, while somebody who lets plants flop any which way is relaxed? Is that what you're getting at?"

"Yeah." He ran his other hand across his chin as he contemplated Karen. It made a rasping sound that shouted *male* and sent a shiver through her. After a moment he made a decision of some kind and said carefully, "I was interviewing somebody. He grows dahlias..."

"Henry Lyons."

She had the sense she'd disconcerted him. "Is he the only dahlia fanatic around here?"

Karen looked away. She ran her finger over the damp side of her water glass. "No, probably not. He, uh, came into the nursery the other day." She hesitated. "I've known him for a couple of years, but now... Oh, shoot, I can't help thinking about Lisa and Chelsea every time I see a man who happens to be tall and brown-eyed. Especially when he dated one of them."

"Two."

She turned her head sharply. "Two?"

His voice was expressionless. "Miss Pyne and Miss Cahill."

"Chelsea I knew about, but Lisa, too?" Karen drew a long breath. "Then it *was* Henry's dahlias that got you thinking."

Neal took a sip of his coffee. "Uh-huh."

"Well." Karen gave it some thought. "Yes, I suppose you could draw some conclusions. I'm just not sure what they are. I think my earlier point is valid. Somebody who is a neat freak, really big on organization, isn't going to have a cottage garden." She waved her hand. "Too messy. The cottage-garden kind will probably have books stacked all over inside his house, too. Maybe he won't care if the breakfast dishes don't get in the dishwasher before dinnertime. But as to kinds of plants..." She trailed off, then realized he must have an idea of his own. "What was it you were thinking?"

His big shoulders moved in an easy shrug. "I've seen dahlias at the fair. They're pretty big and gaudy. I got to wondering whether a person who is basically lacking in confidence would overcompensate by choosing something so..."

"Tasteless? Unnatural?"

That slow smile curled his mouth. "Yeah. I was trying to think of a tactful way of putting it."

"Oh, why? I'm never tactful." Damn, it was hard to resist that smile.

Which widened, becoming wicked and mischievous in a way that let her see the boy he'd once been. "No," he said in that rough voice, "I guess 'tactful' isn't a word I would've applied to you."

But she was already thinking. "So your theory is that confident people go for a subtler effect. I suppose that means the gardeners who write those books on the effects of foliage are bursting with confidence. And...oh, Lord." She stopped, her eyes widening. "It gets worse. What about Japanese gardens, with a few twisted trees and lots of raked gravel?"

"I guess those gardeners cross right over into being arrogant," Neal said, shaking his head as though in sorrow.

"Ye gods." Karen pretended to look horrified. "I love hydrangeas. You know, with those huge bluish purple heads? And the old roses with all those petals packed in and that fragrance that knocks you out at a hundred yards?" She finished gloomily, "I must be crying out for attention."

His laugh was rueful. "Sounds pretty damn silly put that way. Forget my theory."

"No. Maybe I *am* trying to get attention."

His face went still. "You have mine."

Her heart gave an uncomfortable bump, which she decided to ignore. "Now *I'm* trying to be serious," she said, her frown reproving. "Of course it's possible that our gardens say something about us. Doesn't everything we do? I just don't see how it's going to help you catch a rapist."

The grooves in his cheeks deepened. "Hell, I don't know how, either. I guess I'm desperate."

Chilled, Karen said, "There hasn't been another rape?"

"No. Not unless the victim didn't call the police." He took his hand from behind her to rub the back of his neck. "It's been almost two weeks. The three rapes were within a week of each other."

"Maybe he isn't a local. Could be he's moved on."

Neal grunted. "Or maybe you were right and all the attention *has* scared him off."

Despite Neal's generally unrevealing face, she read his expression without any trouble. "Why don't you think so?"

"Because he's nuts," Neal said bluntly. "A rational man might be scared off. Right now this town has more guns per capita than Tombstone during the shootout at the OK Corral. But a man who puts women through hoops like this son of a bitch is doing, who rapes them and hurts them, isn't rational. He's got this urge inside, and it's dragging him along, making him feed it. He's not going to stop now." Neal shook his head. "He can't."

Karen felt a squeeze of fear that kept her silent. She didn't know if she was glad or sorry when Abby and Michael came back to the table.

"Dad, can I have some more quarters?"

Neal glanced at his watch. "Nope. We'd better get this show on the road. Your sister will never forgive us if we're not in the front row."

Actually they ended up three rows back. The auditorium filled quickly for this first of four performances. When Neal showed no inclination to chat, Karen tuned into the conversation of some teenagers in front of her.

The boy half sat on the back of a seat in the front row, so that he faced Karen. His baggy pants hung low on his hips. He wore—Karen counted—four gold hoop earrings in each ear. Plus one in his eyebrow. The girl, sitting directly in front of Karen, kept flipping her long wavy dark hair over her shoulder.

"So, wha'd'ya think?" the boy asked. "I mean, afterward, we could, you know, go do something. Like..." He pumped his hips graphically.

Karen, waiting for the girl's response, resisted the impulse to cover Abby's eyes.

"God, Chris," the girl said. She tossed her hair over her shoulder. "I mean, my *parents* are here."

Really. Karen sneaked a look around. Did she know the parents? If so, she might suggest they send their daughter off to a Swiss boarding school.

When she glanced at Neal, she lost interest in the teenagers. The police chief was scanning the crowd, his gaze stopping to assess each man. His face was completely expressionless.

Unsettled, Karen looked toward the stage just in time for the lights to dim.

The curtain opened to a barnyard setting. After a few rustles and catcalls, the audience settled into silence. In the darkness, Karen almost forgot that it was Neal's shoulder brushing hers, his forearm sharing the armrest, his low chuckle at Wilbur the pig's antics. But not quite.

Krista was extraordinarily good, especially considering that she was a shy fourteen-year-old and a newcomer to town. In black tights and with her face blackened, she ruled over Wilbur and the other animals, her intelligence and sweetness shining through, just as Charlotte's did in the book. There was obviously more to Neal's daughter than met the eye, Karen realized thoughtfully. For the first time, she wondered about the girl's mother—Neal's wife. All Karen knew was that she was dead.

After the curtain calls, still applauding enthusiastically, Abby said, "Come on, let's go backstage."

"Lead on," Neal said. He was grinning like any proud father. "Hey, she was good, wasn't she?"

"Wonderful!" Karen told him. "The whole production was amazingly professional. I'm really impressed with what Harvey's done with these kids."

Waiting for an opening to join the crowd that filtered out to the hallway, Neal raised a brow. "You mean, he doesn't have to show *Wolf* to get them to shape up?"

"Not unless he wants them to see Jack Nicholson at work."

Neal stepped out into the aisle and waited for her to go ahead. Abby and Michael had already inserted themselves into the crowd and disappeared toward the exits. In Karen's ear, Neal murmured, "Tell me Harvey doesn't happen to be six feet tall and have brown eyes."

"You haven't met him?"

He casually put a hand on her lower back to steer her. "Nope."

"He's about five five, chubby, with flaming red hair and bright blue eyes."

"Thank God for small favors. No pun intended." They emerged into the relative openness of the wide hall, and Neal looked around. "Okay, now where?"

"I don't know if they'll actually let us in, but we can try. This way, I think."

Nobody was bothering to guard the door. Backstage was a wild celebration, kids laughing and talking and doing improvisational dances as they gloried in their successful opening night. Cleaning off her makeup, Krista accepted congratulations with quiet smiles. It took her only a minute to be ready to go.

She climbed into the back of Neal's car with Abby and Michael.

"You were fabulous!" Abby enthused. "You should get an agent. I bet if you auditioned, you could act in some commercials and stuff. They pay tons! Maybe you could even be in a series. Like Beverly Hills 90210. Think how cool that'd be." She stopped, apparently to marvel at the idea.

Krista said softly, "Thanks. But I don't think I'm that good."

"What do you mean, you're not that good? You're *great*. Wouldn't you like to live in Hollywood and be a big star?"

"I lived in L.A. I like it here. I don't want to go back."

Glancing at Neal, Karen saw a fleeting oddly intense expression cross his face. It made her wonder what he and the kids had given up to come here. Or what they had run from.

He took Karen and Abby home, insisting on walking them to the door. Abby wanted Krista to come in, but Neal squelched the idea.

"I have to work tomorrow," he said gruffly, and his daughter settled back in her seat without argument or apparent resentment. Karen wondered what it was like for a girl that age to be motherless.

When Karen unlocked her front door, Neal stepped in behind her. He stiffened at the thump that came from the direction of the kitchen.

"Don't worry," Karen said. "That's just our cat hopping off the refrigerator to come and say hi. She's, um..."

Maggie strolled into the entry hall.

"Obese?" he suggested.

"Plump and cozy."

"Ah." He glanced around, and Karen was reminded that except for picking her up this afternoon, he'd never been here before. "I don't suppose you'd like me to look under your beds and in your closets before I go."

Abby batted her eyelashes. "I'll go look under my own bed. Thanks for dinner, Mr. Rowland." She gave her mother a saucy smile and pretended to yawn. "Night, Mom," she said, and disappeared into her bedroom. The door closed firmly.

Karen could have killed her. She gritted her teeth and, ignoring her daughter's desertion, said, "I think I'll check out my own closets, too. But thanks for the offer, Neal."

He frowned. "Are you being careful?"

She met his eyes. "Yes. Don't worry."

His mouth twisted, and then before she could step back he took her chin and lifted it. She blinked, parted her lips to say something—God knew what—but before she managed a sound Neal was kissing her. Hard. Hungrily.

She knew herself well enough to understand that she'd wanted this, been waiting for it. With a soft needy sound she kissed him just as hungrily, clutching at wide shoulders as he groaned and backed her against the wall.

By the time he lifted his head, they were both breathing in shallow gasps. His eyes glittered down at her, and his voice scraped her eardrums like his shaven jaw had her soft skin.

"We need to take this up another night."

He didn't bother to wait for her response. Probably figured she was bowled over, just because she'd let herself warm her hands by the fire for a minute, so to speak.

His only other remark was a command, barked over his shoulder. "Lock up."

Karen stuck out her tongue at his back.

She also threw the dead bolt.

CHAPTER SIX

NEAL RARELY FOLLOWED his impulses without question, but he didn't bother arguing with the one that sent him to the deli for two sandwiches, muffins and pop, then directed him to the Cottage Garden Nursery. He needed a break from staring at those damned charts. Karen Lindberg might irritate him, but she was smart and observant.

And sexy. If a man's idea of sexy wasn't softness and sweet acceptance. Which Neal's always had been.

At the outdoor tables a white-haired woman wanted to help him.

"Thanks," he said, "but I'm looking for Karen."

She waved toward the building. "In the office."

The office was a tiny cluttered corner room heaped with catalogs, one wall covered with a bookcase filled with tattered gardening books. He found Karen hunched over a computer, frowning fiercely at the screen. Her bangs stuck straight up from fingers having been run through them. Mud smeared one cheekbone, and the hands resting on the keyboard had dirt embedded around the fingernails.

None of which diminished the qualities that had drawn him here. She was a woman of intelligence, energy, passion, even anger. Nobody could react passively to her. When she didn't make him mad as hell, she tweaked some sexual chord in him. He kept imagining what she would be like in bed. Her ability to make him feel alive was damned seductive.

Only because he needed a change, he tried to tell himself. Because he couldn't face a woman who reminded him of his wife.

But something told him it wasn't that simple.

Trying to wipe the frown off his face, he asked, "Lunch?"

She whipped around, clapping a hand to her chest when she saw him. "Oh. You."

He would've been insulted if he hadn't understood what she meant. "Jumpy?"

Ms. Flowerwoman wrinkled her nose at him. "Wouldn't you be?"

He leaned against the door frame. "I don't think you need to worry in broad daylight when you have employees around. Doesn't fit his—"

"Pattern. Yeah, yeah, I know." Her chair squeaked as she stood up. "Trouble is, three women doesn't seem like a big enough sample to me. Maybe by the time he rapes ten women, some variation will have shown up."

That had occurred to Neal. But he said only, "I don't like you being here alone."

"I'm not very often."

All it took was once, but she knew that. And he didn't want to think about it.

He lifted the bag that held the food. "Have time for a break?"

Karen's smile, for once uncomplicated by mockery or cynicism, reminded him of her daughter's: sweet enough to be unintentionally tempting. "Oh, bless you. I'm starved. I forgot to pack a lunch." She stabbed a button on her computer and the screen went blank. "I have a table out behind the greenhouse."

Along the way they passed a white-haired man who was laboriously lifting a heavy potted plant onto a flatbed cart. Neal nodded toward him. "Do you want to wait on this customer first?"

"Hmm? Oh, no, that's Bill. He works here."

Neal could almost hear the creaks as they passed the elderly man, who was bending down for another plant. "Good God," Neal murmured out of one side of his mouth. "Are you robbing the nursing home?"

Karen grinned, leading the way into a long greenhouse filled with flats from which tiny seedlings of some kind emerged. "The seniors center," she informed him. "I've been relying on teenagers for extra help, which I think is a contradiction in terms. If I've ever heard an oxymoron, it's the words 'teenager' and 'help.' For everything useful they do, they foul up twice. Or don't show at all. Anyway, I was talking to a neighbor who must be eighty if she's a day, and she still has the most beautiful garden. She moves slowly, but she's death on weeds. Light bulb. I called the seniors center, they had a dozen names, and I have three new part-time employees. None of them wants to work enough hours to require benefits, I tell them what to do and they do it without elaborate instructions, and they're all knowledgeable enough to advise customers."

She and Neal emerged from the warm damp greenhouse to a small cobblestone courtyard furnished with a wrought-iron table and chairs. Spiky daisylike flowers bloomed profusely in pinks and purples from tall clay pots.

Neal pulled up a chair. "Maybe I ought to call the seniors center. Think they could provide a few good cops?"

"Darn right. Unless they had to chase a bad guy on foot. But maybe they would never get into that position, 'cause they'd use their brains, instead of brawn, in the first place. Less testosterone." She watched, bright-eyed, as he opened the bag. "So, what's on the menu?"

"Raw meat," Neal said dryly. "We cops need a steady diet of blood to keep up that hormone production."

She tore her gaze away from the food. "Don't tell me I hurt your feelings?"

"Nah." He handed her a turkey sandwich. "My feelings don't get hurt easily." He took out two cans of pop. "Cola or orange?"

"I've already had my fourth cup of coffee. I'll take the orange."

Handing it to her, he said, "Tell you the truth, I always hate to send young cops out on the street. That first year or two, they're dangerous. Maybe it is hormones."

Ms. Flowerwoman gave an odd twisted smile. "No twenty-year-old, female or male, thinks very clearly. Didn't you do dumb things?"

"Volunteered to go to Vietnam. Doesn't get any dumber than that."

"You volunteered?" she said incredulously. "Why on earth . . . ?"

It wasn't his favorite subject. "I told you my brother was killed over there," he said briefly. "I wanted vengeance."

Her eyes were unnervingly steady. "Did you get it?"

"Hell no." He nodded at her sandwich. "Food okay?"

She took the hint. "It's great."

His weariness was catching up with him. He ate slowly, not feeling hungry but knowing he should be. He tilted his head back to enjoy the sun on his face, and his eyes kept wanting to drift closed. Too many late nights, too many sleepless hours once he did get to bed.

For the first time he could remember, Karen was restful company. He could feel her gaze on him, but she seemed to have no inclination to talk. Maybe that daughter of hers talked her out. Maybe she'd opened the nursery for the solitude.

Still, she was the one who broke the silence at last. "You have nice kids," she said in an idle way that didn't demand any more response than a grunt.

But then, he was the one who'd come calling, so he figured he owed her more than that. Sitting up, he took a long swallow of pop in hopes the caffeine would jolt him awake. "Yeah, I do, don't I?" He surprised himself by opening a door he always kept firmly closed. Gruffly he said, "Sometimes I don't think I deserve them. I hope if there's a heaven up there, their mother got the credit."

Very softly Karen asked, "Do they miss her terribly?"

Wrenched by unresolved feelings of anger and loss, he cleared his throat. "God, I don't know. I suppose they do, but it's been two and a half years now."

Karen watched him, tiny creases between her brows. "Are they why you moved here?"

"Yeah. Small-town life. No crime." His laugh was mirthless. "I wanted to have more time for them. Instead, I'm lucky to get home early enough to say good-night."

And it was taking a toll. Not with Krista; gentle like her mother, she'd never been a problem. But Michael hadn't wanted to move and wasn't at an age to recognize the greater good. Neal remembered promising damn near anything in return for cooperation and a positive attitude: he would coach his son's soccer team, teach him to rope, help him build a computer. He hadn't crossed his fingers behind his back, but he might as well have. Soccer season was halfway over now, and Neal had barely managed to attend Michael's games. Preoccupied with the rapist, he'd been a lousy father. But if he didn't nail the bastard, his daughter might be one of the victims. Catch-22.

Karen's eyes held unexpected understanding. Even gentleness. "You can't be two people, no matter how hard you try. And believe me, I've tried."

His curiosity stirred. What kind of man had Karen Lindberg loved? Had she shredded her husband and then discarded him? Or were her prickles belated defense against a man who'd hurt her?

"Doesn't Abby see her father?" Neal asked.

"Two weeks a year." The gutsy woman sitting across from him tried to smile, but it didn't quite come off. "Funny thing is, she's a nicer kid than some I know who have two parents. So who can tell?"

Her vulnerability rocked him; he didn't want to think of her as needing anyone else. "Maybe it's different when a parent dies."

Karen crumbled her muffin, concentrating on it, instead of him. "In a strange way, I wonder if it might not be easier. That abandonment isn't voluntary. And with divorce, we don't let our kids grieve openly; instead, we keep telling them that really Mom and Dad both love them, that they'll still have two parents." Her own laugh was no more convincing than his. "How often does that happen?"

He thought of the kids he'd seen in the line of duty: the sad faces, the scared faces, the dead faces. "If a kid has one parent who loves him, he's lucky."

"There you have it." Her smile was wry. "Your kids are lucky."

"I'll be sure to tell them that."

The silence was less peaceful this time. He knew what was coming.

"Are you getting anywhere?"

They'd had this conversation before. He answered just as he had the last time. "I don't know. I can't even say I've got any real suspects. Half a dozen men have earned a closer look, but I can't find anyone with priors. Except maybe a kid at the high school, but . . . oh, hell." He scraped his chair forward so that he could prop his feet up on another one. "He ought to look like a good suspect, but my gut feeling is that he's not the rapist. The whole thing's not his style."

He half expected Karen to jump all over him, want a good reason he hadn't hauled in a seventeen-year-old with a rape prior.

Instead, not looking at him, she said, "I don't suppose you can give me his name."

Neal told himself this was why he'd come. In a town the size of Pilchuck, it wasn't any secret who he'd talked to. What he needed now was to hear the gossip, the things no one else would tell him.

"You know everybody. Can we talk about some of these people? Confidentially?"

Her clear eyes met his. "You mean, you want the dirt."

"I want the dirt," he agreed.

"And me to keep my mouth shut."

"I don't want a minor who was never charged with a crime to be labeled a rapist."

She mulled it over, nodded.

"Mark Griggs."

"His father's an SOB."

"So I hear."

Karen brooded for a moment. "I don't know Mark well. Thank God. Jeez, what if Abby fell for someone like him?"

Neal didn't hesitate. "Forbid the relationship."

Her laugh held real amusement. "You've got to be kidding. Talk about asking for it!"

Grimly Neal said, "What, you'd let him cuff your daughter around? Maybe rape her?"

The laughter fled. "Did he really?"

"Girl recanted," Neal said tersely. "Without her testimony, there wasn't enough to take him to court. I'll tell you, though, nobody I talked to had any doubt about it."

"Creep." Karen pressed her lips together and thought some more. "But date rape is...opportunistic. I've watched him play football. Mark isn't... patient."

"My feeling exactly," Neal agreed. "A little needling and he explodes. The bastard we're looking for is stalking these women. He's waiting until the perfect moment. I just can't see a hotheaded, overmuscled kid being our man."

Karen shook her head firmly. "No."

Neal named other names. She told him what she knew and what she'd heard. Most of what she said confirmed his own hunches; none of it seemed relevant to a violent perverted crime.

They talked about the two victims whose names she knew. Their relationships with coworkers, with men. If Karen was privy to any dirt about them, she didn't share it. His instincts said there wasn't any. Those two, along with the third victim, were exactly what they appeared to be: attractive, friendly, decent women.

"Was there anything different about the first rape?" Karen asked at last. "Or the woman?"

"She's a little older than the other two. Thirty-six. Divorced, and has a teenage son. That sets her apart to start with. The others live alone. She doesn't. But the boy plays select soccer, which means he's gone a lot. He was at a tournament in Yakima the night she was attacked. She usually goes, but she'd had to work that Saturday. The boy drove over with a teammate's parents." Anger and frustration tightened Neal's voice. "Somehow the son of a bitch knew she was alone. He walked up and rang her doorbell. She opened the door and he was in before she could react."

"He already had on the mask?"

"Yep. Her front porch is screened by shrubs. Can't be seen well from the street. He could've been buck naked and nobody would have noticed."

Karen gave a small shudder that tightened his gut, took away the abstract in what they were talking about. She fit the profile: pretty, single, knew everybody in town. "Everybody" meant the rapist. What if he was stalking Karen already?

She didn't appear to notice his sudden tension. Instead, she asked thoughtfully, "Everything else was the same? Her description of him?"

"Navy blue knit ski mask." He had those damn charts memorized. "Brown eyes. Tall. Black sweatshirt and jeans. Running shoes, white with a black stripe."

"Color-coordinated."

"Except for the ski mask."

"True," she conceded.

"One oddity." He frowned, remembering. "She said she kept catching a whiff of something sweet. 'Sickly sweet' were her words."

"After-shave?"

"She says not."

"On his breath? Maybe whatever he'd had for dessert?"

Neal sighed and ran a hand over his jaw. "Hell, she might have been tasting her own dessert coming back up her throat."

He glanced her way in time to see her hide revulsion. And no wonder. Damn. He'd been talking to her as if she were another cop.

"I'd better go," he said abruptly, taking his feet off the chair and gathering the trash.

In a very small voice that brought his head up sharply, Karen asked, "Did he . . . did he kiss them?"

Considering what the bastard *had* done to those women, a kiss was a hell of a thing to be Karen's breaking point. But he could see why it might be. Sex was biological, uncivilized, at its heart still almost brutal. But a kiss was something different. Personal. As often tender as passionate.

The distress in her wide blue eyes made him swear as he shoved his chair back and stood. "No. He didn't kiss any of them."

"Oh." She nibbled on her lower lip. "I suppose, with the ski mask..."

He spoke roughly. "Rapists don't usually kiss the women." Instead, they force them to do unspeakable things. But she already knew that, too.

Karen sat very still for another moment, her head bowed, gathering her poise. By the time she looked up, she was herself again. The angle of her chin defied him to acknowledge her moment of weakness.

"I'd better go," Neal repeated.

She gave him a sassy smile. "The lunch was great. The conversation lacked something."

"I wouldn't say that." He sounded stiff. "You were very helpful." Good God. Were his feelings hurt?

"I'm sorry." She came around the table, her eyes soft. "I didn't mean that the way it sounded. I was, um..."

"Making light of something you wish wasn't deadly serious. I know." He had an itch to touch her, didn't argue with this impulse any more than he had the one that had brought him here. Trouble was, he could see in her big, china blue eyes that she felt the itch, too.

His hand brought her chin up even higher, slid irresistibly down her slender throat as he bent his head. His mouth was almost touching hers when she muttered, "I must be nuts."

He kissed her, lingered, lifted his mouth. "I'm that bad?"

Breathless, she said, "You're a cop."

This time her lips were softer, welcoming under his. When their mouths parted, she drew in a shaky breath.

He explored her small neat ear. "So?"

Even in a whisper, she could sound pugnacious. "My parents had to bail me out of jail when I was sixteen."

He kissed her closed eyelids, her cheekbones, her jaw. She was so damned fragile, small high breasts flattened against his chest, narrow back straight under his splayed hand. Deceptive packaging, he thought. And asked flippantly, "Murder your boyfriend?"

"An antiwar march." She tried pulling away from him. "I threw a rock at a policeman."

He laughed, couldn't help it. "What do you weigh, maybe 110 pounds? Bet he felt like a bully."

"He *was* a bully. He was using his stick on this Vietnam vet in a wheelchair."

"What's your point?"

"My point?" She yanked free and glared at him, her gaze outraged. "He deserved more than a rock!"

"I'm not that cop," Neal said patiently.

Karen blinked. Emotions flitted across her fine-boned face. At last she said stubbornly, "I don't let other people decide for me what's right and what's wrong."

It finally sank in. The kiss had panicked her. She was trying to convince him that he didn't want her.

"Will you have dinner with me tomorrow night?" he asked.

She stared incredulously at him. "I don't think you listened to a word I said."

Neal crossed his arms. "Now my feelings *are* hurt. I take it that cops are supposed to like spineless women who wouldn't know right from wrong if it tickled their painted toenails."

"That's not what I said."

"Damn right it is." He distanced himself, hardened his voice. Made sure he saw the prickles more than the fragility underneath. "I'd like to get to know you. Obviously you already know me. Forget I asked."

He was brushing by her when she grabbed his sleeve. "Neal."

He stopped, muscles locked, and waited without looking at her. Good God. He was acting like a sixteen-year-old whose dream girl had refused his invitation to the prom.

"I'm sorry. I don't know what gets into me. I guess I *want* to believe my own prejudices. It's...unsettling to have them thrown in my face."

"I won't push you," he said.

"I'm not afraid of you."

He turned his head. "Aren't you?"

She struggled some more. "You're just...unexpected for me."

His tone was dry. "Lady, you aren't exactly in my game plan, either."

"Then why...?"

"Damned if I know." He moved his shoulders to release his tension. "I've already said let's forget it. Thanks for the conversation."

Her voice stopped him before he'd taken two steps. "I'd like to have dinner with you. If you don't mind going to the school-board meeting first."

Neal turned. She was smiling. And damned if that smile wasn't another challenge.

"Last meeting before the election. It's time you take sides, don't you think?"

"The police chief doesn't take sides," he told her. None of his intense relief could be heard.

"But a parent does."

He wanted to kiss her again. Didn't quite dare. "I wouldn't mind seeing you in action a second time," he said lazily. "There's a certain thrill to the spectacle."

Her chin rose another fraction of an inch. "Six-thirty?"

"Six-fifteen. We want front-row seats."

"I WENT BACK to work today," Chelsea said.

The telephone receiver braced with her shoulder, Karen squirmed into a clean bra. Her laciest. "How did it go?"

Her friend was silent for a moment. Then, "I cried. It was the dumbest thing, but there they were, twenty-four little faces all looking up at me, all of them grinning, and suddenly I realized tears were running down my cheeks. I probably scared the daylights out of them."

Karen closed her eyes. "Oh, Chelsea . . ."

"I made a joke out of it. Which mostly worked, except that Jason—he's the attention-deficit kid who drives me so nuts—picked me a bouquet of dandelions at recess. Can you believe it?"

Karen had to blink fiercely to keep from crying herself. "That's sweet."

"Maybe he's turned over a new leaf. He was so co-operative the rest of the day."

Karen had to laugh, though her throat stung. "The eternal optimist."

"How can a kindergarten teacher be anything else?" Chelsea asked logically enough.

"You have a point." Karen resumed her hunt for a runless pair of nylons. "So, are you home or still at your parents?"

She was immediately sorry she'd asked. The life left Chelsea's voice. "I'm afraid to go home. I tell myself I won't be once the police catch him, but... I just keep remembering how helpless I felt."

"Why don't you stay with Abby and me for a while?" Karen offered on a sudden impulse. "You'd have to sleep on the pullout couch, lumps and all, but you could pretend you're still broke and in college."

Her friend gave a watery chuckle. "That's as nice as Jason's flowers. Bless you, but no. You and Abby are a family. And it's not as though I don't have my own family right here."

"To drive you crazy."

"Well, there is that. I'll call if I get really desperate."

"Okay," Karen conceded. "But the offer's open any time. I mean that. And you know Abby adores you."

"Mmm." A smile sounded in Chelsea's soft voice. "Have fun tonight."

"Have fun? Oh, Lord." Karen focused on the panty hose dangling from her hand. She gave a panicky glance at the clock. "I'd better get a move on. I don't want to be late to the school-board meeting."

"Right. Or your romantic dinner with our esteemed police chief."

"The things I get myself into." Karen was gathering up one leg of the panty hose. "See you, Chels."

Five minutes. She squirmed into the hose, dropped a dress over her head—a dress, for God's sake!—and applied makeup with a freer hand than usual. For once, thank heavens, her hair cooperated, and she'd earlier applied polish to finger- and toenails. Gazing at herself in the mirror, she decided that this was as good as it was going to get. After all, he wasn't twenty years old, either.

Which was not necessarily a bad thing, she realized the moment she let him in. Why did a few lines age a woman, when all they did was add character to a man's face? A young man's beauty was closer to androgynous. Nice, but less primitive in its effect on a woman. Neal had the bulk of a male in his prime, and the deep grooves from nose to mouth and between his brows that hinted at suffering. The Neanderthal look must be growing on her, because her body's reaction to the sight of him was all positive.

Positive, that is, if the idea of an affair with the police chief had been a good one. She hadn't made up her mind about that yet.

As if her mind had anything to do with the way he made her feel.

His gaze flicked over her, leaving Karen's nerves quivering at its passage. "Pretty," he said at last, that extra roughness in an already gruff voice. "You surprise me every time I see you."

She tried to make light of his compliment. "Telling me I clean up better than you expected?"

"I wasn't sure you'd bother."

He understood her too well. She would have dressed up for the school board, but not this much. The red silk dress was for him.

"I try to be gracious in defeat," Karen said wryly.

He grinned, dazzling her. "I have yet to see you defeated."

"Wait'll after the election."

"I'll believe it when I see it." He glanced around. "Abby home?"

"No, she's spending the night with a friend. I didn't like the idea of leaving her alone." Karen picked up her purse. "Shall we?"

He waited on the porch while she carefully locked the front door. He opened the car door for her and closed it once she was settled in. Being treated like a dainty feminine creature flustered Karen. When he slid behind the wheel she said the first thing that came into her head. "What do you do with your kids? Are you comfortable leaving them alone?"

"Under normal circumstances I would be. They're good kids. Krista has been baby-sitting for other people for more than a year. But this last month I found a grandmotherly type who lives down the road. She stays with them nights when I'm gone."

Karen imagined Abby's reaction. "Krista doesn't resent being baby-sat?"

He raised his brows in surprise. "Resent? Krista? She doesn't question me."

If those weren't famous last words, Karen had never heard any. She only hoped she'd be present the day he discovered that even good little girls eventually kicked over the traces.

When he pulled into the nearly full parking lot in front of the district office building, Neal asked, "Anything special about tonight's meeting?"

"I go every month," Karen said. "Somebody has to keep an eye on 'em. But tonight's ought to be especially interesting. Were you here when we had the last bond issue on the ballot?"

Backing into a narrow slot, he said, "No, but I hear it failed."

In the silence when Neal turned off the ignition, Karen said, "Well, it failed because the district is determined to build the new middle school here in town. Because they have the land, it would be cheaper to put it here, which is why they're so stuck on the idea, but there are also plenty of drawbacks. Access is limited, and traffic is already a problem on Hawthorne with the elementary school there. With most of the growth north of town, it makes sense to put a school there, instead. People have been saying that, but the board doesn't want to hear them. So the issue has been put to the vote twice, and it's failed twice. Tonight they're to decide whether to try again or go back to the drawing board."

On the way in, she and Neal greeted people. Karen was glad to see the turnout; in fairness to the board, they'd been acting partly in a vacuum. The initial failed ballot was a shock all around; the district usually passed levies.

This politicking stuff was getting easier, she decided by the time she and Neal sat down on metal folding chairs. Not that she'd been doing any lobbying. All she'd done was chat, smile, introduce Rowland and ignore her opponent in the upcoming election.

Dennis Shafer was a local businessman who currently headed up the Chamber of Commerce. On both fronts, he and Karen clashed. He wanted economic development; she liked their small town because it was small. He was vociferously behind the school administration whatever they did, no matter the idiocy of the action. Karen was on the superintendent's blacklist.

The meeting heated up fast. The chairman, Harold Glover, gazed at the packed room over half-moon

reading glasses and said, "Well, I assume you folks are
here to give an opinion on the question before us—
whether to put our levy request on the ballot again
unchanged. Unless the other board members have an
objection, I suggest we open the meeting to the floor
without further ado." The other members shook their
heads. In the audience, hands shot up. Harold nodded to a woman halfway back. "Carol."

Carol lived on Hawthorne and was sick to death of
kids on their way to school trampling her flower beds
and breaking branches off her shrubs to make swords.
"They eat all the junk out of their lunches on the way
to school and drop the wrappings on my lawn," she
said plaintively. "A middle school would double the
foot traffic!"

"And the bus and car traffic." Another speaker
rose. "We already have a rush hour morning and afternoon."

Further increasingly angry opinions were proffered: traffic flow to the elementary school had been
poorly designed, which the board didn't want to admit, and with no other road access, a second school in
the same general location would double the nightmare.

The sole woman on the school board, Sandy Diehl,
leaned forward to her microphone. Her tone was patronizing. "I understand that the residents don't like
the traffic, but we have to remember it's confined to
two hours or less a day. And, correct me if I'm wrong,
there have been no accidents or even an unusually
large number of traffic tickets being given. Our parents aren't speeding down Hawthorne to deliver their
children to school."

A distinct growl came from somewhere in the audience. Karen figured the time had come for intervention. She raised her voice. "We have our police chief in the audience tonight. Perhaps he would comment."

She should have felt guilty, but didn't. Neal gave her a look, but rose to his feet. "As you know, I wasn't here last spring. I can only comment on these first few weeks of school. It's true that we haven't issued many tickets in that vicinity. We've been fortunate and not had an accident yet."

Sandy Diehl started to smile. Her satisfaction died stillborn when Neal continued.

"Which is not to say that before and after school hasn't turned into a headache. With heavy car and bus traffic and no crossing guards at most corners, kids are at risk. We do see speeding, although so far we're only issuing warnings in hopes of encouraging cooperation, instead of forcing it. Speaking for the police rather than as a voter, I'm hoping that new school goes in elsewhere." He sat down to a flurry of applause.

Karen leaned toward him and whispered, "Way to go, Chief."

"I'm not an attack dog," he muttered back.

"Hey, I didn't know which side you would come down on," she pointed out quietly.

Amusement lurked in his eyes. "I think you did."

She tuned in to the goings-on in time to hear Sandy Diehl remind the audience of the cost of building on the site the school owned versus the cost of acquiring land and going through the process of environmental-impact statements and permits.

"In a time when voters are increasingly reluctant to raise their taxes, I think the district is obligated to be cost conscious."

Karen stood up. "The board seems to have forgotten that the district owns a nice piece of land given by the developer of Beaver Creek Estates. Environmental-impact statements have already been completed. With the larger piece, we could build the playing fields our community needs, there are several roads to provide access, and that's where the growth in the district is taking place."

"But for the foreseeable future we'd be busing kids who can now walk. Increased transportation costs—"

"Could be offset by building the new bus barn on the land we own here in town, rather than having to buy more acreage. An alternative would be to build a new elementary school at Beaver Creek and remodel the existing building into a middle school, which would leave it centrally located."

Board members shot off figures; Karen retorted with her own. Dennis Shafer got into the act, attempting to put her in her place as a "mother who doesn't understand the complexities of the budget or state regulations." With a pleasant smile, Karen asked him when he'd employed more than two people or supervised a budget bigger than his print shop's. Threats were freely flung around: two of the school-board members were up for election this fall, and the levy could be soundly trounced again. Vicky Thomas stood up to sweetly remind the board that the Parent Group provided most of the manpower for drumming up the necessary votes; if they weren't behind the levy, the board might as well not bother submitting it.

Joining the applause, Karen said under her breath, "I swear that woman's growing on me."

In the end, the board agreed that an alternate site needed to be studied, and they appointed a committee. Karen would normally have stuck around to make sure they didn't pull a fast one in conducting other business, but tonight she was ready to go when most of the crowd stood up to leave.

The minute they walked out the door into the still-light evening, she started to get cold feet. She'd never really been alone with Neal, excluding the lunch out behind the greenhouse. So, okay, they were attracted to each other. If she was honest, she'd admit that the attraction was part of what made her edgy. But they were adults; they didn't have to act on it.

And, yeah, he'd been willing to come to the board meeting tonight. That showed a little give on his part. It didn't mean she should put blinders on. He'd let drop a few too many hints about his basic nature, such as tonight's comment about his daughter: *She doesn't question me.* Karen wondered what she was doing dating a man who obviously thought that the world was right because his daughter knew better than to question him. Had his wife?

Karen wasn't altogether sure whether her misgivings were finally crystallizing, or whether she was just plain scared. When he touched her, she felt out of control. She wasn't sure that, once he kissed her, she would do the smart thing.

Whatever that was.

Neal was a silent presence beside her as they crossed the parking lot. Karen shook a few more hands, told some of the newcomers to the school wars that she was glad they'd come and debated points with a couple of waverers. When he was greeted, Neal inclined his head, looking as if he'd have been more comfortable tipping a Stetson. To Karen, he didn't say a word until they reached his car.

Then he held open the passenger door and let his gaze rest on her face. "Tell me, Ms. Lindberg, do you ever quit fighting?"

CHAPTER SEVEN

APPARENTLY SHE NEVER DID quit fighting, Neal discovered.

Karen's instant reaction was to stop dead on the sidewalk and thrust out her chin. "I take it that's a criticism," she snapped.

"Aren't you jumping to conclusions?" He motioned toward the car's open door.

She crossed her arms and didn't budge. "Then what was it?"

The hell if he knew. He was too torn between admiring her willingness to take on the world and a chauvinistic belief that women should nurture, not engage in battle.

So he told her another small part of the truth. "I wish my wife had known how to fight."

It wasn't what Karen had expected to hear. Perplexity creased her brow as she scrutinized his face. Once she'd forgotten to be annoyed, the angle of her chin became less pugnacious. "Are you going to explain that?"

He moved his shoulders uneasily. "You can't really want to hear about my marriage."

Who was he kidding?

She gave a Cheshire-cat smile. "I'm nosy."

Neal leaned against the car and contemplated her. "All right," he said at last. "But I'm nosy, too. Goes with the trade."

Karen's inner debate showed: her curiosity about him against her reticence about her own past. Letting out a gusty sigh, she conceded, "Fair enough, I guess."

He again nodded at the open car door. Karen scooted in, treating him to a glimpse of long shapely legs before she pulled her hem down.

It took no more than that to awaken a vivid sexual image: those legs wrapped around his waist. He carefully closed her door and headed around the back of the car, swearing under his breath. What was his problem? Too long without a woman? Or did Ms. Flowerwoman alone have a talent for strumming the right chords?

Funny, too, because she didn't appear to try. Tonight was the first time he'd seen her in clothes that had been designed to tempt a man. Not that it mattered. Even when she wore jeans and a sweatshirt, he liked what he saw. He found it erotic that she was built on a scale to contrast with his body. Despite her obvious strength and competence, her underlying bone structure was delicate, and she was light on the padding. Those small breasts would fit in his palms; her waist could be spanned by his hands. She would ride him like a jockey did a Thoroughbred.

"Hell," he muttered before getting in behind the wheel.

As he started the car she asked, "Well, what did you think about the meeting?"

Thank God for small favors, Neal thought. This kind of conversation he could handle.

It stayed at that level all the way south on the interstate to the hillside town of Edmonds. They had apparently come to an unspoken agreement to hold off on the personal stuff. He'd chosen a restaurant with a spectacular view of the Puget Sound waterfront. As the waiter seated them by the window, a green-and-white car ferry backed away from the dock to make its trip across the sound to Kingston. Farther out on the breeze-riffled blue water were sailboats and a huge tanker following the shipping lane.

Neal and Karen had no sooner ordered than she took a sip of her Margarita and said, "You first."

"Why me?" he stalled.

"Because you're the one who was dropping provocative hints."

Provocative. God. How had he gotten into this? He was tempted to evade. But damned if he didn't realize he *wanted* to spill his guts to her. He had to find out whether she would end up despising him or going all tender and sympathetic.

Neal cleared his throat and said, "I'm going to sound like a bastard. Probably not for the first time." His fingers were drumming on the table, and he self-consciously curled them into a fist. "My wife—her name was Jennifer, actually Jenny, that's what I called her—uh, she was a lot like Krista. Looks, too."

"Pretty," Karen said softly.

"Yeah, she was pretty." But not by the end. Nothing about her death had been pretty. Neal turned his head to gaze blindly out the window and gave the bare facts as if by rote, "She died of cancer. Breast cancer, to start with. They didn't get it all and it spread. The whole thing was unbelievably fast. A year, and she was dead."

Even the words were stark and ugly, and he cursed himself for starting this. But it was too late.

Karen studied him with grave eyes. "And you think she didn't fight it. Is that what you meant?"

"Damned right that's what I meant!" He clenched his teeth. He had never said this aloud, and he was astonished at the anger that unfurled into a jagged blade in his chest. Explosively he said, "She knew she was going to die from the moment they found the lump. At first the doctors were optimistic, but nothing anybody could say convinced Jenny. She took to crying a lot. Dropped out of the things she'd been involved in. Hardly ever left the house." He remembered his anguish and her seeming indifference to it. She was the needy one, with no comfort for herself, much less for him. He would come home from work and find her just sitting there on the living-room couch, no dinner on, and he would wonder if she had moved all day.

Shaking his head to rid himself of the memory, he told Karen what he'd figured out. "It wasn't even terror. It was resignation. She was just waiting for the end. By the time they found out the cancer had metastasized, I was already living with a ghost." A grimace twisted his face, and he bowed his head. His voice was hoarse. "One time I, uh, yelled at her to live while she still had the chance, and she just flinched and wept some more. Hell." He took a couple of slow deep breaths. "Why didn't I just hold her and keep my mouth shut?"

"Because you were angry." Thank God, Karen didn't sound soft and tender. More brisk, as though nothing ever shocked or disgusted her. "Because you were two different people. She was mourning what she was going to lose, and you were refusing to believe she'd lose it."

"Yeah." He shoved fingers through his hair. "That's about it. The kids—I've never said any of this to them. Hell, sometimes I think her way might have been healthier for them. Maybe she was getting them ready to let go. If they'd listened to me, they would have believed she wasn't going to die."

He hadn't even noticed that somewhere in there Karen had reached across the table to hold his hand. He was squeezing back so hard it must hurt.

"I retract what I said the other day. About divorce being harder for kids." Karen's eyes were so blue he couldn't look away. "I was wrong. At least it's not final. I know Abby dreams that someday things will be different. That Geoff will come begging for another chance and she can graciously agree to let him be a better father. But Krista and Michael—"

She broke off as the waiter arrived with salads, but made no move to pick up her fork or pull her hand free. When the waiter was gone, Karen asked, "How did you survive?"

"I don't know. No." He let go of her hand. "That's not true. You want to hear the worst part?"

She nodded, those fathomless blue eyes never leaving his face. He hadn't a clue why he was telling her all this, but now that he'd started, it was all just rushing out, the roaring waters breaking down the dam.

"It was a relief." There. He'd said it. "I mean, Jenny dying. The last few months, they were hell. She was suffering, and the kids and I tried to be there for her, tried to pretend nothing was wrong, that we were managing fine, but, hell, it wasn't fine. I was angry all the time and hiding it, the kids felt selfish if they did anything but come straight home from school and hold their mother's hand, the house was a mess, I'm a lousy cook..." He was actually able to laugh, if without much humor. "I'm a better cook now. I guess that's the silver lining."

"I get the feeling you're closer to your kids than most fathers are."

"Yeah." Amazing. His lopsided smile felt as if he meant it. "We made it somehow. I try to talk about Jenny to the kids so they don't forget her. Not formally, just mentioning her when it's natural. You know."

"I'll bet that was hard at first." She glanced up. "Oh, Lord. Here come our dinners, and we haven't even started the salads."

They assured the waiter that no, everything was fine, and let the conversation become more casual as they ate. But Neal didn't find it easy to switch gears. He felt the way he did when he was about to close a case, tense, senses hyperalert, some part of him standing back and watching events as though from a distance. Evaluating. Telling him when to move. When not to be a damn fool.

No judgment was in this time. Not yet. He kept picturing the tired angry woman who'd let him in to Chelsea Cahill's house, who'd have done anything for her friend, even defied the cop she'd called. He'd been grateful she was there, and irritated that she didn't jump when he said jump. But even then there had been a sexual jolt, a knowing they'd be good together in bed.

That knowing had never eased up. It gripped him in the gut every time he saw her. Now it was complicated by everything he knew about her and by everything she knew about him. He hadn't talked to anybody the way he had to her tonight in longer than he could remember. It made him uneasy, wondering what she saw when she looked across the table at him. Wondering whether she was any happier than he was about the way things were developing between them.

One thing he could do was erase the advantage she had over him. Neal waited until they were sipping coffee to say, "Your turn."

"My...?" Her gaze flitted nervously away. "Oh. You mean the history of my life."

"Yeah, this is equal opportunity, remember? I tell you a story, you tell me one."

Without the cynicism he sometimes saw in her eyes, she looked ridiculously young. There had been times her years had shown: when she carried the invisible weight of other women's anguish and terror. But right now, with her silky blond hair framing her elfin face, she could have played Sleeping Beauty waiting for her prince. He didn't suppose in her book the prince had a rifle rack on his pickup or made a living catching bad guys.

He almost gave a grunt of amusement. Truth was, Ms. Lindberg would probably sell the prince the brambles and tell him to forget the rescue. She wasn't the kind to lie around snoozing while a man took charge of her life.

"Okay, okay," she said, frowning in a way he thought was cute. Not that he was foolish enough to say so. "I've already told you about the protest marches."

He nodded.

"Well, the thing is, my parents are conservative." Karen's nose crinkled as she thought about that.

"Which is putting it mildly. My dad thought all the longhairs—his word, not mine—who were out protesting should be hauled off to boot camp and shipped to Vietnam." She had a faraway look in her eyes. "Roger, my brother, he was a jock, but a top student, too. He did a couple of years of college, then wanted to take some time off. Big mistake. He was drafted, and he went. Scared to death." She made a small helpless gesture. "Literally, as it turned out."

"Tell me about it," Neal muttered.

Her eyes were suddenly sharply in focus. "I'm sorry. I forgot..."

He shook his head. "This is your story. Not mine."

Bitter regret showed on her face. "He shouldn't have gone. Not Roger. You know what he wanted to be? A teacher. Elementary school. He really liked kids." She stopped abruptly. "Anyway, I had a high-school teacher who gave a bunch of us rides to marches. Until I got arrested."

"Caught some flak for it, did he?"

"A pun?" Her quick smile faded. "Yeah. He lost his job. So guess what?"

Neal didn't even have to reflect. "You protested that, too."

"You've figured me out." She didn't look as if she was sure how she felt about that. "I organized a sit-in. Amazingly enough it worked. So I got hooked. *I* could make a difference. I haven't quit since." She shrugged. "End of story."

He set down his coffee cup. "You skipped the part about Abby's father."

Karen affected surprise. "I didn't know you wanted to hear it."

Neal held her gaze, letting her see how serious he was. "I figure there are a few basics we should know about each other."

She got prickly on him. "Should?"

He raised an eyebrow. "Weren't you curious about my marriage?"

Appealing to her essential honesty worked every time. The chin lowered and she made a face at him. "Yeah. I was curious. Okay." Karen visibly collected her thoughts. "Geoff. We met in college, at Cal. Berkeley. We were both idealists, activists. Out to change the world. Now I wish I had a degree in horticulture, but then I majored in sociology, of all the useless things. He went on to law school. I worked to put him through. He became a public defender, protecting the underdog." The acid in her voice gave Neal an idea where this was going. "We had Abby. Geoff won a fairly spectacular case, and a San Francisco law firm offered him a job. The high road to a partnership. He was still going to do pro bono work, he said. We owed it to Abby to move from a crummy rental. We could buy a house. So we did. Seemed like after a while he was spending his time defending corporations that had evaded taxes. I kept opening my mouth on issues the firm didn't want to be associated with. My name was connected with some causes. The partners asked Geoff to muzzle me. He tried."

"Idiot," Neal commented with no particular heat. "He should have known you never quit fighting."

Her wicked grin did more than the sight of her long legs had to make him eager to see what would come of their good-night kiss. "I made a lousy corporate wife."

"You didn't marry a corporation."

"Turned out that way, though." Karen paused a beat. "You never know what you're getting into."

Neal recognized that they were no longer talking about either of their past marriages. "You were young when you got married. Me, too. College students can't be sure they know what they want. You and I—" he shrugged lazily "—we have a pretty good idea. Even if we do still get taken by surprise now and again."

"No kidding." She sounded wry.

Neal figured the moment had come. "Ready to go?"

Her expression turned wary. "As ready as I'll ever be."

He took care of the bill and escorted Ms. Flower-woman out to the car. Earlier they'd watched the sun set in shades of orange and violet. It had left a cool fall evening in its wake. She shivered a little in her skimpy dress, and he laid an arm across her bare shoulders as he unlocked the passenger door. She gave another shiver, but he felt the difference. It rocked him to his core.

What conversation they made on the way home was desultory. Neal turned on the radio to a country-and-western station, not loud, just a gentle wash of ballads about lost love and second chances. Sounded about right to him, wrapped as he was in awareness of the woman beside him, her soft breaths, her occasional surreptitious glances.

A foot-stomper by Clint Black came on as the car headlights pierced the purple darkness on Karen's street. From beside Neal, she spoke for the first time in ten minutes. Tartly. "Let me guess. You really do spend Saturday nights line dancing."

Neal grinned. "You're wrong there. I don't do the same thing as a dozen other people are doing. I'd rather surprise 'em."

He wished he could see Karen's face when she said thoughtfully, "Maybe that's why I like you."

He turned the car into her driveway. The headlights momentarily illuminated her carport and a fleeing cat before he turned lights and engine off.

"Would you like to come in?" Her nonchalance almost convinced him.

"Thank you. I would," he agreed. Damn. His palms were getting as sweaty as they had the first time he'd taken a girl out.

Karen was already slamming her car door and hurrying up the walk, heels clicking, when he came around the car. Ten feet away from him and she'd already almost disappeared. It wasn't the first time he'd noticed with disapproval those enormous shrubs that ringed her porch and lined the driveway, arching woody arms over the narrow brick path and leaving deep shadows between.

"Wait!" Neal ordered sharply.

She stopped so suddenly he almost ran her down with his long strides. Voice hushed, she demanded, "What's wrong?"

"Do you know how dangerous it is to have all these damn bushes concealing your place?" The words came out more harshly than he'd intended. "How the hell do you know if somebody is behind one before you pass?"

She released her tension in an exasperated harrumph. "You scared me! I thought you heard something."

Trailing her onto the porch, Neal said, "Hell, somebody could be standing three feet away and I wouldn't see him. What if you were alone?"

She unlocked the front door. "If I was alone, I'd go in the side door from the carport. No shrubs. But since it takes us right through the utility room and past the cat litter, I figured I'd do the romantic thing and bring you in the front way. After all, I have you here to protect me."

"And here I thought you were never romantic." He let the front door close behind him and leaned back against it.

Her eyes shied away from him. "It was a nice dinner. I thought you deserved better than cat litter."

She wanted to keep things light. His heart had begun hammering uncomfortably hard in his chest. It was too soon to feel the urgency he did, and he knew he had to rein himself in. That didn't mean, however, he had to play any more games.

"I want to kiss you," he said roughly.

She set down her purse and faced him, and he was shaken to see the same urgency in her eyes. Karen answered just above a whisper. "Yes. Please."

A couple of steps and he had her in his arms. She wound her own almost fiercely around his neck and stood on tiptoe, meeting his mouth with the same hunger he felt. It was insane; too much, too soon, but already he was groaning low in his throat, yanking her tightly against him, where she couldn't fail to notice that his body wanted a hell of a lot more than a goodnight kiss.

Her taste was like her personality: tart with a dash of sweetness. Nothing cloying about Ms. Flowerwoman, nothing submissive. Her tongue tangled with his in an erotic duel; tension quivered down her narrow arching back. Her breasts were flattened against his chest, and already her hips lifted in instinctive seeking.

He couldn't stop. Damn, Neal thought dazedly. He had to. She hadn't invited him farther than her front hall. Another groan ripped from him as he lifted his mouth from hers.

"Don't leave yet," Karen said raggedly. She moaned as he kissed her throat and then bit the lobe of her ear, taking the tiny hoop earring into his mouth and flicking it with his tongue.

If he was going to stop, it had to be now. He tried to raise his head and she tugged it back down, meeting his mouth with desire headier than the wine he'd sipped with dinner.

He wrapped his hands around her hips and lifted until she was where he wanted her, then he backed her against a wall and kissed her savagely. He couldn't think, didn't want to. He only wanted . . .

"Where's your bedroom?" he growled.

Her lips were red and swollen; her eyes had a glassy look. "Down the hall," she whispered, and he snatched her up. They made it, barely, Neal kissing her the whole way, her hands kneading his arms and shoulders, her legs wrapped around his waist. One dream come true.

His blood was thundering in his ears, and he was so hard he felt as if he had a nightstick shoved down the front of his pants. He lowered her onto her bed, and as fast as he could peel off her panty hose, she was unsnapping his shirt and pulling down his jeans. Kneeling between her pale thighs, Neal kissed her again while reaching around her to unzip the little red number. He was shaking he wanted in her so badly, but damned if he'd make love to a woman with his pants around his ankles, however hot he was for her.

He sat up and cursed as he tried to kick off his boots. Ms. Flowerwoman just lay back and tormented him with fingernails moving up his spine, blue eyes smoky with desire, and her breasts, creamy white and pink-tipped, bare above the red silk twisted around her waist.

Naked at last, a condom clumsily applied, he rolled on top of Karen. God, she was beautiful. Small, lithe, brazen. Her feet curled around his calves and she looked up at him with something close to a challenge. "What are you thinking?"

His laugh was husky. "What the hell do you think I'm thinking?"

The smokiness in her eyes had cleared while he'd wrestled with his boots; now the blue was in sharp focus. "Wondering why you're in bed with me?"

"I know why I'm in bed with you." No wondering here. He was at the gates of heaven; he could feel her slick heat. If he moved only a little, he would be inside her, reveling in her shivers, her snug grip. Possessing her, if only for this short time.

But she was still talking. Talking, for God's sake!

"We shouldn't be doing this."

He backed off a little, just enough to kiss her breast. "Why not?" he murmured against the soft scented curve, before he drew the tight nipple into his mouth.

Her back arched and her answer was breathless. "Do we even like each other?"

"Damned if I know," he said, and thrust.

She gasped. Her eyes widened, then drifted closed as she accommodated herself to his length and breadth. Muscles quivering, he held still, giving her a chance to react. He didn't expect any retreat, and he was right. Her hips rose, her muscles tightened, her eyes went dreamy again and she whispered, "Oh, yes."

He was lost. He kissed her frantically as he pushed deeper still, pulled back, buried himself in her again. She made little sounds and clutched him and arched and kissed him back with need as desperate. Part of the time he was on top, part of the time she was. They tangled with the covers and damn near fell off the bed. At the end she cried out. She sounded surprised, exultant, and it was his name on her lips. Something in the way she said it brought him to an explosive climax, one that went on forever, like dying might, leaving him changed at the other end.

They lay together afterward, legs still entwined, sweat cooling and second thoughts held off by languor.

"So that's why," she murmured, her breath tickling his damp chest where her head rested.

"Part of it," he agreed, his voice a rumble to his own ears. With one hand he stroked from her shoulder to her hip and back again. He liked the feel of her, the sharp edge of her shoulder blade and pelvic bone, the curve in between, the delicacy of her frame and muscles. His first thought was that her body didn't go with her character, but then he wasn't so sure. The sharpness was there, all right, and the curve of waist and hip represented her softer side, the compassion that made her ferocious in defending the underdog. He found himself smiling and turned his mouth against her hair, which was downy as a baby's.

He'd never had sex like this. Not with Jenny—she'd gained satisfaction from their lovemaking, but she'd never demanded anything for herself. Neither had any other woman he'd taken to bed before his marriage or after his wife's death.

And, in not demanding, none of them, not even his wife, had given as unreservedly. He'd made love to women before; for the first time, though, he'd made love *with* one.

Karen had taken him on a ride as wild as any on the wickedest Brahman coming out of the chutes. He had a feeling that a man who loved her would willingly climb right back on if he hit the ground.

Half-appalled, he wondered why the idea sounded so exhilarating. He'd never liked feeling out of control. He needed to hold the reins. With Karen, there weren't any reins to hold.

His sweat had dried and he felt cool except where Ms. Flowerwoman was draped over him. Time to go home, he thought, though a part of him wanted to lift her back on top and start the ride again. His body stirred at the image, though his brain was telling him to think this over before he got thrown.

The sound of an electronic beep made him jerk. Then ice seemed to form in his veins. Swearing, he sat up, shedding Karen who rolled onto her back.

"Telephone?" His voice was taut.

"Right there. On the nightstand." She scooted up until she leaned against the headboard, the bedspread tugged to cover her nakedness. Her eyes were wide and dark.

He grabbed the receiver, punched the number and identified himself. "Rowland here."

The county dispatcher said, "You've had another rape in town. The victim called right away."

"Where?"

He committed the address to memory, along with the fact that a pair of his officers had already responded.

Two films played in his mind, first separate, then mingling like a double exposure. His own fierce joining with Karen seemed to haze into the brutal rape that had happened too close to the same time. Neal felt sick. Fighting for detachment, he hung up the receiver and reached for his pants.

CHAPTER EIGHT

"WHAT IS IT?" Karen spoke to Neal's broad back. She wanted very badly for the call to be about something routine. A stolen car. A window shattered to set off an alarm at one of the businesses along Front Street. But when Neal went still at her question, she knew.

His voice was brusque. "Another rape."

"Oh, Lord," Karen whispered. She saw Chelsea's face, swollen and bruised, her brown eyes terrified, hopeless. Lisa, fighting to pretend nothing had happened to her, desperate to bury the horror.

Anger came rushing on the heels of Karen's shock. "This can't go on! There has to be something we can *do!*"

Neal stood to shrug into his shirt. For the first time since he'd picked up the phone, she saw his face, and the sight knotted her stomach. His eyes smoldered, his jaw muscles vibrated with tension, and his mouth was a thin line.

"Just what the hell do you suggest?" he asked tautly. "Do you think we haven't tried?"

She'd been clumsy, Karen realized. She wouldn't think about why it was so important that he understand she wasn't criticizing him. "I know you have," she said. "That's not what I meant. It's just that we— the community—ought to be able to do something to help. Instead of waiting for the police to take care of us."

In the middle of tucking his shirt into his pants, Neal lifted his head with the sharp awareness of an alarmed animal. "That's what we've been hired to do."

Karen sat up, forgetting to clutch the sheet to her breasts. "Yes, but we don't have to be helpless. In the old days, people weren't. A hundred years ago, you'd have deputized half the men in town."

Neal shook his head and muttered an obscenity. Sounding disgusted, he said, "So they could all shoot first and ask questions later? That's what the constitution is designed to prevent."

"But—" Karen stopped herself. This was no moment for a philosophical debate. Something told her that her talking was a cover, anyway, to keep herself from thinking about the rape. About who the victim was this time.

Neal was sitting on the edge of the bed pulling on his socks and boots when she took a deep breath. "Is it . . . someone I know?"

He didn't even look at her. "I'm sorry," he said distantly. "If I can tell you later, I will." He stood. "I'll feel better if you come along right now and lock the door behind me."

Her robe was in the closet. Her red silk dress, which had been shed along the way, had vanished. She'd probably find it tomorrow wadded up among the sheets. Karen hesitated, then slipped out of bed naked. Goose bumps shivered down her spine, though she wasn't cold. Maybe it was the way Neal looked at her without saying a word or moving. Just looked, his eyes dark beneath bunched brows, the set of his mouth that of a man under intense strain. Karen grabbed her robe from the hanger and quickly wrapped it around herself.

On bare feet, she went ahead of him down the hall. Neal opened the front door, bent his head and gave her a quick hard kiss. "I'll call you tomorrow," he said gruffly, then disappeared down the dark walkway. She waited until she heard his car start, then closed, locked and bolted her front door.

She should be tired, would be tomorrow, since she had to be at the nursery early to accept a delivery, but right now she was too keyed up, too restless, to sleep. Trailed by Maggie, Karen prowled through the house making sure that windows were locked, that she couldn't see anything moving outside. How many times in the past month had she checked these same latches?

With a sick feeling in her stomach, she wondered if the woman who'd been raped tonight had checked *her* windows over and over again. And all for nothing.

At last Karen was back in her bedroom. Maggie hopped onto the bed, sniffed, and leapt off so quickly it was as though her feet had been singed. Most nights she slept at Karen's feet. Tonight, her behavior suggested, the bed had been fouled.

"Yeah, well, you've been neutered," Karen told her. "So what do you know?"

It took her ten minutes to remake the bed, untwisting sheets and blankets and rescuing her dress. She was mildly shocked by the condition of the bedding; she couldn't remember ever participating in a sex act quite so... unrestrained. She'd enjoyed making love with Geoff, though decreasingly so as he became more buttoned up, more starched. But oddly enough, their lovemaking had been considerably more conventional than tonight's main event.

She hadn't intended to let things go quite so far with Neal. Not yet, anyway. She'd been taken by surprise when he kissed her. Swept away. Karen sat on the bed and smoothed the pillow with one hand, frowning as she realized how thoroughly she'd let herself be dominated and how erotic that had been. Appalled, she wondered if she'd been harboring some secret wish to find a man stronger than she was.

Maybe it was just circumstances and her sense of self-preservation that made her body react so positively to him. Danger was loose in this town, and the police chief meant protection, safety. A woman was programed to choose a man who could take care of her.

That thought was even more abhorrent to Karen than the last. She'd never wanted to depend on anybody. Now not only she but every other woman in this town waited passively for men to protect them.

Well, so far the police had failed. Was every woman who didn't have a man of her own supposed to come up with one, and fast? Was that why she'd succumbed so easily tonight?

But what could a man do these days that a woman couldn't? Carry a gun? Karen frowned and propped pillows against the headboard so that she could lean back. No, somebody might get shot by accident. She didn't like or approve of guns. Two-thirds of the violent crime in the country occurred because a gun was handy, not because a criminal had bought one to use to kill. Domestic arguments going too far, children playing with the revolver from Daddy's closet, teenagers daring each other. No, guns weren't the answer.

Karen heard a thump and tensed. The refrigerator began to hum and she relaxed, her mind turning back to the problem.

What was the answer? What could women do to protect themselves?

Eventually she turned off her bedside lamp and slept, but fitfully. Every small noise in the otherwise silent empty house awakened her. Her dreams were muddled and nightmarish, made up of ski masks and cowboy boots and her red silk dress twisted into a garrote. But nobody had been killed yet, she realized in her dream, and then was confused.

Her mind converted the alarm clock's whine to a woman's scream, and she sat bolt upright at the same time as her eyes opened. Awareness came, and she groaned and turned off the alarm. Even after a shower, her face reflected in the mirror was puffy and heavy-eyed. If Neal had spent the night, one look at her this morning and he would have made his excuses and fled.

"See?" Karen told herself. "Women can scare men."

Instead of amusing her, the idea nudged a memory. Something she had read. Women coming together to protect each other.

Over breakfast, Karen dredged the memory from her subconscious. Seemingly unstoppable, a serial rapist had terrified a neighborhood in Miami. At last the women had banded together and formed patrols. The intention had been not so much to catch the rapist as to scare him off. Make it impossible for him to stalk a lone woman. She couldn't remember what happened in the end, whether the police had caught him at last or whether he'd just disappeared, but she remembered reading of the women's satisfaction.

It could work here, too, she realized with rising excitement. The first three rapes, at least, had taken place within the city limits. The town wasn't large. If enough women could be organized, patrols could be spread out so that they covered every block, the routes altered to remain unpredictable. They could have several shifts, so that the patrols were on the street from nightfall until the early hours of the morning. No weapons; they would carry cellular telephones, she decided, so that the police could be summoned in minutes.

As she got ready to leave for work, Karen examined the idea from every angle and liked it better by the minute. If groups patrolled their own neighborhoods, they would know where single women lived and could keep an especially sharp eye out for them. With luck, their constant presence would frustrate the rapist. At the very least, the women would be empowered; they would be doing something to take care of themselves.

Just as she was going out the door, the telephone rang. Karen hurried back to answer it.

"Hello?"

"It's Neal," he said unnecessarily. "How are you?"

"I'm fine." She swallowed. "How...how is the woman?"

"Not good." There was a pause. "She has a broken jaw and several broken ribs."

Pure rage squeezed the air out of Karen. "The bastard," she said fiercely. "Why? Why did he hurt her?"

"I don't know, and she's in no condition to tell me. Maybe she wouldn't dance. Seems that's the most important part for him."

"God." Karen closed her eyes and leaned her forehead against the cool wood of the kitchen cabinet. "Did you learn anything new?"

"Nothing yet." He suddenly sounded tired, even defeated. "The victim isn't in any state to talk."

"Have you gotten any sleep?"

"Later." She heard him exhale. "I'll let you go. I just wanted you to know that I'd rather have stayed last night."

"You're saying you're not the 'thanks, ma'am, I've got to run' type?"

"Something like that."

"It never crossed my mind that you might be."

"Good." There could have been a smile in the one word. She'd accomplished something. "I'll talk to you later," he said.

"Wait." Karen straightened. "I had an idea."

"An idea." Neal sounded wary.

She didn't let that dim her enthusiasm. Quickly she explained. "If we see something," she concluded, "you could have an officer there in minutes."

"That's the most harebrained plan I've heard in years!" he said scathingly. "What are you trying to do, make it easier for the bastard? Offer him a selection? Hell, he wouldn't even have to break into a house to find a woman to rape!"

She shouldn't have been surprised at his reaction. She'd always known he was a chauvinist. She'd just forgotten. Deliberately blocked the knowledge from her mind. Funny, what physical attraction could do.

But he'd been reasonable about some topics. She didn't want to assume anything, just because he had short hair and wore a badge. After all, his nature— hell, his *job*—was to protect and defend. He might regard her suggestion as criticism of his ability to do just that. She should give him a chance to get beyond that first instinctive reaction and not lose her own temper too quickly.

"Maybe I didn't explain myself very well," she said. "The women would patrol in groups, maybe three or four together. They could take dogs on leashes, carry flashlights. If every group had a cellular phone—"

"I don't care what they carry," Neal interrupted, his voice completely inflexible. "We've got a nut running loose, and you want to send women out on the streets in the middle of the night. The answer is no. Don't even think about taking this any further."

"You'd like to believe that women are completely helpless, wouldn't you?" she snapped. So much for keeping her temper.

"It's been looking that way, hasn't it?"

Steaming, Karen retorted, "At least *I'm* proposing action that might work. Do you have an alternative to suggest? Something besides the tactics that are obviously failing?"

She heard him swear just as she slammed the receiver down. The telephone was already ringing again by the time she stormed out the front door.

With autumn advancing, business would be slow at the nursery today. She'd have plenty of time to make some phone calls of her own.

LISTENING TO the unanswered rings, Neal swore again. Surely to God Karen would have the sense not to go ahead with her foolhardy scheme. But the cold chill crawling up his spine reminded him that he knew better. Ms. Flowerwoman was an activist to her core: gutsy, stubborn and impetuous. What he ought to be hoping was that the other men—the husbands and fathers and boyfriends—would succeed in vetoing the plan.

Reluctantly he hung up. Right now he didn't have time to run out to the nursery, but as soon as possible, he had to talk some sense into her. She imagined her scheme would be as simple as a neighborhood watch: folks keeping an eye out for one another. Instead, her plan would stake women out like goats for the slaughter. They might be safe if they stayed in groups of four or five. But what if not enough women came on board and Karen planned the patrols with three each? And one didn't show? The one with the dog, of course. The other two wouldn't want to go home; they'd feel committed. From that point on, a man who stalked women as successfully as this bastard had wouldn't have any trouble somehow separating the two.

Another way of looking at it was that she would be inadvertently forming a vigilante group. Karen was figuring no weapons. How long would that last? Some men would want to join the patrols. At the very least, husbands would insist their wives pack a pistol for protection. On a black night, how hard was it to work up to a nervous state? Pools of darkness between streetlights, the rustle of the wind through the big maples, a stray dog knocking over a garbage can, a lone set of headlights slowly approaching. A hand might reach for that pistol, just for reassurance. Fingers might tighten on it, ready for the first threat.

Under enough pressure, even trained police officers sometimes fired when they shouldn't. Sure as hell, some nervous Nelly was going to pump out a few rounds before common sense caught up with her terror.

Wearily Neal rubbed a hand over his face. He glanced around the police department at the state of controlled hysteria. Already phones were ringing off the hook. The morning *Herald* had managed to find room on the front page for news of the latest rape, this one, they reported, the most brutal yet.

Neal was infuriated that they'd managed to learn all the details, but he knew there wasn't a damn thing he could do about it. There never was. Too many people liked the feeling of importance that passing on inside knowledge gave them.

Last night's victim, a young hairdresser named Toni Santos, was barely out of high school. She'd been found by her roommate, who was supposed to have gone to Port Townsend for the weekend with her boyfriend. But they'd had a fight, and instead of getting on the ferry with him, she'd made him take her home. The TV had been on when she let herself into the shabby little rental. With a shudder, she'd admitted that she almost tripped over Toni, sprawled on the living-room floor. Toni's nose was bloody, the side of her face purple and grotesquely swollen, every gasp for breath a whimper. She wore a spandex exercise top and nothing else.

The broken jaw was now wired shut. She wouldn't have been in any state to talk yet, anyway. Pain and shock had dulled her ability to respond to outside stimuli. When she was awake, she stared at nothing, her eyes empty.

But the roommate was ready and willing to tell everything she knew about Toni. The victim had no current boyfriend; she'd dated half a dozen men the past year, not one of whom was on Neal's list culled from the other victims. She had probably been doing aerobics when the rapist broke in through the back-bedroom window. Over the music, she wouldn't have heard the glass shatter. A Jane Fonda tape was in the VCR, automatically rewound. The roommate said Toni had several different aerobics tapes and exercised faithfully every day.

Like the first victim, Toni Santos didn't live by herself. Somehow the rapist knew her roommate's plans, knew that this was one sure night Toni would be alone. The question was, how many people had she or the roommate told?

THE NIGHT WAS DARK, even the yellow glow of street lamps muted by a damp mist. A dog barked in some backyard, but Karen couldn't tell if it was two houses or two blocks away. The mist deadened sound, distorted it. She shifted the umbrella to her other hand and aimed her flashlight around the corner of a hedge. In its narrow beam, she saw nothing but empty driveway and garbage cans beside a garage door.

Across the street something moved, and beside Karen her daughter sucked in a breath. Before Karen could turn her own flashlight in that direction, Joan spotlighted a cat jumping over the fence. The general relaxation made Karen as angry as the momentary spurt of fear had.

A month ago she wouldn't have hesitated to walk down her street at ten at night. Now she wouldn't have stepped foot out her door alone. Instead of the comfortable shape of familiar trees and houses, she saw the darkness between them. She resented the way her heart leapt into her throat at every sound, the wariness she had to feel at every approaching car.

It was past time she and all the other women reclaimed their neighborhoods. And she wasn't alone in her thinking.

Virtually every phone call Karen had made met with enthusiasm. Her first contacts suggested other names, who suggested yet others. By late afternoon, she felt like a general planning a campaign. Her lists of names and phone numbers grew. On a map of the town spread out on her desk, she drew bold red lines marking patrol sections. For each section, Karen put someone in charge. By nightfall her troops were ready to fan out, armed with no more than flashlights, family dogs and phones.

Her own group consisted of herself, Abby, Joan from next door and Chelsea Cahill, still staying with her parents only a few blocks from Karen's house. Chelsea, sounding more like her old self than she had since the assault, had insisted on coming.

"Do you know how... how *small* I've felt?" she asked when Karen called. "And how mad?" Her voice shook. "I think if I could kill him, I would. Sometimes the anger just builds and builds until I could explode, and all the while there's nothing I can do. This gives me something."

Joan had brought her dog, a spaniel mix who sniffed his way delightedly down the street, lifting his leg on every handy telephone pole or car wheel.

"I won't call him a guard dog," Joan admitted ruefully when they met out in front of her house, "but he probably has better hearing and smell than we do.

Once in a while he can even sound ferocious. Besides, he likes walks."

"It's a good idea to bring him," Karen said. "I've been thinking that maybe we should get a dog."

"Really?" Abby asked. "Cool! Except I bet Maggie would hate a dog."

"Maggie hates all other four-legged creatures. And most two-legged. But she could adjust."

"Can we go to the animal shelter tomorrow?" Her daughter sounded as bouncy as ever. "If we got a puppy..."

"I had something in mind that could look and sound at least a little bit dangerous right now."

Even Abby fell silent as headlights approached and passed. There it was again: that insidious apprehension that Karen so hated. Every situation had become potentially fearsome. She didn't *want* to be afraid of a lone male customer, of the creak of a tree branch scraping another in the wind, of a car doing nothing more than driving down the street. She would not accept having to live that way.

"Why couldn't we have a nice moonlit evening to start?" Joan asked suddenly, her voice just a little too loud. "This fog gives me the creeps."

Abby scooted a little closer to her mother. Now their shoulders bumped with each step. Nobody said anything for a minute.

Until Chelsea made a surprising contribution. Quite solemnly she recited, "'From ghoulies and ghosties and long-leggety beasties and things that go bump in the night, Good Lord, deliver us!'"

"Amen," Joan said. Her flashlight probed a driveway while Karen's and Chelsea's arced across the house's front yard, the beams briefly revealing shrubs and the trunks of trees and a red tricycle. Nothing moved but the mist.

"Let's talk," Abby suggested, her words rushed.

"Sure," Chelsea said as quickly. "Tell us how school's going."

Karen's daughter never had any trouble thinking of things to say. With only a little encouragement, she rambled from algebra—boring—to boys, beginning with the one who wanted to go out behind the gym "and do it." Joan stopped dead on the sidewalk.

"Don't boys even *pretend* to be romantic anymore?"

Abby sounded a little depressed. "Not really."

Karen saw a window of opportunity—to quote the catch phrase—and slipped into it. "You date, Chelsea. Are the guys in their twenties and thirties any better?"

Chelsea didn't answer immediately, which made Karen feel guilty for putting her on the spot. Maybe Chelsea didn't want to think about men at all. But she sounded natural enough when she said, "No, I haven't been propositioned quite that crudely, but, yeah, lots of guys think because they took you out to dinner, it means—" her head turned as she glanced at Abby "—umm, that they've earned more than good-night kisses."

"Harry's sounding better all the time," Joan muttered, referring to her potbellied husband.

Constantly sweeping her flashlight from side to side, Karen said, striving to sound casual, "Chels, didn't you date Henry Lyons, the ophthalmologist? Is he a jerk, too?"

"You went out with *him?*" Abby said incredulously. "But he's getting bald."

"Some men start losing their hair when they're still in their twenties, even their teens," Karen felt obliged to point out. "A man can be bald and sexy."

"Sean Connery," Joan said, and Chelsea and Karen murmured heartfelt agreement.

"But he's old."

"Well, Henry isn't," Chelsea said. "He was okay. We just didn't really hit it off. He liked jazz clubs and these chic little restaurants on Broadway in Seattle. I like pizza and a movie without subtitles. I guess I'm just lowbrow. The kicker was that I couldn't picture him volunteering in my class. There's no way he'd fingerpaint or help some five-year-old blow her nose. He might get his hands dirty. You know what I mean?"

Karen knew exactly what she meant. Watching him wandering through her nursery in his Levi Dockers and Ralph Lauren polo shirt, she'd come to the depressing conclusion that *he* would never have dirt under his fingernails. He probably bought one of those ridiculously expensive organic soaps that upscale gardening catalogs sold, kneepads so he didn't dirty his pants and goatskin gloves to protect his hands.

"Surely," Joan persisted, "there are high-school boys who still have some remnant of chivalry."

They'd come to the end of the street and turned now to make their way back along a different route. Abby seemed to have forgotten her nervousness. She told them at length about Brian the Cool, who had scored a touchdown that afternoon in the big game against Stanwood High. "When he was running off the field afterward he smiled at me and gave me a thumbs-up. He'd taken his helmet off, and he was all sweaty and he looked so, so..." She stopped as if at a loss for words.

Sexy. Not for worlds would Karen have said it aloud.

"Masculine," Joan supplied.

Chelsea didn't say anything, and Karen gave her a sidelong glance. How did she feel, deep down inside, when they talked about men and sex and dating? She'd sounded matter-of-fact enough about Henry Lyons; maybe too carefully so. What would happen the next time a man kissed her or put his hands on her breasts? Would the near-violence of the sex act forever recall that one horrifying experience?

So far, Chelsea didn't seem to want to talk about those kind of feelings, and Karen hadn't pushed. She sure wasn't going to push tonight, not with Abby all ears. At fourteen, her daughter was already more sophisticated and knowledgeable than Karen would have liked.

"Steph thinks all the boys are so immature," Chelsea said finally, half a block farther along. Stephanie was her younger sister, a senior in high school. "I didn't believe her until I chaperoned the dance a while ago. Trust her to stick me with something like that. But then, she couldn't have volunteered Mom or Dad. She knows they'd have a stroke if they heard the way kids talk these days. Every other word is an obscenity. My kindergartners have bigger vocabularies!"

"It's just a cool way to talk," Abby said nonchalantly. "I mean, nobody says stuff like that around their parents."

"Except for an occasional slip," Karen pointed out dryly.

Abby ignored that. "Steph's lucky to have a big sister like you. I saw all the guys asking you to dance. I mean, my *mother* is going to chaperon. No offense, Mom, but it's totally humiliating."

...*all the guys asking you to dance.* Oh, my God, Karen thought, barely hearing her daughter's last comment.

"Chelsea, when did you chaperon the dance?" Amazing how calm she sounded.

But not calm enough. Or else Chelsea, too, had stumbled over the reminder. Chelsea turned, as though in slow motion, the streetlight overhead revealing the dawning horror on her face. "It was... it was before..."

"How long before?" Karen asked urgently.

She was peripherally aware that Abby and Joan were staring at them, but she focused on Chelsea, who said in a harsh whisper, "Four days. Afterward, I couldn't have chaperoned. I couldn't have stood watching everybody dance." She was shaking her head, over and over. "I can't watch."

"Then the dance was the Friday before. You're sure?"

Now her head bobbed. "I never thought... I forgot all about it. I didn't tell... Not the police, not anybody." Her face crumpled in confusion and distress. "But he wasn't a teenager. I'm sure of that."

Karen took Chelsea's hands. "Are you? Think about how grown-up some of the seniors are. They're as big as men. Anyway—" she pressed her lips together "—there must have been adults at the dance, too. Teachers or fathers or... I don't know. Was there a band? Were they kids? Did anybody help them set up?"

Chelsea squeezed until her fingernails bit into Karen's palms. "I don't know. Oh, God, I don't want to think about it."

Karen turned her head. "Abby, you've been to most of the dances. Did Lisa Pyne ever chaperon one?"

She knew even before her daughter spoke. Abby made a hiccuping sound of shock, and Joan instinctively wrapped a protective arm around her.

"Yes. It was the week before she got sick. I mean, before..."

Before she was raped. Karen heard herself say steadily, "We'd better call Chief Rowland. Right away."

HE WAS STARING mindlessly at the TV, at a cop show of all things, when the phone rang. Neal muted the television's sound and picked up the receiver.

"Yeah?"

"Neal."

He knew her voice immediately, knew from the electric tension that something had happened. He sat up so suddenly the recliner snapped upright. "Are you okay?"

"Yes, it's not me."

"Then who—?"

"Nobody. I mean, nobody else has been raped. It's just that Joan—she's my next-door neighbor—and Abby and Chelsea and I were talking. And something came up."

She told him, then, in a few quick words. Chelsea Cahill had chaperoned the high-school dance the Friday before she was raped. The very next Friday, Lisa Pyne had chaperoned the dance. Two days later, she was raped.

"Why the hell didn't Miss Cahill think to mention it?" He was on his feet now, prowling back and forth within the reach of the phone cord. He was as irritated at himself as at anybody. Chelsea Cahill *had* vaguely mentioned volunteering at some high-school "function." That was how she'd put it. Function. Couldn't she bring herself to say the word "dance?"

He should have pursued it, usually would have, but she must have said something else that sent him haring off in another direction, now forgotten.

Neal shook his head. "I asked her whether she'd been dancing in the recent past."

"The thing is, she didn't dance," Karen told him. "Her sister asked her to chaperon, and she spent all her time patrolling the washrooms and out behind the gym."

"Did anyone ask her to dance?"

"Dozens of guys, according to Abby. Chelsea can't remember exactly who. Joe Gardner, she thinks, probably the other male chaperons and a bunch of the older boys. It wouldn't have to be one of them..."

"No," he said grimly, "but chances are good it was."

Sounding hesitant, she said, "But if the other rape victims chaperoned, too..."

"They didn't," he said. "If they had, this would have popped up sooner. But there's got to be a connection." He was already thinking. It wasn't too late for him to call Kathleen Madsen and Toni Santos's roommate tonight. Then if Mrs. Feeney could stay with Krista and Michael, he could interview Chelsea Cahill again.

"Ask Miss Cahill if I can come by to talk to her tonight. I have to have names of who was there."

He heard a muffled discussion. Then Karen came back on the line. "She says okay. She'd rather you came here to my place, since she's staying with her parents right now. They've probably gone to bed, and she doesn't want to alarm them."

"No problem. I've got to make a couple of phone calls first. Karen, thanks. This feels like the break we needed."

Neal's tiredness had vanished. His first phone call was to Mrs. Feeney, who in a sleepy voice agreed to come over. His second was to the roommate.

"Yeah, Toni went to the dance last week," she told him. "She only graduated this spring and she still has friends there. She didn't stay very long, though. She said it was boring."

"Did she happen to mention names? Anybody she danced with? Or who wanted her to dance?"

"I don't remember," the roommate said. "I'm sorry. The thing is, I didn't go to school here. So I wouldn't have known who she was talking about, anyway, you know? Sometimes she'd go on and on about high school, but I'd just kind of turn down the volume and nod a lot. It's just not *interesting* when names don't mean anything, you know?" she asked again, probably hoping for reassurance.

He knew. Neal tuned his own kids out sometimes for the same reason. He felt guilt at the realization, but—as usual—he didn't have time for it.

"If you remember her mentioning anybody, please call me," he said. "It's important."

"Sure. Okay."

He got lucky again. Kathleen Madsen, too, was home.

"No," she said. "I haven't chaperoned any dances. I swore off doing things like that."

Grasping for straws, he said, "Have you chaperoned them in the past?"

"I'm afraid not." She sounded apologetic. "My family has been so involved in soccer it really eats up our time."

Neal thought it over. Kathleen Madsen was the reason he hadn't made the connection in the first place; the occasional parent-teacher conference was the most she had to do with the schools, she claimed. Could she have become a target for a different reason than the other three women?

No, damn it! he thought in frustration. The bastard had made her dance, too. In every way, the assault on her matched the pattern. She *had* to be linked to the other women. There must be a common trigger.

"You haven't been anywhere near the high-school dances? Dropped your son off, picked him up, turned down a chance to chaperon?" Neal ran out of ideas.

"I did drop Kurt off once." Kathleen Madsen sounded almost surprised to hear herself say it. "I remember getting out of the car to talk to another mother. In fact—" the words were coming faster now "—I actually parked and wandered on into the gym. I suppose I hung around for twenty minutes or half an hour. I talked to quite a few people. I even turned down a few invitations to dance." She fell silent, then said quietly, "How odd. I'd completely forgotten."

Elation gripped Neal, but he kept his voice even. "And do you remember when this was?"

Now she spoke so softly he could barely hear her. "I'm looking at the calendar. It was September ninth.

The night before I was attacked. I know because that was the first football game of the season. I didn't go, but Kurt did."

Very gently Neal said, "What I need you to do, Ms. Madsen, is try to remember who asked you to dance. And who might have been angry because you said no."

CHAPTER NINE

NEAL CLOSED his notebook. "If you think of anybody else..."

"I'll call," Chelsea agreed. She had been sitting stiffly on the couch, her hands folded tidily in her lap. Now, like a schoolchild released from the classroom by the bell, she jumped to her feet and backed toward the door. "Listen, I'd better go," she said quickly. "I don't want to worry my parents. Karen, thanks. I'll talk to you later."

"Wait!" Karen exclaimed, hurrying after her into the kitchen. "You can't walk home alone. Let me grab my jacket."

From behind her, Neal said calmly, "I'll walk Ms. Cahill home."

He was back in five minutes. When Karen wordlessly proffered a beer, he accepted it and followed her into the living room. Since she hadn't expected company tonight, the room was in its usual state of disarray. Abby had dropped her book bag on one end of the couch, Karen's bank statement and bills were spread over the coffee table, and a bouquet past its prime had scattered dried flower petals on the dusty top of the piano to join a pile of overdue library books. One chair was stacked with campaign posters she hadn't yet distributed. Home, sweet home.

Neal didn't even look around. He flung himself into the biggest easy chair, opened his notebook and took a swallow of beer. "Is your buddy really having trouble remembering," he growled, "or doesn't she want to?"

Karen understood his frustration, because she'd felt some of it herself. Chelsea had been mulish, every name dragged out of her, none given willingly.

Pushing the book bag onto the floor, Karen curled up at the end of the couch. She made herself be fair. "I think she's put up a giant mental block. Maybe subconsciously she'd rather not know who he is. Or else she's just plain scared that somehow he'll find out she's helping you." She frowned. "The other thing is, since she doesn't work at the high school, she wouldn't know any of the newer teachers or even lots of the parents. She really may not remember names."

He grunted. "Most victims start healing when the rapist is identified and charged with the crime. Fear of a faceless monster who could be anyone is what's debilitating. Can't she see that?"

"How can you or I know how she feels?" Karen asked. "We're not victims."

Yet. The word might be unspoken, but she could tell from the way his jaw muscles worked that he was thinking it, too. Nothing but luck separated Karen from the women who'd been assaulted. She hadn't stayed to talk on those occasions when she'd dropped off Abby at a dance; Joe Gardner hadn't buttonholed her until he'd already lined up chaperons for the first six weeks.

Luck.

It was the memory of Abby hopping out of the car and waving goodbye that made Karen say thoughtfully, "I wonder if Abby could help. She's really very observant. If it hadn't been for her, this whole subject wouldn't have come up."

She'd sent Abby to her room when Neal arrived earlier. Her daughter hadn't appreciated being treated like a child, as she put it, but Karen wasn't about to take a chance on her hearing some graphic detail about the rape. And even though Karen wanted Abby to be careful, she didn't want her thinking that every male teacher or friend's father might be a brutal rapist. Abby's final comment on the expulsion had been to slam her door so hard the vase on the piano had wobbled. Since then, silence had fairly vibrated from her bedroom.

Neal took another swallow of beer and let his head fall back. "If you think there's any chance she'd remember something Miss Cahill didn't, I'd like to talk to her."

"Abby?" Karen called. "Could you come here for a minute?"

Abby's voice was muffled by the distance and closed door, not to mention a pouting lower lip. "Why?"

"Because I'm telling you to." Karen's automatic rejoinder triggered vague memories of her youthful self swearing never to say that to her own children. Of course, she hadn't understood then how exasperating a teenager could be. *She* had thought she was eminently reasonable.

Besides, as tactics went, it worked. The door opened and Abby sauntered into the living room just slowly enough to be insolent without crossing over to defiant. "Yeah?"

With that gravelly voice, Neal took over. "Your mother tells me you have a good memory. I could use your help. What we're looking for now are names. Chaperons, older teenage boys—" he spread his hands "—anybody you can remember who was at the dances."

"You mean, just the guys?"

"No, women, too. What I'll have to do now is compile lists. Go to people I already know were at a particular dance and get them to remember who *they* saw. And then go to those people. So I'll want to interview women, too. But it's true that mostly I'm interested in the guys."

"Umm..." To her credit, Abby quickly forgot her hurt pride. She wandered in and sank gracefully into a cross-legged position on the floor, her elbows propped on the coffee table. "It's hard to remember who was at which dance, if you know what I mean."

Neal nodded encouragement. Karen remained silent.

"Some of the teachers come to almost every one. Like Mr. Gardner. And, umm, Mr. Morris and the principal, Mr. Bradley. And Ms. Pyne. She came to the first couple. Until..." Abby gulped.

He didn't let her linger on the memory. "Let's start with the second one. Miss Cahill was there. Think back. What else comes to mind about the evening?"

Abby's fine-boned face looked unnaturally solemn as she concentrated. "Well, I remember all the guys wanted her to dance. Because she's so pretty. I wish I was tall like her. But she just laughed and shook her head whenever anybody asked. With the boys she'd joke. You know, stuff like telling them to go after someone their own size. Once she got mad. Mark Griggs—he's this senior who plays football, and he's such a jerk—anyway, Mark came on really strong with her." Abby's cheeks turned pink and she sneaked a glance at her mother. "He said he was plenty big to do her, and he kind of grabbed his crotch." Her lip curled. "He's just so gross."

"Why hasn't he gotten expelled yet?" Karen muttered.

Abby took her question seriously. "I think some of the teachers are scared of him. One time I saw him come out of Mr. Bradley's office, and he was smirking, like he'd gotten away with something. Everyone I know thinks it's because he's such a good football player. If they suspended him or something, he'd miss a game and they might lose."

Bradley was a worthless little slimeball, but Karen had the sense not to say so and interrupt Abby's train of thought. Neal was scribbling away furiously without even lifting his head.

"Okay, what about parents? Do you remember any?"

He took her through every dance, week by week, and Abby amazed Karen with her detailed recollections. Probably this was the kind of stuff that filled her memory cells so that there wasn't room for algebraic formulas or historical facts.

In the end he slapped his notebook shut and said with satisfaction, "Well, at least now we have a limited number of suspects and a reason for the once-a-week time schedule."

"Yes, but he skipped a week," Karen pointed out.

"If Abby is right, that week the dance was chaperoned by two couples and a few male teachers. No single women."

"Which would suggest," Karen said slowly, "that he doesn't look at married women in the same light."

"Maybe doesn't even ask them to dance. That's worth checking out. It would be suggestive if one of the teachers, say, asked each of the single women but not the married ones."

"Or maybe he wasn't *at* the dance the one week."

"That would be an interesting coincidence, wouldn't it? Nobody leaps out on Abby's list, but there are bound to be a few additions and corrections." His smile was feral. "Abby, you've been a big help. My job would be easier if everybody had your memory."

She should have turned pink again with pleasure. Instead, she nibbled on her lower lip. Hesitantly she said, "Umm, maybe you've thought of this, but, well..." She nibbled her lip again. Just when Karen was about ready to shake it out of her, Abby concluded in a burst, "Today's Friday, you know. There was another dance tonight after the game."

Neal swore and looked at his watch. "How late do they usually break up?"

"Maybe eleven-thirty or twelve. Something like that."

He was already on his feet and shrugging into a jacket that hid the black holster at his side. "I can still make it over there," he said.

With his dark brows drawn together and his mouth a forbidding line, he was a cop, not the man Karen dated. She knew he must be irritated at himself for forgetting what night this was. But mostly what she saw on his face was unrelenting grimness. If they were right, the rapist was at the high school now. Probably he'd already chosen his next victim, piqued because she'd refused to dance with him. That was what mattered.

She'd have sworn Neal had forgotten her entirely, except that he stopped at the front door and turned back to frown at her.

"Do me a favor and forget the patrols," he said brusquely. "This is no time for women's lib."

Just when she was feeling charitable toward him, he had to blow it. *Women's lib.* Karen rolled her eyes. "Boy, you really know how to say the right thing, don't you?"

"What's that supposed to mean?"

She shook her head. "Never mind. Go."

"Damn it, Karen, I'm not trying to antagonize you!" He wrapped one large hand around her wrist. "I asked a favor..."

She didn't yield an inch. "That was asking? What's an order sound like?"

He glowered down at her, the planes of his face harsh. "Why the hell can't anything to do with you be easy?"

"Because I'm a difficult woman," she suggested, only partly tongue in cheek.

"Damn right," he muttered, and kissed her.

His lips were surprisingly tender, considering his mood. Maybe he *liked* difficult, she thought fuzzily, even as her blood heated and she swayed toward him. Karen heard him groan an instant before he deepened the kiss and pulled her tightly against him.

Just as suddenly he let her go. "Hell, I don't have time for this." He sounded disgusted with himself. "Lock the damn door behind me." Neal stopped again halfway out. "And one more thing. Don't let Abby tell anybody what she told me tonight. You were right. She *is* observant. That's not something we want the SOB to realize."

The idea of Abby becoming the focus of the rapist's attention was a chilling one. And it would be just like her to chatter away at school about everything she'd told the police chief. With a crawling sensation, Karen remembered that the last victim was only nineteen. What was to say the next one wouldn't be younger yet?

She leaned her forehead against the door, took a couple of slow deep breaths and followed Neal's order to lock up—or had he considered it a polite request?

When Karen returned to the living room, Abby was lying flat on her back, staring up at the ceiling.

"Time for bed," Karen announced.

Her daughter didn't move. Karen waited.

It came out then, in a small flat statement. "He must be somebody I know."

Karen pushed aside some envelopes and sat down on the coffee table. She reached over and took Abby's slender hand in hers.

"Yes. I'm afraid so."

"What if it's someone I like?" Abby sounded so young then, a small child crying out her terror. When she sat up, Karen took her in her arms, her lips brushing the top of Abby's blond head.

"Let's just keep our fingers crossed that it turns out to be someone you don't know well or someone you don't like."

Abby nodded, sniffed and with the back of her hand scrubbed tears off her cheeks. "It could be Mark Griggs. I wish it would be him!"

Karen studied her. "Do you really?"

Abby shrugged, but her gaze evaded her mother's. "Why not? He's a creep! Everyone says he is."

"What I hear is that his home life isn't so good. That his dad's an alcoholic who hits his mother and probably Mark, too."

Her daughter lifted troubled eyes. "Really? But...if people have treated him like that, wouldn't he know what it feels like?"

"You'd think so, wouldn't you?" Karen sighed. "But you have to learn how to relate to people, and I guess he hasn't."

"Oh." Abby was silent for a long moment. "I hope they catch the guy soon. Whoever he is."

"Me, too." Karen gave her daughter a compulsive hug. "Me, too."

DAMN. IT SHOULD BE easy now. He knew how and where the rapist chose his victims. Trouble was, the lists of potential suspects and victims were still too long.

Neal scowled as he slammed the squad-car door and strode toward the high-school gym. Saturday morning, and the first time he had seen the lot deserted. Not quite; one pickup was parked illegally beside the yellow curb. Presumably it belonged to the man he was here to see.

Actually the place wasn't as empty as it had appeared at first sight. A couple of joggers circled the track, some boys were playing one-on-one basketball on an outdoor court, and a washroom door stood propped open by a custodian's cart. From inside came clangs and then the sound of running water.

Neal was here to meet Joe Gardner, the one man everyone was certain had been at every single dance. He was also the man who'd talked the administration into holding the dances despite problems with them in past years, who'd recruited the chaperons, and who was officially in charge. Last night as the dance was breaking up, they had arranged to meet this morning. Gardner said he had to get into his office to compile an accurate list of chaperons.

Sure enough, the locker-room door opened silently under Neal's hand. Inside it was dark and silent, rank on rank of high metal lockers giving the room a secretive feel. Only the smell was unmistakable, no different from what Neal remembered from his own long-ago school days, made up of damp towels and sweaty socks.

A wall of windows separated staff offices from the locker room. Only one was lit, the door to it standing open. The teacher/football coach was hunched over an electronic typewriter, stabbing at it with two fingers, mumbling to himself.

Neal cleared his throat. "Mr. Gardner?"

The teacher glanced over his shoulder and waved toward a seat. "Yeah, yeah, I'll be done in a minute. Sit. Help yourself from that thermos if you want coffee."

Neal didn't. The espresso bar two doors down from the police station had spoiled him. He sat, studying Joe Gardner.

Young. Maybe thirty, tops. Short, light brown hair streaked with blond, brown eyes, six foot three, give or take a little. Bulging muscles, emphasized by a snug T-shirt and the kind of form-fitting shorts cyclists wear. Gung ho; he'd expect the boys in his classes and on his football team to give it their all. Definitely a man women would describe as big and strong. No question he could force a woman to do anything he wanted her to.

But, damn it, he was almost too big. A woman who'd been assaulted tended to remember the attacker as larger than he really was. Kathleen, Chelsea and Lisa had all agreed that the man was tall, but they hadn't described him as huge. They couldn't have failed to notice the PE teacher's powerful biceps and thighs.

At that moment, Gardner ripped the paper out of the typewriter and swung around in his office chair. His expression was friendly. "Here's the list I promised you. According to my calendar, that's who was at each dance. We have a great staff here at the high school, so I haven't needed all that many parents. Usually two or three. I've got parents lined up for the next few weeks, too. Let me know if you want their names."

Neal didn't even want to think about the next Friday, or his few alternatives. Right now, he just hoped to God he'd be making an arrest by then.

"Mr. Gardner," he said, "you're one of the few people who's been at every dance." He paused deliberately, interested when the teacher didn't react. Gardner's square-jawed face stayed open and interested. Was the guy that good an actor? Neal wondered. Or just innocent? He continued, "If you can spare the time, I'd like to go over this list and compare it with what I've heard from other people. Catch any inconsistencies. Maybe I can nudge your memory a little."

"No problem," the coach said promptly. "I tell you, I don't like to think of some wacko circulating among a bunch of fifteen-year-olds. And after all our efforts to keep these functions drug- and alcohol-free."

"We've discussed the possibility that the 'wacko' could be a kid," Neal reminded him neutrally.

Gardner was shaking his head before Neal finished the sentence. "I don't believe it. I won't say some of these boys don't have problems. We talked about Mark Griggs, for example. But he's not that bad a kid. He's got guts. I ask him for more effort, I get it. He has a lousy situation at home. That doesn't make him a rapist."

"No, it doesn't," Neal agreed. "But I have to consider him. To the best of your recollection, was he at every dance?"

"No." The coach leaned forward, elbows on his knees. "See, I've been thinking about that. Most of the older boys don't come. Maybe they did the first week or two, looked over the crop of freshmen girls, but a school function like this is pretty tame for them. I don't remember seeing Griggs more than a couple of times."

"Did he dance?"

Gardner frowned in thought. "Got me. I'd be surprised if he did."

Neal pulled out his notebook and pencil. "Let's move on to the adults for now. Why don't we start with the teachers and administrators. Appears you have a pretty faithful group."

"I'm damned lucky." Gardner grinned ruefully, looking more human and less bionic. "God knows we spend enough time during the week rousting smokers out of the john and trying to knock some sense into the heads of those kids. But these are people who really care about them."

Give him twenty years and that enthusiasm will be burned out, Neal thought cynically. Which'll be a pity.

Starting at the top of his list, he said, "Frank Morris."

"Math teacher. Fortyish. Single. I've wondered..." His face stiffened. "Forget I said that."

If a man didn't marry, somebody always wondered. In this case, Neal would be just as glad to find out Morris *was* gay.

"What I'm looking for," Neal said, "is somebody who hates women. Not somebody who is sexually uninterested in them."

Appearing discomfited, either about the topic or his own slip, the football coach shoved his chair back and put his snow white Nikes up on the desk. When he clasped his hands behind his head, powerful muscles flexed.

After a moment he grimaced. "Frank's an odd duck. But... mild, you know what I mean? Maybe socially inept. I get the feeling the high school is his life. He stays late every day, comes to all the games, volunteers to be faculty adviser to the newspaper and the computer club—" He broke off. "I hear he's actually sold some computer games. Smart."

Not an atypical description of a rapist. But, hell, every high school probably had half a dozen teachers that would fit the same description. Hell, the man might like teaching because it gave him summers off for his sideline. Maybe he genuinely liked kids.

Frowning, Neal moved on. "Peter Merck."

"Chemistry and biology. This is his second year. I don't know him well. He's also trying to get a horticulture program up and running. You might ask Karen Lindberg down at Cottage Garden Nursery about him."

"I'll do that," Neal said, inclining his head. "Any idea where he came from, age?"

"Eastern Washington." The young coach shrugged. "Thirty, thirty-five. Wife's a flight attendant. Out of town most weekends. That's why he volunteered."

Neal made a note: check wife's flight schedule. Her absence on all four relevant nights would be suggestive. The fact that the chemistry teacher was relatively new here interested Neal, too. It was possible the rapist had lived in Pilchuck his entire life, and something just in the past few weeks had pushed his dislike of women into active hatred and a need to humiliate them. But it was equally possible that the assaults had begun only recently because the rapist hadn't been here before; perhaps a string of similar assaults had ceased wherever he came from.

Neal didn't let his face show his thoughts. "Carl Bradley."

Gardner's feet thumped to the floor and he sat up. "You don't seriously think—"

"No, I don't." True as far as it went and easier than explaining that even U.S. senators had been known to sexually abuse women. Neal kept his voice bland. "But according to your list, he *was* here. Every week except September thirtieth." He didn't have to point out that Bradley had missed the one dance that wasn't followed by an assault.

Gardner didn't like the spot he was in; his reluctance was obvious. But either eagerness to get himself off the hook or genuine desire to help kept him talking.

"He's been here a year or two longer than I have. Say five, six years. Doesn't have a lot of teaching experience, I understand. On an administrator track from the beginning. Before he came here, he was a vice-principal at a middle school. He's not always popular with the kids or parents, but you could probably say that about anyone in his position."

"What about with the teachers?" Neal asked out of curiosity, not because it was particularly relevant.

Gardner reached for a neon yellow rubber ball and began squeezing it in one hand. "He's behind the football program a hundred percent. I've got no complaints."

A nonanswer. Neal let it drop. He and the coach went over the half-dozen fathers who'd chaperoned at least one dance. None were great prospects, but at this point all were possibles. One of them might well have driven his son or daughter to the other dances and hung around himself for half an hour each time without provoking comment.

Neal's lists from other sources mentioned adults not on Gardner's list, including one father who apparently had not been a chaperon the time he asked Kathleen Madsen to dance. She swore he'd been kidding, that he had no more intention of staying than she did, but then she didn't remember anybody who had sounded very serious or appeared even mildly peeved by her quick departure. Shit, Neal thought. The rapist might not have asked her to dance at all! Maybe he'd been mad because she hadn't noticed him. Maybe he'd only chosen her because she was a woman and he'd overheard her tell someone that her son was going to Yakima the next day for a weekend tournament. In that case, the attack would have depended on opportunity rather than a personal grudge.

At two dances, local bands had played, Gardner explained. A custodian had been on hand in case of electrical problems, but the duty had been rotated. Otherwise, a CD player was used.

With the feeling he hadn't learned a hell of a lot that was new, Neal flipped to a clean page in his notebook and said quietly, "Mr. Gardner, I'm sure you understand that I have to ask you some personal questions."

The coach squeezed the ball so hard his knuckles showed white, but he gave a terse nod.

"You've taught here four years?"

"This is my fifth."

"Before you came here?"

"I was getting a master's degree in phys ed."

"And where was that?"

"WSU in Pullman."

"Married?"

"No."

"Do you live alone?"

The ball was getting a workout now, first from one hand, then the other. "Yes," Gardner said shortly.

"Did you dance on any of the Fridays we're discussing?"

"Yes." The ball was moving faster and faster.

Neal let his voice harden. "Did you dance with Kathleen Madsen, Lisa Pyne, Chelsea Cahill or Toni Santos?"

"Lisa. I asked Chelsea, but we got distracted. I don't know the other two women."

Neal pushed a little harder, and they established that, yes, Joe Gardner knew Kurt Madsen, thought he'd recognize the boy's mother, but he didn't remember seeing her at any of the dances. He didn't teach girls' PE and claimed to have no idea who Toni Santos was.

Neal gave him a moment to sweat before he said, "Mr. Gardner, can you tell me where you were on the evenings of Saturday, September tenth, Tuesday, September twentieth, Sunday, September twenty-fifth, and Thursday, October thirteenth?"

"Jesus, you're serious," he said incredulously.

"Did you think this was a game?"

The young coach bowed his head, shaking it. "Of course I didn't! It just never occurred to me that I was a suspect." He gave a bitter laugh. "Suspect. God. I'm probably your best bet! I suppose I arranged the damn dances for my own ends."

"Mr. Gardner, you are no more a suspect than any of the other men on these lists." Neal tapped the piece of paper the coach had given him. "If you can produce a witness to your whereabouts on any of these nights, I can cross you off. Believe me, that's my goal."

Gardner shook his head a couple of more times, apparently still in disbelief, then sat up and reached for his desk calendar. "Yeah, okay. Give me the dates again."

On the night Kathleen Madsen was raped, he claimed to have been sleeping out in the Snoqualmie area of the Cascade Mountains. He'd gone rock climbing alone. Running agitated fingers through his short hair, he said, "Maybe somebody saw my car parked up there. Or...hey! I met some other climbers on my way out Sunday. Think you could find them?"

"Did you know them? Or did they say where they were from?"

Gardner's momentary excitement evaporated. "I don't think so. We talked about the route they were taking up Chair. I recommended a different one."

"If we really need to find them, maybe they'd remember." At the moment, there was no way Neal could devote resources to finding some anonymous climbers who might be from anywhere to verify the alibi for a man who was only one of a dozen suspects. "Right now, let's concentrate on the other dates."

But the other dates turned up nothing. The football coach had been home alone.

"Mr. Gardner, I appreciate your time," Neal said at last, rising to his feet. "I'll be in touch with you before Friday."

Pete Merck lived the closest. It was still early enough in the morning that he came to the door yawning and bare-chested. "Yeah, sure, come on in," he said.

This conversation was more productive. It developed that his wife flew three weekends out of four. The previous weekend had been the fourth. He and his wife had gone to Friday Harbor in the San Juan Islands for a romantic getaway.

"Your name is on the list of chaperons for that Friday," Neal said.

The chemistry teacher, who seemed an easygoing type, said, "Yeah, but I told Joe on Thursday morning that I couldn't make it. He must have forgotten. He said he had plenty of people. Carol and I left right after school, stayed in a bed-and-breakfast in Anacortes, then caught the morning ferry."

The clincher was that he'd also driven his wife to Sea-Tac Airport on the Thursday night Toni Santos was raped. Back at the station, Neal called the airline, who confirmed Carol Merck's arrival time and found somebody who'd seen her kiss her husband goodbye. There was no way he could have made it back to Pilchuck in time to commit the assault.

Neal sat in his office thinking about what he ought to do next. Speak to Carl Bradley and Frank Morris, assuming either were home. Track down the five or six fathers he hadn't yet interviewed. With luck, they'd all be home mowing their lawns or kicking a soccer ball with their kids.

But first... "DeSalsa?" he called.

The young Hispanic officer appeared in the doorway. "Yeah, boss?"

"Make sure Darlene Nelson really left town. Then talk to Carla Taft," Neal ordered. "See if you can't change her mind. Failing that, maybe she'll let you spend the night outside her bedroom door. I'd rather you didn't take your eyes off her."

Two single women had chaperoned last night's high-school dance. Neal had talked to both in the parking lot. One, a school secretary, had agreed to visit her brother in Olympia for a couple of weeks. The other was a one-on-one aide to an autistic kid. He would be lost without her, Miss Taft had told Neal, her eyes soft and anxious. She'd be careful. Besides, she had faith the Lord would protect her.

Neal subscribed to the "God helps those who help themselves" philosophy. He failed to convert her. For someone with such a gentle, round face and china-doll eyes, she had a will of iron.

Now DeSalsa leaned a shoulder against the doorjamb. "You really think he'll go after her?"

"Damn it, yes!" Neal exploded. He rolled his shoulders and moderated his voice. "I think he'll go

after someone. She's the obvious next target unless she
agrees to a nice vacation."

"Yeah, okay, I'm on my way." The young policeman had the sense not to try to point out the flaws in
his superior's reasoning.

God knew, there were plenty of them. Yeah, Ms.
Taft was the obvious choice, but there was no saying
the bastard wouldn't go after one of the older teenage
girls, instead, or some mother who'd done no more
than drop off a son or daughter and stay for a minute
to chat with other parents the way Kathleen Madsen
had done. Or he could attack someone he'd spotted at
an earlier dance.

Neal's best guess still was that the victims had all
turned the rapist down when he asked them to dance.
But he wasn't going to want to quit raping, even if the
dances were canceled. That angry destructive need
would push him to choose his victims in a different
way. If he was a teacher, he might decide some woman
teacher or aide hadn't been nice enough to him in the
faculty lounge. If he was one of the fathers who
worked at the nearby factory, as half the county
seemed to, he might follow some coworker home because she hadn't heard him say hello when they passed
in the hall.

Or he was going to get pissed off because women
were walking the streets with their flashlights, thinking they could stop him. A man who hated women
would feel as if they were taunting him, even trying to
emasculate him. He'd want to show them how powerful he was, how easily he could humiliate them.

Neal swore under his breath. He didn't have time to
sit here brooding. He'd see if he could catch Frank

Morris at home, then stop by Karen's and try again to talk her out of those damn fool patrols.

But first he'd call home.

A minute later his daughter said tentatively, "Will you be here for dinner, Dad?"

He glanced at the clock. Almost noon. "I'll try," he said. "Do you have anything planned for the day?"

"Nothing special. Except—" her voice gained some eagerness "—I thought maybe I'd make dinner tonight. Mrs. Feeney says that's okay. I found this new recipe..."

"Then I'll be there," he promised. "Can you aim for six-thirty?"

"Sure," she said. "But if you're busy and don't get home, that's okay."

"Thanks, sweetheart." He had to clear his throat. "Once I catch this...creep, I'll make it up to you and Michael. I'm not due for vacation yet, but we could go for a long trail ride. Maybe even an overnighter. What do you think?"

"That would be fun," Krista said. She didn't remind him how many times he'd made similar promises, or question whether he would catch the rapist. She was just like her mother, he thought on his way out to the car: smart and talented, but also sweet and compliant.

He could undoubtedly thank Ms. Flowerwoman for the fact that he wasn't sure he liked that idea.

Frank Morris lived on a cul-de-sac in a neighborhood that was only about ten or fifteen years old. His was one of the smaller houses. It stood out from the others only because the yard was so scrupulously cared for. Velvet green lawn, precisely edged, roses perfectly spaced to each side of the front walk, house freshly painted. Neal didn't get the feeling the man loved to garden; only that he required tidiness in his surroundings. Which, for a math teacher, stood to reason.

Morris answered the door immediately. Brown-haired, brown-eyed, he was one of those people that made up fifty percent of the population: so ordinary, he'd never stand out of the crowd.

"Chief Rowland." He didn't look pleased, but he stood back. "Come in."

Neal followed him into the living room. Spartan, it held no books, no bouquets, no ashtrays or cigarette butts; the pillows were carefully spaced on the couch. The room was devoid of personality. Presumably Morris did his living elsewhere in the house, a den, maybe, or a family room.

Turning to face the math teacher, Neal said, "I wonder if I might have a few minutes of your time."

Morris's mouth twisted, but he said stiffly, "Please, sit down. I take it you're still of the same mind as last night—that the rapes are connected with the school dances."

"Yes, I am." Neal pulled his small notebook from his shirt pocket. "Have you been thinking about who you saw at each occasion?"

He frowned. "Yes, in fact I made some notes. Let me find them." He was gone only a minute, returning with a pad of paper from which he tore a couple of pages. "I think they're legible," he said, handing them over.

Neal glanced at the scrawled pages. Nothing new, though the lists were detailed, agreeing in most particulars with Gardner's. Again, not surprising that a math teacher's thoughts were clear and well organized.

It was difficult to picture such a man having, much less indulging in, violent physical appetites. How had Joe Gardner described him? Mild, socially inept. Morris was technically tall enough at perhaps five foot eleven to match the profile, but his lankiness and rounded shoulders made him unimposing.

Neal watched him closely. "Mr. Morris, on the occasions when you served as chaperon, did you yourself dance?"

The man blinked several times. "Well, let me see... Perhaps once or twice. To tell you the truth, I'd feel like an idiot out there most of the time. I don't know how the kids dance to some of that music."

"Do you recall who you danced with?"

Unlike Joe Gardner, Morris was smart enough to see where this was going. "Has somebody accused me?"

Neal explained again that he hoped to get a clear picture of who was where at all times. "I'm also hoping to eliminate some of you as possible suspects. If I can winnow my list down with these preliminary visits, it would be helpful."

The teacher gave a short nod. "Very well."

He admitted to having danced a couple of times with women chaperons: one a mother, the other a young foreign-language instructor. He supposed he might have asked other women; the only one who stuck out in his mind was Lisa Pyne.

He sounded genuinely troubled when he said, "I wouldn't like to be associated in her mind with something so ugly just because I'd asked her to dance."

"I understand she danced several times and probably turned some other men down," Neal said. "She's not likely to associate the assault with any one of you."

A muscle twitched under one eye, and Morris gave a jerky nod.

Questioned, he conceded that he knew Chelsea Cahill because they'd been on a district-wide curriculum committee together, and that, yes, they'd talked briefly the evening she chaperoned the dance. He knew Kurt Madsen, but wasn't sure he'd recognize Kurt's mother. Toni Santos hadn't been a very good student and wasn't especially memorable.

Unemotionally Neal asked, "Do you remember seeing her at any of the dances?"

Morris shook his head. "No. But, good God, the music is blasting your eardrums and the gym's dark except for a strobe light. And frankly, I wouldn't have thought anything of it if I *had* seen her."

When asked, he thought that Mark Griggs had been at several of the dances, though he wasn't sure which. On the Saturday night Kathleen Madsen was raped, Morris had gone to see a concert at a new jazz club in Seattle. "I might still have the ticket stub," he offered.

For the other three nights, he had no alibis. Again, not surprising.

Frank Morris was still standing in his doorway watching when Neal backed out of the driveway. Carefully sandwiched in Neal's notebook was the ticket stub. On his agenda for tomorrow was finding out whether the club had any record of their ticket holders. According to Morris, it was a small place. If Neal could track down some of the concert goers, he could show a picture of the teacher; with luck, someone would recognize him.

Chances were, Morris was as innocuous as he looked. But there was something about his stark living room and compulsively edged lawn, something about the fact that he had bought only one ticket to the concert and had kept the stub, that sat uneasily with Neal.

But no more uneasily than the idea of those women out walking the streets tonight. Neal looked at his watch. Time to stop at the nursery and talk some sense into Karen.

Not that she would listen, he thought ruefully, signaling to make a left turn. She was too damned pigheaded.

But even arguing with her had a certain appeal. Why else did he feel the first lift he'd had all day just because he was on his way to see her?

Maybe pigheaded was too strong, he decided. Gutsy sounded better. Even that wasn't a quality he'd ever admired in a woman. But something in him had changed when Jenny conceded to death long before it had come for her. He'd discovered he wanted a woman who loved him enough to fight.

And one thing you could say about Ms. Flowerwoman. By God, when she loved somebody, it would be with every ounce of passion and determination in her. She would go out fighting.

He wouldn't mind knowing it was for him.

CHAPTER TEN

WHY WERE MEN all so bullheaded?

"Good question," Karen said aloud.

Brooding, she swung her hammer and drove the stake into the ground. Her campaign poster was a satisfyingly eye-catching blue-green. Karen Lindberg for Pilchuck School-Board Position No. 3, it declared. A Better Education for Our Kids.

The intersection was a busy one, where her message would reach plenty of commuting voters. Standing back, she was pleased with the effect. Hers was larger, more readable and appealing than the one a few feet away that blared her opponent's name in neon orange.

She resisted the temptation to "accidentally" knock Dennis Shafer's sign down. If people weren't smart enough to figure out who was the better candidate, they deserved what they got, Karen told herself with a sniff.

She slid back in the Civic and tossed the hammer onto the seat beside her. Okay, where next?

Putting the car in gear, she headed for the freeway exit. The country road was quiet on a Sunday afternoon. Hard to believe it was already mid-October. Alders and vine maples were turning vivid orange and yellow, with drifts of fallen leaves crunchy and dry beneath. This was one of her favorite times of year.

She could put her garden to bed for the winter, pruning and mulching and tidying, beginning the anticipation of spring. Business would slow down drastically at the nursery in the next month; in fact, after the middle of November she stayed open only weekends through the end of December, selling live Christmas trees and wreathes and garden ornaments, then closed altogether until the middle of March. Though she used the time for ordering and starting seedlings, the winter always felt leisurely to her.

But her mind didn't seem to want to settle into deciding whether she should start offering some of the more exotic annuals, as well as the usual marigolds and pansies and geraniums. She was to debate with Dennis Shafer this week, too, but planning what to say didn't interest her much, either.

Part of the trouble was her uneasy awareness that she—and everyone else in town—was waiting for the rapist to make another move. Or for the police to arrest him.

It made her anxious and mad as hell. And she bitterly resented having Neal tell her repeatedly that she and all the other women should go home like good little girls, lock their doors and be careful not to open them to the big bad wolf.

"You don't know what you're setting in motion," he'd told her yesterday, grimly, during one of his fleeting visits, which he probably imagined were furthering his romantic cause. "What are you going to do if a couple of you catch the son of a bitch? Hold him politely at flashlight point?"

"I'm not polite," she said waspishly. "Haven't you noticed?"

"Damn it, Karen, this could be life and death!" he snapped, those heavy brows bunched together. "Somebody is going to get hurt!"

"Somebody has already been hurt. Four somebodies. And they were all women." She tasted the acid that seeped into her voice, and she forced herself to speak quietly. "Neal, don't discount our efforts. If the police work with us, we'll be stronger."

What she resented most of all was his response. He muttered an expletive and bent his head to kiss her. For the first time, she yanked free and stepped back. Holding her chin high, she said, "I don't like wondering who you think you're kissing. Because I know the woman you want isn't who I really am."

It was also the first time she'd struck a blow close enough to home to make him flinch. Then his jaw muscles tightened and he asked in a gritty voice, "What are you running from? Is the idea of a man wanting to protect you so bad? Is that what scares you?"

"What scares me," she said bitterly, "is how close I just came to getting involved with a man who thinks of me as little more than a child. It may be news to you, but all women don't equate being coddled with true love."

That did it, of course. His face froze, and after issuing another dire warning of what would happen if she didn't back down, he stomped out.

That was when she discovered what scared her the most: she wanted to call him back, to apologize, to acquiesce.

Her pride hadn't let her, and she was grateful. Somehow she'd forgotten that love had a way of weakening a woman. There was a reason she'd sworn off it.

But now, getting out of her car with her hammer and another campaign poster, Karen wondered.

Was she really defending the right of women to take an active part in their own defense? Or was she using the issue as a shield to protect herself from her own feelings for Neal? The feelings that scared the daylights out of her?

FIVE RINGS, six rings, seven. No answer.

Growling under his breath, Neal hung up the pay phone. Had Karen gone into hiding?

The high-school quad was empty but for a few students who apparently weren't bothering to go to class. A girl who didn't look a day older than Krista was snuggling up to a big overmuscled senior Neal had seen sauntering by earlier with Mark Griggs. A woman from the office hurried across the paved quad, clipboard in hand.

Neal turned away. He was done here, though far from satisfied. His instinct said the son of a bitch was on this campus right now. The high school was where it had all begun, where the bastard fueled his sexual anger. Neal's money was on a teacher or student.

Yeah, but which one? He didn't like Bradley, the principal, but it was hard to see him as a rapist. And then there was the fact that his wife swore he'd been home at the times of all four rapes. The way her gaze had bounced nervously between her husband and Neal had made Neal wonder, but chances were it was true.

The math teacher, Frank Morris, was an odd character, but odd didn't necessarily equate with sick. Gardner was the one who stood out. But Lisa Pyne had danced with him. If a refusal had triggered the other rapes, why had he also chosen her as a target for his brand of revenge? The inconsistency didn't sit well with Neal.

He was grateful Carla Taft, the aide to the autistic boy, had finally succumbed to pressure and agreed to get out of town for a week or two. At least that was one weight off his mind.

A big student bulletin board hung on the wall by the entrance to the office. Reflexively, Neal scanned it as he passed. A poster for the next theater production took up one corner. Krista would be working on sets for that one. Notices of cars for sale, mothers looking to hire baby-sitters, somebody wanting to sell some concert tickets...

He was two strides past the bulletin board when a square white notice registered in his brain. He spun around, hoping he'd been wrong.

Shit. No such luck. Somebody was trying to organize a high-school branch of the foot patrol. Girls could escort other girls home at night and add their numbers to the existing patrol.

The shock came when he reached the phone number and contact name. His home phone number. Krista Rowland.

Rage rose in him with the force of a tidal wave. It was Karen he wanted to get his hands on, but his daughter was closer. How could she do something so goddamn idiotic and without discussing it with him first?

He turned back toward the office, but just then the bell rang and a human flood poured out into the quad. Anger barely held in check, he searched the crowd of students for one particular dark head.

She passed so close to him he almost missed her. She was walking with several other girls, all giggling. Krista was the quiet center, her expression grave as she listened; she possessed a calm unnatural for her age.

A pang of sadness didn't stop him from calling, "Krista."

She turned, the surprise altering to an uncomplicated smile. "Dad!" she exclaimed, before saying something to her friends, who glanced back but then went on.

Bucking the tide, Krista was almost to him when her gaze slid guiltily away, touched the bulletin board, came warily back.

Most disconcerting was the fact that she was enough of an actress to hide the wheels turning in her head. By the time she reached him, her face was brightly inquiring. "Dad!" she said. "What are you doing here?"

He crossed his arms. "Right now, trying to find out what my daughter's name is doing up on that bulletin board."

Krista flushed, but also lifted her chin in a way Karen had made familiar to him. "I volunteered to be the clearinghouse—you know, like Ms. Lindberg." She spoke quickly, breathlessly. "As long as I've done my homework, Mrs. Feeney doesn't mind if I'm on the phone a lot, and I'm mostly home. We—some of the other girls and I—we were talking about it, and we thought the whole idea was really great." His daughter was winding down, but seeing the expression on his face, she said defiantly, "You're the one who always says girls can do anything boys can. I've heard you!"

He asked implacably, "Why didn't you tell me what you had in mind?"

Students were parting to go around them, some of them turning to stare. Krista hugged her books. "When? You're never home anymore."

He had to have wandered into a nightmare. "Damn it, what do you want me to do?" he growled. "Sometimes the job has to come first!"

"I know that!" Her eyes were huge and blue, angry even, although the rest of her expression was pinched and scared. "But you're still not home!"

"Don't try to tell me you couldn't have found a minute to talk to me."

"I wanted to do something myself!" she cried. "Something that made *me* feel useful. Well, now I am! It's important. Don't you understand?" Krista whirled and ran, the pile of books still gripped to her chest.

Shell-shocked, Neal stared after her. He couldn't remember his gentle daughter ever yelling at him. She was the one he'd been able to rely on during this hellish past few years. She'd grieved, of course, but if she felt anger, it wasn't at him. Michael had acted out at school, but never Krista. Michael had fought the move, but Krista hadn't.

She'd changed. Now—now of all times!—she had to choose a dangerous way to rebel, to prove to herself and her new friends that she was her own person. Recharging his anger, Neal told himself that the old Krista would never have dreamed of doing something so foolhardy, so downright stupid.

The thought of a couple of fourteen- or fifteen-year-old girls—of Krista—walking the streets at eleven at night with no more protection than flashlights or the family beagle was enough to mix terror into the anger brewing in Neal's chest.

His daughter had changed, all right. And he knew who to blame.

He turned on his heel and stalked toward his squad car. Ms. Flowerwoman might be in hiding, but he was going to dig her out.

BY THE TIME Abby was off to school Monday morning, Karen felt restless enough to decide to go to work, even though the nursery was closed on Mondays and she usually went in late. Despite the temptation to stop for a doughnut, she skipped it. She simply wasn't in the mood to deal with other human beings, good, bad or anything in between.

Leaving the Closed sign turned out on the gate, she parked inside by the greenhouse, unlocked and began her chores with watering the tables of shade perennials and ground covers that were under a shed roof.

The phone rang half a dozen times that first hour, but Karen ignored it. Let the answering machine pick up the calls.

She enjoyed the quiet on these days when the nursery was all hers. An occasional car passed, but on one side was a dairy farm and on the other fields of corn stubble. Between greenhouses, Karen could catch glimpses of a curve of the river, brown-green and low at this season.

She checked, sorted and labeled boxes of daffodil and tulip bulbs that had arrived from the Skagit Valley grower. With satisfaction Karen noted that they were top quality, as usual: large and plump, clusters rather than the single skimpy bulbs sold by most nurseries and mail-order suppliers.

By the time she reached the greenhouse where she would start annuals in trays, she had regained the serenity that gardening in all forms had always offered her. She misted the rose starts along one wall, then began counting trays and four-inch black plastic pots.

It was too bad more gardeners didn't recycle their pots, she thought; like many nursery owners, she took them back, but ninety percent of the customers just tossed them in the garbage.

She was frowning at a pile of burlap used for bundling bare-root plants when the door at the far end of the greenhouse flew open.

Her heart jumped into her throat and Karen swung around. In that moment of sick fear, she realized she hadn't even brought the cordless phone with her.

But it was Neal, wearing his uniform, who filled the doorway, who strode toward her with lowered brow and set jaw. He was in a temper, she realized instantly, so angry he didn't speak until he stopped just in front of her. Then his voice was like raw gravel against bare skin.

"What the hell are you doing here alone?"

"I'm closed today."

"Parking that car of yours where it can be seen looks like a dangerous invitation to me. But then, you like fights, don't you?"

"Are you picking one?"

"No." Was that contempt in his dark eyes to match his scathing tone? "Since you don't answer your telephone, I came to let you know that two members of your foot patrol were assaulted last night."

A wave of shock, near dizziness, threatened Karen's hard-kept calm. "They were hurt? Who was it?"

"Gretchen Williams and Marta Peters. Mrs. Peters is fine. Ms. Williams was treated and released at the hospital. They were lucky. A couple of drunks were cruising for some action. Two women on a dark street at midnight fit the bill."

"There were supposed to be three."

The look on his face was searing enough to raise blisters. "The third woman couldn't make it. They decided to go, anyway."

"They should have called me."

"Were you answering your phone last night any better than you are this morning?"

"Damn you!" Karen snapped. "Yes! I was there. I'd have joined them if they'd called!"

Neal's mouth curled in derision. "What good would you have done them?"

"Sheer numbers—"

He lashed out with one hand, sweeping a stack of half-gallon pots to the floor. His voice was low and furious. "You think you're invincible, don't you? Well, goddamn it, you could get raped and beaten and shot, too. I've seen what happens to pretty women like you who aren't careful."

"Three of us—"

His rage was both deaf and blind. She might as well not have tried to defend her point of view, because he stormed on, "Doesn't it give you pause to think of all those women out there on your say-so?"

"They're my responsibility. Is that what you're saying?"

"You're damned right that's what I'm saying!"

"Well, let me tell *you* something!" Karen snapped. "Even assuming it is dangerous, Marta and Gretchen are adults who chose to take a risk for something they thought was worthwhile. Believe it or not, women can make that kind of choice, too, you know."

"Hell!" Neal paced away from her and back, his fingers flexing as though he wished they were around her throat, tension radiating from him in palpable waves. "What is it with you, lady? I believed you went to the newspaper because you thought it was right. Now I'm starting to wonder whether maybe you just like to see your name in print. Or do you imagine yourself as some kind of heroine? Joan of Arc? Only, somebody else might burn at the stake in your place."

She felt a wave of adrenaline that made standing here quietly taking whatever he wanted to dish out the next thing to impossible. Answering anger pressed at her temples until they hurt, but she realized dimly that something was wrong here. He should have been saying "I told you so," not attacking her with bitter personal accusations. He'd felt betrayed when she'd gone to the *Times,* but then his anger had been cold. This time it was white hot.

Very quietly, ignoring the way her head ached and her teeth ground together, she asked, "What are you really angry about?"

He'd swung around to face her, and now raw emotion shivered through his eyes and twitched a muscle in his cheek. "You've gone too far this time. I just came from the high school. I found out that you seem to have inspired—or should I say, recruited?—a bunch of high-school girls to join your group of martyrs in the making. I didn't like what you were doing before, but you were all over twenty-one." His voice rose steadily until he was shouting. "But now you're involving kids. You've got my daughter thinking she's some kind of wonder woman, and, by God, I won't stand for it!"

The extra decibels shattered Karen's control like fragile glass. She yelled back, "There aren't any high-school girls in my patrol except Abby! If a group of them started their own, I don't know anything about it!"

Neal stuck his face about six inches from hers and said from between clenched teeth, "But they're out there, anyway, thanks to you. It was sheer god-damned luck that I saw a notice!"

She held off anger with the dismay she felt at the idea of girls out there without an adult. "I hope you know I wouldn't encourage anything like that."

"Do I?"

Karen counted to ten before she asked, "What do you want me to do?"

"Call the whole thing off. Tell everyone to stay home and lock their doors. Leave law enforcement to the experts."

That did it. "You patronizing son of a bitch. You won't give women any credit at all, will you? Maybe you should keep in mind that even those high-school girls aren't all docile little dolls who march where their daddy tells them to!" That was hitting below the belt, and she knew it, but she was too furious to care.

He snarled at her like a wounded animal. "The whole thing was Krista's idea!"

Krista? Good Lord, no wonder he was infuriated. His sweet obedient daughter had done something behind his back, and—if Karen was reading him right—once confronted, Krista had stood up to him.

"And you think it's my fault," Karen said, getting angrier by the minute.

"I know damn well it is!"

"Maybe—" she gave him a small twisted smile "—you should think about what kind of woman you're raising her to be. Do you really want her to be so compliant she'd let any jackass push her around? Or do you want her to have determination and spirit?"

They stared at each other, his eyes hot and hostile. After a moment he said harshly, "Spirit is a hazardous thing to have if it doesn't come with a little common sense."

"Krista has common sense."

"How the hell would you know?" Neal asked in a dark, dangerous voice. "You have such a chip on your shoulder, you come up fighting no matter what. A man wouldn't dare turn his back on you."

The swift explosion of pain in her chest robbed her of her voice for a moment. When it returned, Karen said hoarsely, "Get out of here. Now. And don't come back."

"Oh, no." He advanced on her as she retreated, his voice thick with controlled violence. "You're not going to slip out of this that easily. If it wasn't for you, those two women wouldn't have been assaulted last night. My daughter wouldn't have decided she had to do something herself. You're going to end this craziness before it goes too far."

Karen stopped dead, let him crowd her, his bulk looming over her. She saw the mask of fury on his lean face through a red haze of her own. "You," she said, flinging the words at him like shards of glass, "can go to hell!"

He growled deep in his throat and then grabbed her shoulders and yanked her against the hard length of his body. She had no time to react before his mouth captured hers savagely, forcing it open so his tongue could invade in a primal notice of his sexual intent.

The horrifying part was that her body responded instantly, powerfully. Instead of kicking his shins or beating him with her fists, she gripped his shoulders and held on. Her mouth answered his with passion as potent, as furious. If he thought he could intimidate her this way, he had another think coming.

That kiss was more like a tornado than an expression of love or sexual passion. It was dangerous and mindless, a spiral of brutal hunger that stripped Karen of pretense and left her feeling the shudder that tore through Neal's big body, the anguish beneath the rage.

Maybe her lips softened or her hands gentled, she'd never know, but suddenly he wrenched his mouth free and, with fingers that bit into her arms, came near to flinging her away from him. Karen stumbled back until she bumped up against the rough wood of a table. She was shaking with fierce emotion, outrage and need and hurt.

Both panting for breath, they stared at each other, his eyes dark with shock. Then a spasm twisted his face. He bowed his head and said hoarsely, "My God, what am I doing?"

Karen wasn't any too happy with herself at the moment. The fact that he'd behaved badly, as well, was no excuse. Acidly she said, "Letting your testosterone rule you. Man must be dominant, right?"

"Wrong." Neal lifted his head to meet her eyes again. The self-loathing she saw there went bone deep. "I've never touched a woman in anger before. It won't happen again." His voice was flat, even dead; he'd tried and condemned himself.

Remorse was one thing, sackcloth and ashes another. In the interests of fairness, she pointed out, "I was angry, too."

He frowned. "Hell, I damn near threw you on the ground and ripped your clothes off!"

Driven by some instinct, she said stubbornly, "I kissed you back."

The frown had turned into a glower. "Damn it, woman! Do you have to argue about everything?"

"I don't want you to walk out of here determined never to kiss me again." There. She'd been honest. The look she saw on his face—the incredulity and desire and something else that made her heart skip a beat—gave her the courage to add, "And I said some crummy things, too."

He said, "I was a bastard," but he also took a step toward her.

"Yes, you were," Karen agreed with some astringency.

"I'm not used to a woman like you." It sounded half-accusing.

Which was probably a good sign. If he was still determined to hate himself, he wouldn't let her have any of the blame.

Karen took a step forward, too. "What about that woman partner you claimed to have?"

"Marie? Compared to you, she was shy and self-effacing." His voice had become husky; the molten glow in his eyes made her think of hot chocolate. No, hot fudge. She would be the ice cream underneath that would melt until they ran together. The image was so unexpectedly erotic, Karen shivered.

He must have seen on her face some of what she was thinking, because he took one stride, putting himself just in front of her. He reached up to touch her cheek, then froze as if he didn't trust himself. Or as though he thought his touch would be rejected. He curled his big hand into a fist and returned it to his side. "I didn't mean what I said."

Despite the fact that she was already melting, some tartness returned to her tone. "Which part?"

A romantic man would have said all of it. He said, "Most of it. You're right. Those two women are adults. They made their own decisions. And Krista... Krista's my responsibility, not yours."

"We're all scared for our children."

The creases in his cheeks deepened. "I was scared for you. When I got called last night, I figured you were one of the women. *God.*"

Just like that, he was kissing her again. The urgency was still there, but this time she felt his need for reassurance. And, oh, she wanted to give it.

And more. Karen let her head fall back when Neal's mouth traveled down her throat. Her hands were trying to burrow their way under his shirt without much success; the thick heavy belt he wore defied her.

I must be stark, raving mad, she thought.

Lady, you're not in my game plan, either, he'd said.

"Damn," he muttered against the base of her throat. "We've got to stop."

Shutting out her doubts and fears, she whispered, "Why?"

His head came up sharply. "We're both supposed to be at work."

"Even cops get ten-minute breaks, don't they?"

His hands captured her small breasts. "Is that an insult?"

"Well . . . twenty minutes."

Neal chuckled, but his hands also stilled. In a carefully level voice, he asked, "Do you mean it?"

Karen couldn't remember the last time she'd felt shy. This time she had good reason. Here he was in his crisp uniform, carrying a gun, and she was suggesting they have sweaty sex on a heap of rough burlap. How do you tactfully say only if you want to? she wondered.

It was easier than it might have been, once her bashfully lowered gaze noted strong evidence to suggest that he did want to.

She hesitated only another second, then peeled off her T-shirt. Damn the torpedoes.

The effect was gratifying, even if her breasts were a size-B cup. Neal's eyes blazed and he said huskily, "You have a way with words." Then his hands spanned her waist and moved slowly, sensuously upward.

"Thank you." Karen reached for his belt buckle. "I try."

His thumbs gently rubbed her nipples. "I've never been seduced on the job before."

"Me, either. Love among the blooms." One by one, she freed the buttons of his khaki shirt. She hoped her hands weren't dirty enough to leave spots. People might wonder.

He was making the job tough, because at the same time he was trying to peel off her jeans. Karen tossed his shirt onto a table, hearing the clank of his badge hitting wood. Then she stepped out of her rubber boots to help. A second later she was naked. At least it was warm in here, if humid.

She gave a mildly uneasy glance toward the door at the far end of the greenhouse. "I hope nobody comes looking for me."

Neal gave a wicked grin and dropped his own pants on the table. "If they do, they'll see a couple of bare butts and make themselves scarce."

Karen gave a choked laugh. Truth be known, there was something rather thrillingly sinful about the idea of making love here. She would never look at her greenhouses the same way again.

Neal's gaze moved thoroughly over her, and hers over him. As a general rule, men looked pretty silly naked. Just as well men and women usually did their grappling in the dark under the covers. But she had to admit that Neal was an exception. He was a fine, up-standing—the pun pleased her—example of his sex. He had lovely broad shoulders with enough muscle to make a woman shiver, but not so much to suggest that he spent time thinking about the definition of a par-ticular muscle group. Well-developed chest, flat stomach, narrow hips and long lean legs. And then, of course, there was the upstanding part. Large really didn't have anything to do with a woman's pleasure, but it was nice, anyway. Maybe because it suggested an especially powerful arousal.

All for her.

When their eyes met again, his burned. Her insides cramped pleasurably. Hot fudge.

He wrapped those large hands around her hips and pulled her up against him. She wriggled a little, and felt his chest muscles quiver under her touch.

"Well," he said, only a little roughly, "which one of us gets to be on the bottom? The floor looks damned uncomfortable."

Karen slid her hands up his back. "I had that pile of burlap in mind."

Neal paused in his exploration of her body long enough to cast a dubious glance in that direction. "I'm not anxious to lose a layer of skin."

"It'll be invigorating."

"You're invigorating enough, thank you."

"Well—" she curled her fingers around his erection "—how about half and half?"

"You're on." He swept her up and deposited her backside down on the burlap, kneeling between her legs. His grin was triumphant, and damned sexy. "You first."

"No fair." Karen protested, just before she pulled him down for a sweet lingering kiss. Somewhere in its midst, she forgot the prickly burlap under her back and felt only the teasing pressure between her legs and the taunting force of his tongue in her mouth. And when the pressure at last became a long deep thrust, she rode it like the steep plunge of a water slide, a gasp of exhilaration and tension building in her throat.

A man of his word, Neal eventually rolled over and lifted her on top of him, where the ride became even wilder. He swallowed her scream at the end and drove into her one last time, his face contorting and her name coming gutturally off his tongue.

What they'd just done together had been so primal Karen wasn't sure she wanted to look him in the eye yet. She let herself sprawl languorously over him, her head tucked into the sweaty curve where his strong neck met his shoulder.

His mouth moved against her hair, and his hand stroked her spine. She felt his pulse beneath her cheek, his slowing heartbeat under her hand. This was one of those rare times she didn't let herself think, only enjoy the sweetness of the moment.

It was too good to last. Unflatteringly soon, she heard his sigh just before he slapped her bare behind and said, "Up and at 'em! Unless you want to take another turn on the bottom."

"Heck, no." Karen scrambled gracelessly off him.

In contrast, Neal rose to his feet with the kind of contained fluidity that made watching him a pleasure. On the other hand, he was also watching *her*, and with the heat of the moment past she was suddenly self-conscious.

Karen grabbed her clothes and started scrambling into them. Out of the corner of her eye, she was aware that Neal was, more slowly, doing the same. She tucked in her T-shirt and zipped up her jeans, then looked around for her boots.

She was in the act of stepping into them when, behind her, Neal said quietly, "I'm going to cancel the dances."

Back to real life with a vengeance, she thought with regret and wryness. What could she do but protest? "But you might never catch him if you do that!"

Neal tucked in his own shirt and buckled his belt, one hand briefly touching his holstered gun. "If it means he never rapes again, I can live with it," he said. "Unfortunately I doubt he'll give up so easily now that he's acted out a few of his perverted fantasies. But we can hope."

Karen hardly listened. The man had to be caught! How could life return to normal if there was no resolution? Chelsea would be left forever wondering, searching faces fearfully. Every woman in town would go to bed nights with disquiet as a companion.

Urgently she said, "But now that you know the dances are his hunting ground, you can set a trap! If you let him try again, you can catch him."

Neal looked at her, his eyes clear and steady. "How?" he asked.

"What do you mean, how? You offer him a tempting target—" She stopped.

"Exactly." His tone was dry; he knelt to tie his shoes. "I don't have any women on the force. If I bring one in from another department, she'd stick out like a sore thumb. The guy's not stupid. He's raping women he knows, however distantly. What am I supposed to do, use some teacher or mother as unwitting bait? What if we screw up and she gets hurt?"

Of course, there was an answer to that, but Karen looked down at the toes of her boots, feeling unaccustomedly tentative. She was reluctant to start another argument, afraid of what Neal's reaction would mean to their relationship. But then, she reminded herself, what was the relationship worth if he persisted in his belief that women had to be protected and guided? If there was to be any hope of a future for the two of them, he had to respect her as an equal.

And so she lifted her head and met his eyes. "I'm to be one of the chaperons next Friday night."

Already he was shaking his head.

"Neal, listen to me," she begged. "I'm willing to take the risk, just as you would be if you were me. I don't want to be afraid every time I hear a noise at night or every time a lone male customer shows up here on a slow day." She held out her hands helplessly. "It's like we're under siege! We can't let him win."

In the silence that followed her plea, Neal stared at her. Though his brows had drawn together and the grooves in his cheeks had deepened, she had a moment of silent hope. At least he'd quit shaking his head; at least he was thinking about her offer.

But not for long. "I can't let you," he said, shaking his head again.

"Why?"

His mouth twisted and he reached out to touch her cheek. "I won't let you put yourself in danger."

"Aren't I the one to decide that?" She pressed her lips together, tried again. "He has to be stopped."

She might as well not have bothered. Neal's hand dropped back to his side, his brown eyes became opaque, and his face set in hard lines. "No," he said flatly.

She stood unresisting when he bent his head and kissed her briefly, careful not to wait for a response. And she only nodded when he said, "I'll call you."

But inside, she felt hollow, so great was her sense of loss. For he'd given her his answer, in more ways than one. He'd just told her he was unwilling to allow her to be a strong individual capable of making her own decisions, of fighting for what was important to her.

What an idiot she'd been to imagine he was falling in love with her! In her book, love wasn't a cocoon offering eternal security. It was a launch pad, and the ship to pick her up once she'd splashed back to earth. Neal must know her well enough to understand that.

Which was why his answer told her a blunter truth. Whatever he felt, it wasn't love. Not the real thing.

CHAPTER ELEVEN

ASSUMING ABBY WOULD HAVE heard about the cancellation at school, Karen asked the minute she had a chance the next day. They were working together to make dinner.

Abby glanced up from where she was chopping lettuce for a salad. "Nobody said anything about it. I mean, you'd think Mr. Bradley would've made an announcement, wouldn't you?"

"Yes," Karen said thoughtfully, "I would."

"But *I'm* not going, anyway," Abby continued. "The whole idea gives me the creeps."

"Good, because I wouldn't have let you go," Karen told her.

Another time, her daughter might have protested being treated like an eight-year-old. Not today. Instead, they worked in silence for a moment, Karen stirring the spaghetti she was heating, Abby peeling a carrot. Then Abby said hesitantly, "This was the week you were supposed to chaperon, wasn't it? You're not going, either, are you, Mom? I mean, it's even more dangerous for you."

"I don't know." Karen turned off the burner and began to dish up. Even if Neal had accepted her offer, she wasn't sure she would've wanted Abby to know what she was doing. In one way, she figured, teenagers felt immortal, invincible. Yet at the same time, their expanded view of the world let them know how insecure they really were, how often dreadful things happened randomly. Abby already had to worry about AIDS, the possibility of nuclear war, flunking algebra, the economy as it would affect her and her own unknown future. She didn't need to add fear for her mother.

So Karen shrugged. "Neal said he was going to have the dances canceled. I won't have to decide."

But when Karen walked in the door after work Wednesday, Abby appeared from the kitchen. She didn't bother with a hello. She looked distressed. "Mom, there *still* wasn't any announcement today."

"Did you ask Krista if she knows anything about it?"

"I didn't think to. Can I call her?"

"If it comes to that, I might as well call Neal."

But she didn't get a chance. Karen took a quick shower to wash off the day's mud—it had poured rain from ten that morning on. By the time she was dressed, Abby had dinner on the table. Then the phone rang twice. Both callers needed Karen to find substitutes for them for tonight's patrols. Karen had to call around until she lined up women to take their places. That left her just time to eat quickly before she and Abby set out.

Dusk was sinking into night by the time they collected first Joan and then, a couple of blocks away, Chelsea, and began their rounds. Already their raincoats gleamed wetly under the occasional yellow street lamp. Because of the rain, Joan had left her dog at home. Karen had tucked her cellular phone into an inside pocket to keep it dry. She held an umbrella in one hand, a flashlight in the other.

Tonight she was in the mood to feel this was all futile. Had they really accomplished anything? Sara Elliott had caught a ten-year-old boy sneaking out his bedroom window at midnight. One group had found a boxful of abandoned kittens, which Kim Lloyd had taken home to bottle-raise. Denise King had called in what turned out to be a minor domestic disturbance after she heard screams and shattering glass. None of it meaningful, unless you looked at it from the kittens' point of view.

Hunching her shoulders against the chill rain, Karen had to remind herself that the women felt good about what they were doing. Look at Chelsea now. Maybe she was still scared, but she was striding out in front, aiming her flashlight at the yawning darkness inside an open garage. Doing something to beat back the fear.

Wasn't that meaningful enough?

They hadn't gone two blocks when headlights speared them from behind. As they all turned, Karen recognized that now familiar twinge of apprehension. *We shouldn't have to be afraid,* she thought for the hundredth time with an equally familiar stirring of anger that renewed her sagging determination.

The vehicle slowed as it approached, blinding her so that she couldn't see it was a police car until it reached the curb beside them.

The passenger-side window slid down.

"Good, it is you," Neal said. Bending, she could just make out his features in the light from the dashboard and the shielded beam of her flashlight. "I need to talk to you," he said.

He sounded tired, not angry. Presumably no fresh disaster for which he could hold her responsible had occurred.

Karen turned back to her three companions, huddled together in the rain. "You guys go ahead. I'll have Neal catch up with you and drop me off in a minute."

Joan was her usual cheerful unflappable self. "Sure thing. Come on, Abby. You haven't told us yet how that algebra test went." The three moved away, Abby sneaking glances over her shoulder.

Karen opened the door, closed her umbrella and gave it a shake before she hopped into the car. "I'm going to soak your seat."

"It'll dry." Neal made no move to kiss her. His fingers were wrapped around the steering wheel, and he was looking straight ahead. Even in the dark, she could make out the creases between his brows.

She waited in silence.

He spoke abruptly. "Are you still willing?"

Just like that, elation rose in her, fierce and wild. He had changed his mind. He hadn't, after all, been able to dismiss her offer. No, dismiss *her*.

She could only nod, but his head had turned and he was watching her now.

"You're sure?"

"Yes," Karen said, almost steadily, "I'm sure."

His voice was flat. "You were right. We have to try. I don't like using a civilian, but you're all I've got."

"How flattering."

"Damn it," he snapped, "why is it you think I'm questioning your worth every time I suggest you're overstepping your areas of competence? I don't know anything about plants. I'm not a nurseryman. I don't pretend to be. You're not a cop. When I say so, you see it as an insult."

"I've never said—"

"The hell you haven't."

He had a way of making her reexamine herself. Was he right?

She began carefully, "All I've ever asked is that you accept my right to choose the risks I take. That you see me as an equal."

Very quietly he said, "I've never seen you as anything but."

Standoff. Or was she afraid to push it just a little further, afraid to find out how personal his fear for her was?

But he'd already gone on, voice stripped of emotion, as he explained that there'd be a policeman secreted inside her house from Friday evening on. It would be better if she could make it publicly apparent that, for at least a couple of nights in the next week, Abby would be away.

Karen nodded. "Her grandmother's been wanting her for a long weekend. I'll set it up for Friday night through Monday or Tuesday. It won't hurt her to miss a day or two of school."

"Good. Spread the word, but don't be too obvious."

She nodded again. They sat in silence for a moment, rain sliding down the car windows, curtaining them from the rest of the world.

Neal made a sound then and turned, hauling her into his arms for a fierce kiss that ended almost as quickly as she responded. The car was already in gear and moving down the street while she was still pulling herself together.

"There they are," Neal said unnecessarily.

Between the rhythmic beats of the wipers, Karen had already spotted the three dark figures ahead. When Neal pulled over to the curb, they turned as one.

Karen's exhilaration had faded, leaving her feeling the first niggling of fear. She reached for the door handle, but hesitated. "You'll make sure I won't be alone."

"Not for a minute."

"Okay." She started to open the door.

His hand on her arm stopped her. "You can change your mind."

She didn't look at him. "You know me better than that."

The bitter sound of his laugh shocked her. "Yeah. I know you better than that."

Karen wanted suddenly, desperately, to fling herself into the safe haven of his arms. Out on these dark streets with Chelsea and Joan and Abby, she was the hunter. Turning herself into the hunted, instead, was a whole other story.

What if the rapist was smart enough to guess that a trap had been set? What if he *didn't* come after her— at least, not this week or the next? Sooner or later the police would figure he wasn't interested in her. Sooner or later, they would pull her bodyguard. With the terror of a rabbit too far from its hole, Karen imagined nighttime with just her and Abby—the first time she heard a thump in the dark house, a shuffle that might be a footstep, the scratch of branches against a window.

In her heart, she'd believed herself to be courageous. Hadn't she always flung herself into the forefront of every fight? But now she discovered a deeper truth. In those other fights, she'd risked very little.

Not her life or her daughter's. Not her chance at a future with the man she was beginning to realize she loved, despite common sense.

But her reasons for taking the risk were still valid. She might become a target, anyway. Or, God forbid, Abby might. The rapist had to be stopped. And Karen could help.

"Then you also know I have to do it," she told Neal, and stepped out of the car, opening her umbrella.

ROGERS STUCK his head into Neal's office. "Chief, did you talk the Lindberg woman into dropping the patrols?"

Neal looked up from the paperwork spread over his desk. Tim Rogers was his bicycle officer. He made afternoon rounds on a ten-speed, an innovation in law enforcement that was a hit with the kids. Parents reported that their sons and daughters were more willing to wear helmets once they'd seen him. Besides, barring a hill or two, Rogers could get around town faster than an officer in a car. But, damn, he looked like a nerd with that funny little helmet perched on top of his rather small head.

What he'd said finally penetrated, and Neal asked, "What do you mean?"

Rogers unfastened his chin strap and took off the helmet. "They disappeared last night. I saw some out early, say eight, nine o'clock. But later—" more of him appeared in the doorway and he shrugged "—nada."

Erickson wandered up behind him. "Yeah, my wife says—" Too late he tried to swallow his mistake.

Neal leaned back in his chair and clasped his hands behind his head. "Your wife?" he prodded.

The young officer squirmed. There was no other way of putting it. "Yeah, she, uh, was hot to join. Said she's gotten nervous evenings with me working, and here was something she could do about it. I didn't like it, but... Oh, shoot." A dark flush crept up his neck, but he looked Neal straight in the eye. "I figured, what could it hurt?"

Erickson should have told him. A month ago Neal would have been unsympathetic. Since then he'd learned how stubborn a woman could be. How sometimes she was even right. So he let it go with a nod, asking patiently, "What did your wife say?"

After a few more twitches and apologies, Erickson got to the point. "Irene said Karen Lindberg called last night, telling her to stay home until further notice. Said she was calling everybody else, too."

Neal frowned, turning his pencil over and over in his hand. What the hell was the woman up to now? She must have gone straight home last night and made dozens of phone calls. Why?

A concession for a concession? She was scrupulously fair. It would be like her to decide that if he was going to give, she should, too.

Or didn't she like the idea of being in his debt? Was this her idea of a payback?

There was only one way to find out. Ask her. He could've picked up the phone, but he'd lose the advantage of being able to see her expressive face. He doubted she had any idea how much it gave away.

Decision made, he dropped the pencil on the unfinished paperwork and stood. "I'll be out for an hour or two," he said abruptly. "When DeSalsa comes in, remind him that I want to see him at about four o'clock. He's taking the first shift in Ms. Lindberg's house. He may go stir-crazy, but he's going to stay until Monday morning, when we'll risk a transfer."

Erickson and Rogers both melted away, probably grateful their weekend wasn't to be spent lurking in Ms. Flowerwoman's spare bedroom. Neal had overheard enough conversations to know that the general consensus in the department on Karen wasn't positive. The young macho guys on his force all figured that she'd declaw a man before she'd let him into her bed, and that she'd pin him down and stay on top even then. Neal wasn't sure they knew he was dating her.

His mouth twitched. Lucky one of them hadn't come looking for him out at the nursery Monday. He might not have had time to explain that only pure chivalry had him flat on his back.

Even though it was one o'clock, he stopped at the deli for two sandwiches and a couple of fresh-baked cookies. If she'd already had lunch, he would have seconds.

He found her giving some pimply-faced teenager hell because he'd been rude to a customer.

The idiot was trying to explain. "I asked her if I could help her, but when I said the fuchsias don't winter over, she acted like I was some kind of dumb shit and told me to forget it. She wanted you or nobody."

Karen planted her hands on her hips. "So you told her you guessed nobody would have to do."

"Well, kind of. I mean, yeah, but..." His voice was rising to a whine. "See, I didn't know where you were and—"

Karen poked him in the chest with one finger. "When you came to work here what did I tell you?"

The boy's eyes rolled like a spooked horse's. "That the customer comes first," he said by rote.

"That's right." Karen gave him a chilly smile. "Mrs. Ludlow is a witch. It also happens that she spends four or five hundred dollars a year here. She's a good deal more important to my business than you are. Is that clear, Josh?"

He nodded dumbly.

"Fine. I'll see you tomorrow."

The kid slunk away and Karen finally saw Neal standing there. "What do you think, did I scare him?" she asked.

"You scared him," Neal agreed. "But why did the customer write him off?"

"We sell *hardy* fuchsias, a dozen or more varieties, and she knew that. They grow into good-size bushes." She tilted her head to one side. "Is that lunch you're clutching?"

"Uh-huh. You busy?"

"Do I look busy?" Karen waved a hand to take in the nursery. A different old man was slowly deadheading roses. Otherwise, everything living was in pots.

Neal followed as she led him to the same courtyard out behind the greenhouses where they'd eaten before. He found that he was strangely reluctant to talk about tomorrow night or her women's patrol, considering that was what he'd come for. Either subject would introduce tension. He told himself there was no hurry; why not relax, eat lunch and enjoy her company first?

As he handed her a sandwich and unwrapped his own, he nodded toward the potted flowers. "You've never said how you got into this."

She looked around, and he could see her eyes lose their focus as she thought about the past. "Chance," she said with no apparent reluctance. Perhaps she, too, would just as soon forget what tomorrow night was to bring. "Or maybe not. Remember the house Geoff insisted we buy for Abby's sake? Well, we bought a new one. Of course, by the time the construction crew was done, the yard could have been a lunar landing site. Scraped bare, rubble all over. I had to landscape, right? I wandered into a nursery, realized I didn't have a clue what I was doing and went to the library, instead, for an armful of gardening books. That was it. I was hooked."

"Most gardeners don't turn their hobby into a career."

Her smile flashed, somehow young and mischievous. "I entered a contest. The kind where you send before and after pictures. I won. *Sunset* magazine did a spread on my garden. A landscaper called and asked if I'd like a job. Abby was starting kindergarten, so I said sure. It was a great experience, but I discovered eventually that I liked the plants better than the design. Most landscape architects love the hard surfaces—you know, the paths, the stone walls, the porch or patio. Plants are just filler. I, on the other hand, kept trying to cram more and more plants into my own garden, just so I could try them. And I couldn't be ruthless about tossing ones that weren't complete successes. Instead, I kept getting rid of lawn until I had almost nothing but flower beds. Forget those hard surfaces, what we were supposed to think of as the 'bones' of the garden. Poor Abby had a swing set on this tiny patch of grass, maybe five feet square. By the time Geoff and I separated, the contest coordinators would have been horrified by my garden. They probably would've recalled my grand prize."

He grinned. "So you satisfied your cravings by starting a nursery, where you could grow everything."

"You got it." She took a bite, chewed, nodded at him. "What about you? Did you play nothing but cops and robbers when you were a kid?"

Neal shook his head. "I was going to be a fighter pilot. Then I discovered I didn't like heights and moved on to road construction. All those big machines, you know."

"Must have thrilled your parents."

"Oh, yeah." He smiled, remembering. "Ever hopeful, Mom suggested I become a doctor. I was only interested if I could cut people open."

"Sounds like the personality of a cop." She ducked when he tossed a balled-up wrapper at her. Straightening, she offered that smile again, the one that stirred his hunger for her. "Just kidding."

"Right," he said dryly. "Anyway, to make a long story short, by the time I enrolled in college I had no idea what I was going to major in, much less do with my life."

"And then your brother died." Her smile was gone.

"And then David died. I went off to avenge him." Neal moved his shoulders, not liking to think about his youthful outrage and the pointless sacrifice he'd nearly made of himself. "Of course it didn't work that way. Eventually I had to find another outlet for all that pent-up idealism. What else but a job where I could 'protect and serve'?"

He expected teasing at least, if not mockery, from Karen. Not for the first time she surprised him. Quite seriously she said, "At first I tried to tell myself you were on a power trip. But even then I knew better, I think." This time her smile was soft. "I *feel* protected."

She might as well have punched him. Here he was, staking her out for the beast. What if he *couldn't* protect her? What if he somehow failed?

Her eyes, searching his, were grave. "Don't worry."

He looked away, ran a hand over his face. His voice sounded hoarse. "Why did you cancel the patrols?"

"Oh. You know." Karen was the one to look away now, concentrating on brushing crumbs from the tabletop into her cupped hand. "Two reasons," she said. "One, we don't want to scare the rapist off anymore. And two—" she stole a brief glance at him "—you're giving me a chance. I thought I ought to give you one."

He nodded, accepting it. "DeSalsa is my best officer. He'll slip into your place Friday evening while you're at the dance. He'll stay until Monday morning. I don't want to take a chance of the perp seeing a shift change. With luck he'll have made a move by then."

"With luck," Karen echoed. Her tone was sturdy, upbeat; but he saw her fingers tremble before she flung the crumbs onto the cobblestones where a bird would find them.

Neal wanted to say again, *You don't have to do it.* Or even, *I won't let you do it.* But if he said the latter, he knew he would lose her as surely as if his precautions failed this weekend.

No, damn it! He shouldn't think that way. The rapist hadn't killed anybody. At worst...

He wouldn't think about that, either.

"I'd better go," he said abruptly, blundering to his feet and bumping the table.

Karen steadied it and stood, too. "Will I see you at...? No." She gave her head a quick shake. "Of course not. What am I thinking?"

"I want you to check in by phone. We'll talk right before you leave for the dance, set up times. And I won't be more than a minute away," he promised. He felt awkward standing here with his hands at his sides, but he was afraid to reach for her, afraid he couldn't let go.

"Be careful," he said uselessly.

"I will." She sounded almost jaunty, but her eyes, huge and dark, gave away the pretense. "Maybe this will all be over in a few days."

"Maybe." He wished he believed it. Would it be so easy? He started to leave.

"Aren't you going to kiss me?" she asked, her voice small.

"I figured you'd walk me to my car." He managed a crooked grin. "Remember what happened the last time I kissed you out in the far reaches of the nursery?"

"Mmm." She came into his arms in a rush. "I don't care."

He did, he realized dimly as he bent his head and captured her mouth. He cared too much. He cared so much he wasn't sure anymore what life would be like without her to raise his blood pressure, one way or another.

NEAL MADE IT HOME by five, leaving the same un-done paperwork strewn on his desk. It had always been his least favorite part of the job. He'd rather kill an entire day in a courtroom waiting for his chance to give two minutes of testimony than write reports.

The city council could damn well wait for this one.

When he walked into the kitchen, Krista gave him a wary look. After Monday, when he'd forbidden her to be in the foot patrol, she'd quit speaking to him any more than she had to. After all, he'd humiliated her forever in the eyes of her new friends. Humiliation, he figured, was better than being in the hospital, fed by an IV, like Toni Santos was.

"Hi, sweetie," he said now, looking over her shoulder to see what she was stirring on the stove. Burgundy beef. "Smells good."

She was careful to turn her face away. "Mrs. Fee-ney made it."

"Where's Michael?"

"I don't know." She shrugged. "Out."

"Could you take a guess?"

Grudgingly she obliged. "Maybe in the barn."

He considered her, his daughter who was halfway to being a woman. She'd changed more in the two and a half years since Jenny died than he'd let himself real-ize. His little girl had breasts now, and the top of her head reached his shoulder. When Michael was a tod-dler, Krista had played mother, but without Jenny—no, even before that, when Jenny first got sick—the game had turned into real life. Krista had had to grow up, maybe too fast. He remembered how lighthearted she'd once been, his sunshine. Now she was solemn, the maturity that had come too soon a burden.

He pulled off his tie and leaned against the counter. "Krista, can we talk?"

She used the excuse of filling a pan with water at the sink to avoid looking at him. "What about?"

"I... probably overreacted on Monday."

Water splashed out of the pan when she set it down too hard because she was staring at him, her expression startled. "What do you mean?"

Neal rubbed the back of his neck with one hand. "I was scared for you," he said ruefully. "That came out as anger. But it isn't just that. Somehow I hadn't noticed that you weren't ten years old anymore."

"You helped me buy my first bra," his daughter said in a stifled voice.

"Yeah. But I let myself forget what it meant."

He was disturbed by her response. She should have felt triumph because he was admitting fault. Instead, her teeth closed on her lower lip and she bowed her head, after a moment mumbling, "I should have told you. I knew I should. I just... I guess I was mad because it seemed like everybody else was more important to you than Michael and me."

He let the grammar pass, took a step toward her and lifted a hand to clumsily stroke her soft dark hair. "I hope you know in your heart that isn't true."

"Yeah." She sniffed.

"I may have been mad—" he felt as clumsy with words as he was with a caress "—but I was proud of you, too. You showed courage and initiative."

Still Krista didn't look up. "Mom would never have done anything like that."

Understanding at last, he took her shoulders and gently turned her to face him. "Your mother," he said steadily, "was a wonderful woman. But Karen is, too. Maybe you can take the best of both. And part of you won't be like either of them. That's as it should be."

Krista's head came up at last. Her mouth trembled and her eyes were drenched with tears, but her voice was hopeful. "You always used to say I was like Mom. I guess I thought I should try to be. That there was something wrong with me if I wasn't."

"Never." He kissed her forehead. "There's nothing wrong with admiring someone else, maybe trying to develop in yourself the quality you most admire in that person. Your mother was a gentle woman. So are you. But I think you're stronger than she was. And I'm glad."

"Really?" She sounded so timid it broke his heart.

He wrapped her in a convulsive hug and assured her, "Really."

Krista clung to him, dampened his shirt with her tears and finally looked up again. "Are you going to marry Karen?"

Her question took him off guard. "What would make you think that? We've only dated a couple of times."

"Yeah, but Abby says you're over there all the time. She says her mom talks about you a lot."

"What does *she* think about it?"

"Abby thinks it would be cool for us to be sisters. I guess she must not hate you or anything."

How comforting, Neal thought. He asked, "How would *you* feel about it?"

"I like her," his daughter said awkwardly. "Ms. Lindberg's... well, she's exciting. You know what I mean?"

"Yeah." He cleared his throat. "I know what you mean."

Funny, too, considering he'd once valued serenity at home above all else. The truth was, a battle now and then added some zest to life.

"So are you?" Krista persisted.

"I don't know," he told her honestly. "I guess marriage is at the back of my mind, but I'm not at all sure Karen is thinking that way yet. So I won't make any promises one way or the other."

"Okay. Daddy?" Just for a second, the sweetness of her smile took him back to a time when life had seemed simpler. "I love you."

Neal hugged her again. His sunshine. "I love you, too," he whispered.

CHAPTER TWELVE

KAREN HOVERED outside the wide double doors to the high-school gymnasium, making sure she had a chance to chat with other parents and the teachers Joe had roped in to help tonight. Already some nihilistic song throbbed from the darkened gym, and she grimaced, then smiled wryly at her own reaction. She remembered her father's bellow. "Turn the music down!" He'd compared Bob Dylan's voice to the buzz of a chain saw.

Amazing how much more reasonable your parents became in retrospect, once you'd become a parent yourself.

"Karen!" someone said. "Dropping off Abby?"

She turned to smile at the father of a boy who'd been in most of Abby's classes all through elementary school. Lord, how she hated suspecting men she'd known for years. "Jim, how are you? No such luck for me—I'm chaperoning. How I get myself into these things, I don't know. Abby isn't even here—she's at her grandmother's for a long weekend—but Joe Gardner buttonholed me ages ago, and I didn't want to let him down."

"Better you than me." He grinned, running a hand over his balding head. "I'd stay long enough to claim you for a dance if I had the slightest idea how you dance to rap."

Nihilism, she realized, had now been replaced by monotony. "Heaven knows," she said, laughing and shaking her head even as she wondered if he was the rapist, would he feel rejected because she hadn't begged him to stay for another song? "Far as I can tell," she continued, nodding at the dark interior of the gym, "nobody's dancing, anyway. The social scene is on the sidelines."

"Speaking of sidelines," said Peter Merck, the chemistry teacher, stopping beside Karen, "anyone know how the game came out?"

As the two men discussed tonight's loss, Karen tried to decide what color eyes Jim Craig had. Unfortunately Pete's were undeniably brown. Jim's, she thought, were hazel. The artificial light was too poor for her to tell whether the color of his eyes was murky enough to be labeled brown.

"Excuse me," she murmured, and wandered over to another group of parents delivering offspring. She was proud of the deft way she let this bunch, too, know she was alone for the next few days.

Eventually Joe popped out of the gym to ask her to check the girls' washroom, and she caught a couple of girls no older than Abby smoking. She made them flush their cigarettes down the toilet and throw away the rest of the pack, then shooed them back out to the gym. By this time, most of the parents playing chauffeur had departed, with only half a dozen adults left to supervise.

Karen made a casual circuit of the gym to identify the others. Pete, she'd already seen. Carl Bradley, she stopped to talk to in a lull between songs.

He was frowning at the disk jockey in front. Local bands had played for two of the dances, Abby had told her mother, but tonight CDs were providing the sound. Requests were being shouted and probably ignored, but Karen couldn't see anything perturbing in the scene.

"Hi," she said, touching his arm. "Busman's holiday?"

He jumped about six inches, then recognized her and forced a smile. "Karen. Joe didn't warn—uh, mention that you were chaperoning."

"Something wrong?" she asked, nodding toward the front.

The frown returned. "Did you listen to that last song? I don't have to allow that kind of destructive crap on school grounds." Karen noticed a tic beneath one eye. "Sorry," he said tightly. "If there's one thing that gets me worked up, it's this violent rap music. I'll pull the plug if I hear any more like it."

Too bad he hadn't felt the same about *Halloween 12* and *Cliffhanger.* But her sympathies were somewhat with him; she didn't like the content of much of the currently popular music, either. Abby, thank heavens, was into country.

"Good turnout," she said.

"Hmm?" He glanced around. "Oh, yeah. Boys outnumber the girls, though. I don't blame the parents, either. If I had a girl, I'd keep her home until the police catch this nut case." His brown eyes were accusing. "You brought Abby?"

"No, actually..." Music blasted out of the speakers, and Karen raised her voice. "She's gone to her grandmother's for a few days."

She wasn't sure he'd heard; he crossed his arms and stood sphinxlike watching the few couples that filtered out onto the dance floor.

Karen wandered on. She encountered Joe talking to a group of boys. They were all laughing, and he gave a high-five to one before coming over to her. With his mouth about an inch from her ear, he yelled above the music, "How about a dance? We can show these kids how it's supposed to be done."

But before she could answer, there was a stir in the crowd nearby. Joe yelled, "Rain check," and plunged right in. As the kids parted, she saw him grab one boy by the arms and haul him off another one. He was yanking the second one up, too, when Karen's conscience suggested she resume her patrol. She might be hunting a rapist, but she had an obligation to chaperon the dance, too.

Joe had suggested regular circuits inside the gym and patrols outside it. Karen's head was beginning to pound, so she made for the girls' locker-room door.

Six or seven girls were clustered in front of the mirrors, but as far as Karen could tell, all they were doing was renewing makeup and giggling. She smiled and said, "Hi."

One who looked vaguely familiar said, "Hi, Ms. Lindberg," and the others chimed in. In the bathroom itself, one set of feet was visible under the stall door, and only the lingering odor of tobacco smoke remained.

The locker room had an exit outside. Karen took it and found herself on a covered cement walkway around the corner from the main doors. A couple was passionately necking not ten feet from her. They were apparently oblivious to the world, or at least to her. As long as they still had their clothes on, Karen figured they weren't her worry, so she passed them. She'd make a quick check of the rear of the gymnasium, then go back in and circulate some more.

She glanced at her watch. Eleven o'clock. She'd call Neal in another half hour or forty-five minutes. He'd wanted her to check in several times, but she'd pointed out that it would look a little strange for one of the chaperons to spend all her time at the pay phone. He'd settled for once, if she would also promise to call him the moment she got home.

"If I don't hear from you by midnight," he'd said, "I'm coming looking for you."

She must have mellowed. Once she would have bristled and assumed he was questioning her ability to take care of herself. Now she was comforted and even warmed to know that he would charge to the rescue.

In the cool night air, with the music no more than a muffled pulse, her headache diminished, but she was more conscious of her edginess. Her brain was sending her body the message that she was in danger, and it wanted to react. Instead, nothing was happening. She had no idea whether she'd talked to the rapist, whether tonight's charade was productive.

The rear of the gymnasium was dark, and Karen hesitated at the corner. Maybe this wasn't such a good idea. A shuffling sound from the darkness sent adrenaline shooting through her, and she started to retreat. But then she heard a whisper, followed by a groan, and realized that another couple must be out here.

Something Abby had told her tickled at her memory. *It's, hey, do you want to dance, and then let's go out behind the gym and do it. Really romantic.*

Good God, Karen thought, her parental indignation mixed with amusement at her own shock.

Chances were, a couple of teenagers were out here "doing it." Did she want to interrupt?

An urgent whisper reached her ears. "Stop. You promised!"

The boy's voice was a rumble. "Come on. What's the big deal?"

Clothing rustled. "You said—"

"Why don't you shut up?"

A desperate cry was followed by the sound of cloth tearing. "Quit it! I want to go back—" The girl broke off.

Outraged, Karen was already advancing when she heard the grunt of male satisfaction.

"Feel it," the jerk said gutturally. "Put your hand on it."

"I won't—" There was a gasp of pain.

Karen's eyes were adjusting to the darkness. A half moon cast silvery light on the pair. The boy had the girl backed up against the gym wall. She was sobbing quietly, her bare breasts and arms pale against the dark background.

Neither heard Karen coming. She marched right up to them and grabbed the boy's arm. "Let her go!" she snapped.

"Who the...?" He swung around.

"Get dressed," Karen told the girl.

"I don't know who you are," the boy snarled, "but this is none of your goddamn business! Get lost."

"And let you rape this girl?" Karen asked icily. "I don't think so. You're both coming with me—"

He shoved her, and she stumbled back. As she retreated, he stalked after her, a huge bulk just darker than the gym wall.

Karen tried to maintain her tone of command. "All I have to do is scream. Now, are you coming with me, or do you want to be in worse trouble?"

His hand shot out, slammed against her chest and knocked her backward. She barely stayed on her feet. Out of the corner of her eye, she saw the girl fumbling into her clothes. Once her white full breasts were covered, Karen called, "Run! Go for help!"

The boy swung back to the girl. "Don't even think about it! I'll make you sorry! You know I will."

The girl shrank against the gym wall and hesitated. Karen sidled a couple of steps toward the corner of the building. Where in God's name were all the other chaperons who were supposed to be patrolling?

She'd shifted position enough so that when the boy faced her again, diffused yellow light from sodium lamps out in the parking lot showed her his enraged face.

Mark Griggs. Tall, muscular, brown-eyed—and fully capable of raping a woman.

Time to scream, Karen decided, and let one rip.

Mark stopped. "Shut up, lady! Shut up!"

The sound of running footsteps was followed by a man's voice. "What's going on?" The white beam of a flashlight pinpointed Mark.

Karen didn't care who her rescuer was. She sucked in a shaky breath and said, "Mark was roughing up his girlfriend here. He didn't like it when I intervened."

The flashlight beam didn't waver. "Griggs, get out here where I can see you."

The boy sullenly went. Karen hurried over and put her arm around the girl. "Are you okay?" she asked.

The head bobbed, and the girl said tremulously, "I guess so."

"I'm glad I came along when I did. What's your name?"

Her voice changed, became alarmed. "You're not going to call my mother or anything, are you?"

Surprised, Karen said, "You're not the one who's in trouble here."

"Yeah, right." Suddenly the girl sounded as sulky as her boyfriend.

So much for being a good samaritan. Karen took a firm grip on the girl's arm. "Come on. We're going to have a little talk."

The girl came, dragging her feet. This side of the gym had a covered walkway, too, well lit. There Karen's rescuer waited with Mark.

Of all unlikely people, it was Abby's algebra teacher who was Karen's white knight. So, Frank Morris wasn't as ineffectual as he looked. No, Karen amended immediately; he wasn't as ineffectual as he'd looked the day of their conference. Tonight he was thoroughly in charge; his expression was stern, and Karen was surprised to realize he was nearly as tall as Mark. The senior was making no effort to break away. Although maybe that was because he had complete confidence in his hold on the poor girl.

"Okay, what's the story?" the teacher asked.

"There isn't any story," the bulky football player sneered. "I was out there with Rita. First thing I know, this woman's yelling at me. I turn around and she starts screaming."

"All innocence, eh?" Frank said skeptically. He lifted his eyebrows. "Ms. Lindberg?"

"I heard Rita asking Mark to stop. He refused. Clothing tore and she cried out in pain."

Mark jerked out of Frank's grip. "That's bull! Rita's my woman. She likes everything I do. Isn't that right?"

A bruise was already darkening the pretty girl's jaw and her head was bowed, but she mumbled, "We were just having a fight is all. I guess I have a temper."

"Rita..." Karen stepped between the girl and her brutal boyfriend. Lowering her voice, she said urgently, "Don't let him treat you like this. Respect yourself. He's on his way to jail if you just say the word."

For a fleeting instant, Rita lifted scared dark eyes to Karen's. Then she hunched her shoulders. "I don't know what you heard," she said lifelessly. "But it wasn't anything like you think."

"Yeah!" Mark pumped a fist in the air. "Come on, babe, let's get the hell outa here."

Karen stood there and watched the bastard hook an arm around his girlfriend's waist and saunter away. Just before they turned at the front of the gym, Mark looked back and gave the two adults the finger.

"He's going to get at least a suspension for that," Frank Morris said.

"A long jail term would be more appropriate," Karen snapped. Anger was boiling up in her, and her mind was already turning over possibilities. If she could find out Rita's last name she'd go see her parents. Maybe, even if the girl wouldn't testify, there was something Neal could do. After all, this time there was a witness. And, boy, would she like to get on the stand!

"He'll end up in jail sooner or later," Frank agreed. "Are you all right? He didn't touch you, did he?"

"He gave me a couple of pushes," Karen said. "Bless you for coming so quickly. I have to admit he was scaring me."

"He's a scary kid." Frank reached into his pocket. He popped the lid off a small container and held it out to her. "Mint?"

The gesture was kindly meant, she was sure. So why did it jolt her?

Her anger drained away as though a plug had been pulled, and Karen was suddenly aware of her isolation. She'd been dumb to get herself into a position where she was alone with one of Neal's suspects. An unlikely one, true, but the eyes slipping evasively away from hers right now were brown, and she'd seen he could be more forceful than she'd imagined.

He took a step forward, and her pulse accelerated. Then he jiggled the little plastic box, and she stared at it, feeling like a fool.

"No, thanks." She moved a surreptitious step to one side. "Uh, maybe we should get back. Joe must be wondering where we've vanished to."

Frank Morris nodded, his brow creasing, his appearance so mild that her momentary instinctive fear relaxed its grip. She was getting paranoid, Karen decided. Considering the circumstances, nervousness was natural, but terror was a bit much.

"This is the last time I do anything like this," she muttered under her breath.

"Excuse me?" the teacher said.

"Nothing." Karen shook her head. "Shall we?"

He escorted her back to the main entrance to the gym, his manner courtly. Karen decided he was a very nice man. As far as she could tell, the only two suspects who *weren't* nice men were the principal and Mark Griggs. And tonight's events hadn't changed her opinion of Mark. He was a creep who didn't take no from a girl. But roughing up a girlfriend was his style, not patiently stalking a thirty-six-year-old woman, as Kathleen Madsen had been. Why would he even look twice at a woman old enough to be his mother?

That left Bradley. Karen would have loved him to be the rapist. If he was arrested, a new principal would have to be hired. Gee, gosh, darn.

But wishful thinking didn't make it likely. Bradley was too self-absorbed to fit the profile. Besides which, he was not only married, he had five children, the oldest three still in the elementary school. It was awfully hard to imagine him scraping up the time, unsuspected, to watch his victims and choose his moment.

"Excuse me," Karen said to the algebra teacher. "I need to make a quick phone call. If Joe's hunting for me, tell him I'll be along in a minute."

"Checking on Abby? She isn't here tonight, is she?"

Karen remembered her assignment. "No, she's gone to her grandmother's in Seattle for the weekend. Until Tuesday, actually. Don't chew me out—I know she shouldn't miss classes, especially yours, but her grandmother begged. She promised they'd do something educational to make up for it."

Frank actually smiled. "I won't fail her for missing two days. We're not covering anything very important."

"Frank...thank you."

His brief show of manly bravado was past. Mumbling, "It was nothing," he sounded very like Abby at her most awkward.

Karen had had the foresight to stick a couple of quarters in her jeans pocket. Outside there was one pay telephone. She had to wait a very long five minutes while a girl tried to talk her mother into letting her stay longer.

The girl's last words were, "But Mom..." A second later she slammed down the receiver and stomped away, presumably foiled by a parent who'd stuck to her guns.

Karen hurried to drop the quarter in and dial. Neal answered on the first ring.

She identified herself and he snapped, "Where the hell have you been?"

She looked at her watch. "It's not midnight yet."

"We agreed on eleven-thirty."

"'Give or take a little' were, I believe, my last words," Karen said. "I'm twelve minutes late. That's a little."

He grumbled some more, then asked. "Has anything happened?"

"I came on Mark Griggs knocking some poor girl around. She was inconsiderate enough not to want to take her clothes off for him. I intervened, he didn't like it, and we had a mildly ugly scene."

Neal swore bitterly. "Has he been taken into custody yet? Why the hell haven't I heard about this?"

"Because said girlfriend denied that any such thing was happening, and the two strolled off into the moonlight. I'd be happy to swear to what I heard, but I have to admit it was dark and I couldn't actually see what they were doing any too well."

"Are you telling me Griggs is long gone?"

"I have no idea," Karen said. "The gym has a strobe light. I could bump into Abby and not recognize her."

"Damn," Neal said. "I don't like you being there."

Karen glanced over her shoulder to be sure no one was listening. "Look at it this way. I ticked Mark Griggs off royally. If he's our guy, he'll be showing up at my house real soon, given his short fuse. That's the object, isn't it?"

Neal made an unhappy sound. "Yeah, yeah. Okay. You made anyone else mad?"

"I've turned down a few invitations to dance."

"Who?"

She listed them.

"If you get another chance, dance with Gardner like we talked about. Only him."

"Right," she agreed. The coach was the only man one of the victims *had* danced with.

"Frank Morris there?"

"He rescued me from Mark Griggs."

Neal's voice sharpened. "Was he following you, do you think?"

"I doubt it," Karen said. "I screamed, he came running."

"Screamed! God almighty—"

"Strictly precautionary," she assured him.

Neal didn't like any of it, including her explanation. Karen soothed him into agreeing not to tear into the high-school parking lot with lights flashing and siren wailing.

"This was a harebrained idea," he said testily. "You have no more defenses than a kitten thrown to the coyotes."

She had opened her mouth to retort when somebody behind her said, "Jeez, is she gonna be on the
phone all night?"

Lowering her voice, she told Neal, "I've got to go.
The women were all attacked in their own houses, not
here, so quit worrying. I'll call you when I get home."

"The second you walk in the door."

"The very second. Cross my heart and hope to die."

"Don't say that."

"Cross my...?" Light dawned. "Oh, you mean the
'hope to die' part." The phrase, she had to admit,
possessed a sharper edge, given her current whereabouts and purpose.

Neal said roughly, "I don't want anything to happen to you."

"Is that a declaration of your affection?" she
asked, trying to sound teasing, not sure she'd suc-
ceeded.

"Something like that," Neal said, and she could
detect no trace of answering lightness in his tone.

"Goodbye," she said softly, and hung up.

She should have felt fortified; instead, she wanted
nothing less in the world than to march back into that
gym and try to attract the attention of a sick, violent
man.

She had to remind herself that this was the only way
to make it end. Once an arrest was made, she and Neal
would have plenty of time to figure out where they
were going with their relationship. She didn't have to
get all weak-kneed and teary-eyed, as though a once-
in-a-lifetime chance was slipping out of her hands
right now, this minute. The worst thing that could
happen tonight, she told herself briskly, was that the
rapist would come calling, and if he did they were

ready for him. The sooner it was over, the happier she would be.

Inside the gym, she almost stumbled over Frank Morris. He stood by the doors, looking no happier than she inexplicably felt. She mimed a greeting and he nodded in return just before a guitar riff ended in silence.

"Is this thing winding down, do you think?" she asked.

He glanced at his watch. "Probably. We're usually out of here by twelve-thirty."

Karen nodded and looked around. The strobe light was gone and the crowd was thinner. A Paula Abdul ballad came on, and pairs drifted out onto the floor to hold each other close and sway in place. She had a sudden picture of herself at sixteen, dancing for the first time with the boy she'd passionately adored from afar. It had seemed like a miracle, a dream, when he'd stopped in front of her and held out his hand.

"Dance?"

Remembering, she smiled, but wryly, feeling an ache around her heart. She didn't even recall that boy's name. She didn't think he'd even spoken to her again, or if he did it had been too late; by then he'd lost the power to move her to agonized longing by the way he smiled or brushed his hair back from his face.

But the memory of the one perfect dance reminded her how painful it was to be a teenager, how exquisitely vulnerable you were.

Of course, she was all grown-up and tough now. It took more than a dance to make her feel as if a layer of skin had been stripped off, as though she could cry from feeling too intensely. Now it took a big man with too-short hair and a glower to beat her father's; it took a dance of another kind altogether, the kind that left a red silk dress tangled with sheets.

She was glad Frank didn't want to talk. Their silence was companionable; she felt safe. Karen knew she ought to go check the girls' washroom again, since she seemed to be the only female chaperon, but before she could make herself move, Joe Gardner, making a circuit of the gym, saw her.

Coming over, he nodded at Frank and grinned at Karen. "How about that dance now?"

Her fragile sense of security vanished, and it was all she could do to smile in return and say, "Sure."

Karen felt a little as though she was deserting Frank. She gave him an apologetic smile as she took the football coach's hand and let him draw her out onto the floor. There she stepped into his muscular arms.

He pulled her closer than she would have liked, then moved slowly, languidly. Karen prayed he couldn't feel the tension vibrating through her or the way her heart thudded. She had a sudden sickening vision of how Chelsea and the others must have felt as they danced, stripped of clothes and pride, for their tormentor. Dear God, what if Joe, tall, muscular, brown-eyed, was the rapist? Did he even now plan how he would humiliate her?

And if not him, who? Was she being watched? Was someone angry because she danced with Joe?

She was scared, suddenly, claustrophobic. She had an overwhelming compulsion to wrench herself out of Joe's embrace and run to her car. It took all of her willpower to stay, to let Joe bend her backward over his arm as Paula Abdul's throaty voice hushed to a whisper and the song ended.

Then he was setting her back on her feet and grinning boyishly. "Hot damn, I like her music! I always make the kids play at least one of her songs."

"I like her stuff, too," Karen said, although she hadn't really heard the music.

They headed back toward where she'd left Frank, but he was gone. Probably doing his duty and seeking out delinquents wherever they hid.

"I'd better make a pass through the locker room," she said guiltily.

Joe waved good-naturedly and said, "I'll go announce that it's one more song, then we'll call it quits."

The locker room was completely empty, and Karen sank down on a bench, leaned her head back against a cold metal locker, and just for a moment closed her eyes. She was drained, shaky, obviously not cut out for undercover work. It was horrible to suspect everyone, to search for the monster behind the mask.

The music ended just as she heard the locker-room door open. It was Joe's voice that called, "Karen, you still in there?"

Her first frantic instinct was to look for someplace to hide. Her second was more rational. He wasn't going to attack her here where anybody could walk in. And where there wasn't any music.

"Yes," she called. "Coming."

"Chase everyone out and lock the outside exit, will you?"

"You bet," she answered, and heard the door shut softly.

The gym was emptying, the parking lot and one-lane access chaos as parents arrived to pick up their offspring and teenagers revved up their cars. Kids were yelling goodbye to each other, girls standing in clusters giggling, boys mock fighting. Karen wasn't sure whether she should stay until the bitter end, but she saw no sign of Joe, so she decided to make her getaway.

On the way to her Civic, she saw half a dozen people she knew, some of whom she had to stop to say hi to. The one that surprised her the most was Chelsea, who was leaning against her car waiting for her sister.

"You let her come?" Karen asked.

"*I* wouldn't have." Her pretty, dark-haired friend was fidgety, looking uneasily around. "But Steph promised to stick like glue to Ron—he's her current boyfriend—so Mom told her okay. She just called, though. Wouldn't you know, Ron's car won't start, so I'm here to get them. Have you seen 'em?"

"No, but the dance is over, so I'm sure they'll be along any second. See you, Chels."

She reached her own car and unlocked the door. Glancing up, she saw that Joe Gardner was now talking to Chelsea. It was strange that he'd singled her out, that he wasn't back at the gym riding herd on the stragglers.

Karen hesitated, not getting in the car, wondering whether her friend would be scared. Surely not—there were still plenty of people around. But she saw Joe take a step closer, laughing as he said something.

And then Chelsea screamed.

CHAPTER THIRTEEN

CHELSEA'S SCREAM went on and on, then died into gasping sobs. As fast as Karen moved, a number of others, mostly women, beat her to Chelsea. They formed a half circle that pinned Joe to her car. Others were pressing in from behind, murmuring, "What's going on?"

Karen pushed her way forward to find Chelsea huddling in Marta Peters's arms. Joe had backed up against the car, hands raised in a gesture of innocence.

"I don't know!" he said. "I didn't do anything! She just started to scream."

"It's him!" Chelsea cried. "Make him go away!"

Murmurs moved through the crowd.

"He said he wanted me to dance! And he smiled..." Chelsea shuddered.

"Is he the rapist?" one voice asked, and several more chimed in. "Is he? Is he?"

Chelsea cast him a look of utter terror. Her head bobbed, and she whimpered, "Yes! Oh, God, yes!"

Stunned by the scene, Karen thought numbly, *I was just dancing with him.*

His hands dropped. "What the hell is she talking about?" he asked angrily. "I'm no rapist! Hell, the woman's a nut case! All I wanted to do was date her!"

Whispering reassurances, Marta ushered Chelsea through a brief opening in the crowd, which closed more tightly around Joe. The murmurs of shock and horror and anger blended together into a bestial sound that had him looking frantically from face to face.

"Why are you listening to some hysterical woman? You know me. All of you know me. Sandra, are you forgetting everything I've done for Colin? God, Karen, tell them! I wouldn't rape a woman! Why would I?"

"Why does any sicko do the things he does?" a voice—safely anonymous—called out.

"He's not going to do them in our town," said a woman, and a growl of agreement swept through the crowd.

An elbow bumped Karen in the side; somebody pressed into her, pushing her forward. She fought to hold back, had a sudden suffocating vision of a riot she'd once been caught up in. But these were people she knew, friends, neighbors. Good, normal, law-abiding people. Somebody had probably already called the police; all they had to do was keep Joe from running.

Yet still she was shoved forward as the crowd grew, as word was passed on and more angry voices joined the chorus. Only a few feet from her, Joe was sweating, his hands braced on the side panels of the car.

Karen looked at him and thought, *He raped Chelsea. He broke another woman's jaw.* But it didn't seem real or possible. *Joe?*

His head swung from side to side like a bull's as the toreadors closed in. "Gayle, you know me. All of you know me! You can't believe—"

"Why would Chelsea lie?" someone asked.

"Yeah, why would she lie?" the chorus agreed, and the crowd pressed forward.

Karen knew mob psychology well enough to be scared. Somebody had to inject some reason before the mood turned truly ugly.

Taking a deep breath, she stepped toward Joe and turned around. She lifted a hand for silence. The rumble died to a murmur, and she said loudly, "Let the police straighten it out! Has somebody called them?"

"What the hell good have the police been?" demanded a man she didn't know.

"You're all crazy!" Joe's teeth showed and his eyes were wild. "I'll talk to the cops and nobody else! None of you have any right to accuse me!"

He pushed off from the side of the car and barreled into the crowd, his head down. Rough hands caught at him, shoved him back. His shoulder slammed against her, and Karen was knocked to her knees.

Above her, Joe swore. "You've all gone crazy!" he yelled, just as a purse smacked the side of his head and he staggered to his knees beside Karen.

Pushing upward, she cried, "No! Stop!" But she couldn't even hear herself.

Rage and helplessness had found an outlet, a scapegoat. Joe flailed with his arms, but another purse connected with his head, a man's fist with his stomach. He expelled air with a sick sound, slammed back against the car. Blood spurted from his nose as another fist struck it. Joe fell heavily, rolling into a ball with his arms over his head as he was kicked again and again.

The sounds were hideous, the grunts, the expletives, the thuds. Karen flung herself in front of him and screamed, "Stop! Stop!" but these faces, contorted, were only distantly recognizable. With shock and horror Karen saw them, women and men she knew, friends, mothers and fathers, gardeners, turned into animals willing to tear and rip and rend only because the others were, because they were angry, because she had taught them that they could act on their own.

A siren was wailing, its voice cut off as a familiar roar of command was followed in seconds by Neal himself. He flung people aside until he reached Karen, who was trying to shield Joe's body.

"Everybody stand back!" Neal bellowed, brandishing his nightstick. "Now!"

Miraculously the sight of the uniform muted the raging mob. Slowly people retreated, opening a space, and Karen gave a sob of relief.

Neal crouched by her, his eyes fierce with the kind of fear she understood, the kind she'd felt the time Abby was pushed by another child from the top of the playground slide and had lain still on the ground.

Hoarsely he said, "Are you hurt? By God, if anybody laid a hand on you—"

"No, it's Joe. They think he's the rapist."

Joe hadn't moved, was still curled in a ball like a child hiding from reality that was too harsh.

Neal sank to his heels. "What happened?"

She told him, quickly. Neal gripped Joe's shoulder and said, "Can you stand up? We'd better get you out of here."

For a moment, the big man was unresponsive, and Karen though he might be unconscious. But then he groaned and wiped blood from his face onto the back of his hand. "Yeah, I think so," he muttered.

Karen watched as Neal helped the coach to his feet. His eyes were dazed and his face bloody. Someone said, "Son of a bitch deserves it!" But when she looked around, Karen saw how much the mob had shrunk. Even now, those on the outskirts were separating themselves from the others and quietly melting away. She only hoped they felt the shame they deserved.

Other sirens were wailing. Two more police cars swung to each side of the crowd, their revolving lights spilling surreal colors on the faces. Officers leapt out to shove their way toward Neal, who was handcuffing Joe Gardner.

Those remaining separated to open a path for the police chief to lead a docile Joe through. Karen accompanied them. Neal spoke to the other cops, who nodded and kept watchful expressionless eyes on the crowd. Their hands rested on holstered guns while Neal helped Joe into the back seat of the squad car and slammed the door. Then he turned back.

"I'll remember who I saw here tonight," he said, raising his voice so everyone could hear. "Whether this man committed the crimes or not, he deserves a fair trial. He deserves the presumption of innocence that every citizen in this nation is guaranteed. I want all of you to go home and think about your behavior. What if someday the accusing finger points to you? Do you want to be tried and found guilty by an angry mob?" His gaze swept contemptuously from face to face, lingering on each to drive home his point. At last he nodded curtly. "All of you, clear out."

Karen stood, her hands at her sides, and watched one head after another bow, before her neighbors and friends turned silently to go. At last, only Marta Peters and Chelsea were left, Marta with a protective arm around the young kindergarten teacher, who was still crying.

Neal came first to Karen. With one hand he lifted her chin and studied her. His fingers slid up her jaw to touch a spot on the side of her face that made her flinch. The spark of pure rage in his dark eyes made her want to go into his arms. Instead, she asked shakily, "How did you know to come?"

"Somebody with some sense ran for the phone when she saw what was happening. Why didn't you do the same?"

Karen felt the sting of tears in the back of her eyes. "I never dreamed something like this would happen." She searched his face for the understanding that eluded her. "How could it happen? They turned into animals! No—" she shook her head "—not animals. Something worse. I think they would have killed him."

Suddenly Neal's voice was raw. "They might have killed you, too, when you got in the way. Did you think of that?"

"No." Blindly she shook her head again, hearing the growl of the mob-beast, seeing faces twisted with hate. "I just couldn't stand there and let them kick him and punch him and..." She shivered. "It was horrible."

Neal's jaw muscles spasmed as though he'd clenched his teeth. Then, instead of offering comfort, he rubbed the back of his neck and turned away. Under his breath he said, "Let's hope to God we've at least got the right man."

He'd warned her, Karen thought, watching him walk over to Chelsea and Marta. He'd told her she didn't know what she was setting in motion. How right he'd been! Tonight she'd seen what she'd so naively, so self-righteously, created. A monster.

And she couldn't blame Chief Neal Rowland if he despised her for it.

SHE DIDN'T KNOW when to retreat or surrender, probably never would learn. A lifetime with her would be a lifetime spent wading into mobs of one kind or another after her. Right now he had to turn his back on Karen, or he would have started kissing her. This wasn't the time or the place, although his hormones didn't agree.

He felt sick, remembering the rush of fear that followed the phone call. Neal had known instantly that there was no chance Karen would happen to be back in the locker room counseling lovelorn teenage girls or knocking a couple of smokers' heads together. Hell, no, she'd be at the center of the action.

Funny thing was, he'd also known she wouldn't be among those swinging their fists. Ms. Flowerwoman had too much passion for truth and justice and the underdog. None of those causes were being served tonight. Mobs were made up of creatures of emotion, not intellect.

Neal thanked the county deputy for coming. Then he turned to Chelsea Cahill.

She was still sniffling, eyes puffy and nose running. Neal was grateful when the other woman produced a tissue and got her to blow her nose. Neither tears nor self-pity moved him to anything but discomfiture. Probably her tears were justified, considering tonight's traumatic experience. He still wished she'd pull herself together.

Damn it, in her position Ms. Flowerwoman would have leveled the son of a bitch with a right hook, not wailed like a cat in heat.

"Ms. Cahill," he said, sounding more patient than he felt, "I'm going to need a statement from you."

She did try, he had to give her that. She blew her nose again, blinked a few times and said on a fresh sob, "It was him. I know it was!"

Without turning, he could feel Karen behind him, listening in uncustomary silence. He didn't let himself reach out a hand to her.

"You're telling me that Joe Gardner is the man who raped you on the night of September twentieth." He put it as clearly as he could. "Is that right?"

Chelsea Cahill's head bobbed vigorously.

"How is it that you recognized him tonight when you were unable to in the past?"

The older woman holding Chelsea frowned repressively at him and tightened her protective arm around her.

"He..." Tears threatened. "He...he was making fun of me. Taunting me! And the way he stood and held his head and even his voice..." She was shrinking, huddling against her self-appointed guardian. Her distress was undeniably real, and Neal had no reason to doubt her. Recognition was a peculiar thing, not necessarily made up of the obvious: hair color, eye color, height to the nearest inch. She obviously didn't expect to be believed, but he'd been a cop long enough, seen enough lineups, to understand exactly what she meant. Joe Gardner might well have loomed above her in precisely the way the rapist had; without saying a word, he might have turned his head or lifted his hand in a particular way.

What Neal didn't understand was why Gardner, so scrupulously careful to this point, would have risked everything for... what? A chance to feed on Chelsea Cahill's fear?

Did it matter? Neal asked himself impatiently. He had a positive ID. Karen was no longer bait. He could get to know his kids again.

"I'll need you to make an official statement and sign it," he said, "but tomorrow would be fine, if that's convenient for you."

She gulped and nodded.

Feeling a need to reassure her, he said quietly, "You can feel safe again."

Her face showed she wasn't convinced, not yet, but he hoped with time she would be. With time, she might almost forget. He was sorry she'd have to testify at Gardner's trial, where her identification of him would be minutely examined and questioned. Thank God there would be corroborating evidence, thanks to the wonders of modern lab work.

He nodded and said, "Good night, Miss Cahill," then turned to find Karen standing a few steps back, staring at her friend, a frown creasing her brow.

Her expression jolted him. "Don't you believe her?" Neal asked.

"Hmm?" Karen started. "Believe her? Why wouldn't I?"

"Then why the look?"

"Look?" She gazed at him in surprise. "I was just thinking. Trying to remember her exact description that night in the hospital."

Uneasiness stirred in his breast. To rid himself of it, Neal responded more forcefully than he felt. "He matches it."

"Yes, but *Joe.*" Her brow crinkled again. "It's just so hard to picture."

He nodded toward Chelsea. "Your friend doesn't think so."

"I know but..."

"Who, then?" He sympathized—damn it, he liked Joe Gardner, too. But he'd have sworn Chelsea Cahill wasn't fingering the wrong man out of spite. She was scared, and no wonder. Tonight she'd put a face to her worst nightmare. And Gardner wouldn't be the first "nice" man to be arrested for and convicted of a heinous crime.

Neal kept his voice unyielding. "Who? Frank Morris? Bradley? Or have you changed your mind about Mark Griggs?"

"No." Karen rubbed her arms as though she was cold. "No, I haven't changed my mind."

"Well, then?"

"I'm sorry. I'm holding you up." She gave a small sigh. "I should be glad, shouldn't I?"

"There wasn't much about tonight's scene to make anyone glad," Neal said roughly. He took a step toward her.

But Karen backed away. *Not the time or place.* She knew that as well as he did.

He stopped. "I'll call you."

She nodded, her gaze not quite meeting his. "Sure. That's fine. Umm, I'll talk to you later, then."

Frowning, Neal watched her go to her friend, touch her arm, talk softly. His gut protested against leaving Karen like this. He'd never seen her so troubled, so vulnerable. For all her prickliness, deep down inside Ms. Flowerwoman had believed in the essential goodness of people—at least, the people she knew and liked. Tonight she'd had a harsh education in reality.

But he had a job to do, he reminded himself. It was time he got on with it. The sooner he booked Gardner, the sooner he could erase Karen's doubts.

In the back seat of the car, the football coach had his face buried in his hands. He didn't look up when Neal climbed in behind the wheel and turned the key.

As Neal pulled away, he glanced in his rearview mirror. Karen and Chelsea and the other woman all stared after him. He swerved to cut across the parking lot to the exit, and Karen was replaced in the mirror by silent spectators standing along the curb. He recognized a few: a couple of the fathers he'd interviewed, Frank Morris, a bunch of teenage boys. Their faces were all unnaturally solemn.

They'd all had a lesson tonight, and they wouldn't forget it.

WHO DECIDED you had the authority to make the moral decisions around here?

She had, of course. Who else? Karen thought wryly. She'd believed she understood people. It was almost laughable now, but she remembered feeling wiser, more sophisticated, than most of the small-town residents. After all, she'd come from the big city; she'd protested the war, seen riots, been thrown in jail for following her convictions. She'd seen more of the *real* world.

Oh, God. Karen bent forward and rested her forehead on the steering wheel. The moment she closed her eyes she saw it all again, the contorted faces, the hate-filled eyes, the purses smashing into Joe Gardner's head, the fist in his stomach. She saw him curled in a ball on the asphalt while people she knew, nice people, kicked him viciously.

She opened her eyes and straightened, dragging in a shaky breath. The carport was reasonably well lit, but still she didn't welcome the moment when she left the safety of her car and hurried to the door, key in hand.

"Don't be an idiot!" she told herself. It was all over. She'd liked Joe, didn't want him to be guilty, but she'd known all along that the rapist had to be someone she knew. Neal was right. Who would she have preferred it be?

None of which reasoning kept her from glancing nervously over her shoulder as she unlocked the side door or from feeling a release of tension once she was in and had thrown the dead bolt. How long would it take before she quit looking over her shoulder, quit lying in bed at night straining to hear every creak of the old house?

Right now she stood, completely still, listening to the silence.

"Hello?" she called. "Anyone home?"

Nothing. So Neal must have recalled the young officer who was to have been here. Well, of course he had, she scolded herself. Why not? Chelsea had been positive; the rapist was in custody.

"Maggie?" Karen tried. "Kitty, kitty?"

No thump or answering meow. Maggie must be out, hunting small night creatures. Karen set her purse down on the kitchen table and wandered into the living room, where she briefly considered turning on the television for company, for distraction.

Tell me, Ms. Lindberg, are you ever wrong?

How terribly wrong she'd been this time. She, in her infinite wisdom, had decided that townspeople shouldn't have to feel helpless. Why? Because *she* didn't like feeling helpless. Because *she* had never liked having to depend on anyone else. For such selfish reasons, she had mobilized her small army, convincing them all that they had the right to defend themselves, that they could take action. The unwritten subtext was that the police were useless, that the townsfolk, banded together, could accomplish what the police could not.

Which made her responsible for the savagery unleashed tonight.

Karen went down the hall to Abby's bedroom and stood in the doorway, noticing with one part of her mind that her daughter hadn't made her bed like she'd promised, that clothes were heaped on a chair, and a bottle of fingernail polish had tipped over to spread a glistening pool of crimson on the top of the dressing table. Most of her attention was on the picture that played in her mind again and again. This time she picked out faces she knew well.

Gretchen Williams, the high-school counselor. A year ago, when a junior at the high school died in a drunk-driving accident, her compassion and care for the kids who'd known him had been boundless. Becky Finch, the hairdresser who cut Karen's hair, gossiping cheerily as her scissors snipped. Marilyn Phelps, the mother of one of Abby's friends, known for her sense of humor.

There'd been a scattering of men, too: Jim Craig, the likable father she'd talked to before the dance; Cliff Jensen, an electrician, who had two foster kids, as well as a daughter of his own; Kurt Mills, the head of the curriculum committee at the high school.

Nice people who were angry.

Karen shuddered. If Neal hadn't come so quickly, if she hadn't been there, they might have killed Joe. Neal was right; guilty or innocent, Joe deserved a fair trial, not death at the hands of a maddened mob formed on the word of a hysterical woman.

What if they *had* battered him to death, only to discover that he *wasn't* guilty, that Chelsea was wrong?

The thought played at the edges of Karen's mind, and just for a moment she put aside her own feelings of guilt. *Could* Chelsea be wrong?

It was true that when murderers or rapists were arrested, neighbors were often stunned. But usually it developed that nobody had really known the murderer/rapist very well. He was quiet, kept to himself, mowed his lawn regularly. He hadn't stirred the surfaces of their lives, so they'd deemed him inoffensive.

In contrast, there were a few, like Ted Bundy, who were charming, smooth, luring victims easily.

Neither description seemed to fit Joe Gardner. He was warm, outgoing, a buddy to the kids and amiable to parents. He maybe admired himself too much; the body-builder muscles must take an awful lot of work, and he tended to wear tight T-shirts and shorts to show them off. How did that fit with a rapist who took such care to ensure that none of the victims saw him undressed?

She went back into the silent living room and sank onto the couch, drawing her feet up under her, grabbing a cotton afghan to tuck around her for warmth. What about Chelsea? Karen wondered, with increasing uneasiness. Once upon a time she'd been rock solid, unflappable, the first person Karen would turn to in a minor crisis.

But that was *before*. Before the night that changed her, perhaps forever. Since the attack, she'd been brittle, quick to tears, nervous. It would have taken very little to frighten her. Had Joe struck an indefinable note of familiarity when he loomed above her talking about dancing? Had he somehow given himself away? Or would any tall, muscular, brown-eyed man have seemed a threat to Chelsea?

But Joe had already been the prime suspect, Karen reminded herself. Although there were other men who might fit, Joe matched the description perfectly. Tall, muscular, brown-eyed.

No, that wasn't quite right. Karen frowned, remembering. Chelsea had hesitated. Her exact words were, "I think he was tall."

Chelsea wasn't the only one to hesitate. Lisa Pyne, too, had been uncertain. "I don't know," she'd said. Then, "He crushed me. I felt smothered, like I'd never escape. There wasn't any point in fighting. I was too small next to him."

Neal, and Karen, too, had assumed the man who attacked her was large. But Joe Gardner, at six foot two or three, must weigh at least two hundred pounds. Karen couldn't imagine that if he'd raped her, she would hesitate about describing him as large. Surely in that situation, a woman would *magnify* his size in her mind!

Karen wondered whether the other victims had sounded more positive. Maybe she was getting herself into a stew about nothing. Still, Neal was a large man himself. He might take the descriptions at face value, never having known a woman's physical vulnerability.

Karen refused to let her uneasiness blossom into fear. But it wouldn't hurt to call Neal, tell him her doubts, ask him to send someone over.

She'd taken the first step toward the kitchen when her doorbell rang.

Neal? Glancing at the clock, she was surprised to see that she'd been home an hour. He'd said he would call, but she had seen in his eyes that he wanted to hold her. And God knows she wanted to be held.

She turned on the porch light and was cautious enough to leave on the chain when she opened the front door. Through the crack it allowed, she saw Frank Morris standing on her front porch.

How bizarre. What on earth could he want? Very aware of being alone, she said, "Mr. Morris. I'm surprised to see you." Understatement of the day.

He seemed to have trouble meeting her eyes. Hunching his shoulders, he said, "I'm sorry to bother you, Ms. Lindberg. I hope I didn't wake up you or Abby.''

Karen knew she'd told him that Abby was at her grandmother's. Obviously he'd forgotten, which put her slightly more at ease.

"No, I hadn't gone to bed yet." She made no move to unfasten the chain or invite him in, not until he gave her a good reason.

He put his hands in his pockets and shifted uneasily. "This must seem really strange. The thing is, I keep thinking about Joe being arrested and I just can't believe he's guilty. I, uh, saw you with Chief Rowland at one of the high-school plays, so I thought maybe you knew him well enough to... I don't know, intervene somehow. Do you have a few minutes?"

He looked so uncomfortable Karen realized what an extraordinary effort coming here like this was for him. Disarmed, she was also grateful that she wasn't the only one having doubts. Still she hesitated, but how could she refuse to let him in? Tell him she was afraid *he* was the mad rapist? Besides, the rapist had never shown his face to his victims. She distinctly remembered Neal saying that he already had the mask on when he rang Kathleen Madsen's doorbell.

"Just a moment," she said, feeling fatalistic, and closed the door to unhook the chain. Then she opened it wide and let him in. He followed her into the living room as docilely as Joe had gone with Neal.

"Please, have a seat," she said. "Can I offer you tea or coffee?"

"Oh, uh, nothing for me." The math teacher chose the chair and sat, but without really relaxing. From his pocket he produced the ubiquitous breath mints, popping one in his mouth so automatically she doubted he was even aware he was doing it. The mints were as much a nervous habit as nibbling on fingernails. In fact, maybe they were a substitute for a habit he wanted to rid himself of. Just as automatically, he held the box out to her.

She'd never liked mints. They were too sweet for her tastes.

Sweet. No, *sickly sweet*. Where had she heard that? Panic rushed through her as she stared at the innocent little box in his hand. According to one of the victims, the rapist's breath was sickly sweet.

Maybe she was getting paranoid. The fact that Frank liked mints was less than solid proof that he was really the rapist. How horrible it would be if he guessed that she was afraid of him.

Better than being a fool, Karen thought.

Obviously she couldn't use the telephone out here; it was right beside him, on the end table. She would make an excuse, go to the kitchen. If he somehow overheard, she could say she'd called Neal so that she could tell him what Frank had to say.

She forced herself to meet his eyes—his brown eyes. "Are you sure I can't get you a cup of something? I'm going to put hot water on for myself."

He looked so inoffensive, so ordinary. "No. Thanks."

Somehow she smiled. "Well, just a minute, then."

He didn't stand or make any move to stop her. She could have deceived herself that she was really calm had her heart not been racing.

In the kitchen she turned on a faucet to cover the click of the receiver and the sound of her voice. Then she went straight to the phone.

But when she picked it up, there was no dial tone. *Oh, God*, she thought.

And then the music started playing, Mary Chapin Carpenter's rich voice, pouring out of the living-room speakers.

He wanted her to dance.

CHAPTER FOURTEEN

NEAL WISHED he felt easier in his mind about this arrest. He'd never liked Joe Gardner as a suspect, primarily because of his size. For the dozenth time in the past half hour he leaned back in his chair and contemplated the football coach.

He was a beefy guy, no doubt about it. Not so enormous as to make impossible the victims' uncertainty, but big enough to keep the issue niggling at the back of his mind. Damn it, a scared woman was bound to exaggerate her attacker's size, even in her own mind; the longer she thought about him, the more monstrous he'd become in her recollection.

Question was, how to reconcile that with the way each victim had hesitated before declaring him tall, powerful?

"For God's sake," Joe said, running a hand over his haggard face, "I was attracted to the woman. I wanted to ask her out! I guess it was insensitive of me, but... Oh, hell. I'd almost forgotten she was one of the women. And the night she chaperoned is the only time we've met." His hand dropped. "She'd promised to have a dance with me. All I did tonight was remind her. Is that a crime?" He sounded beseeching.

Neal kept his face stolid. "Did you touch her tonight?"

"I didn't lay a finger on her, I swear it! I've never laid a finger on her!" The coach yanked at his hair, leaving it spiked. "God. I can't believe this is happening!"

He was too damned convincing for Neal's comfort. To give himself space, Neal stood and went to the coffee machine for a cup—rancid stuff, but the espresso stand was long closed and he needed the caffeine. He took more time than was really necessary to stir in a dash of milk that had been in the small refrigerator too long.

Gardner didn't need any caffeine. He was fidgeting in that hard office chair, staying in constant motion. If his fingers weren't tapping his knee, he was shifting position or jiggling one leg or the other. Wired.

Who could blame him? Neal reflected. He was on his way to the lockup for a crime he swore he hadn't committed.

When Neal carried the coffee over and sat on the edge of the desk, Joe lifted a face so earnest the lines of weariness and fear were momentarily wiped away. "Why would I rape a woman? I mean, I don't have that hard a time finding dates. Usually I'm seeing somebody seriously. Not right now." The chair squeaked as he sat upright, leaned back, changed his mind and braced his hands on his knees. "I just didn't think when I saw Chelsea. I mean, I'd asked her sister if she was married or seeing someone, and she said no, so I figured why not give it a try?"

Neal nodded noncommittally.

As though encouraged, Gardner talked even faster. "The parking lot wasn't dark. There were plenty of people around. It never occurred to me that I'd scare her! I mean, if I wanted to attack a woman, it wouldn't be at the high school. In front of the kids!" His tone was incredulous. "It's crazy," he concluded.

"Yeah," Neal agreed. "It's crazy, all right."

"God." Despair returned the years to his face. "You really think I did it."

"Miss Cahill says you did."

"That's it, then? I'm tried and convicted?"

"Mr. Gardner," Neal said patiently, "as I've said repeatedly, I'd recommend you call a lawyer. He'll explain your rights to you."

The coach slumped, bowing his head for a moment. "Yeah, okay," he said at last. "I'll get myself a lawyer. Let me look at the yellow pages."

Neal shoved the phone book toward him. "You may have difficulty reaching anyone. In the morning..."

Gardner gave no sign of hearing. He was flipping through the phone book's yellow pages so fast that one tore. His hands were trembling and his eyes were bloodshot when he looked up. "I need a cigarette. Hell. I had some in my locker. Tell me you smoke."

"Sorry." Neal stood. "Let me see if I can find you one."

DeSalsa was hanging around in the squad room waiting to transport Gardner to the county jail. Neal sent him off to see if the clerk who smoked had a pack stashed in her desk.

"Top drawer," the young officer said, handing them over with a cheap lighter.

"Remind me to pay her back," Neal said. "Thanks." Joe Gardner needed them a hell of a lot more than the clerk did. Neal tossed the pack to Gardner and lit a cigarette for him, keeping the lighter himself. He handed over an empty plastic cup to use as an astray.

The football coach blew out a stream of smoke. "Thanks. Times like this make me realize how addicted I am." He laughed mirthlessly. "Times like this—I've never had a time like this!" His hand was still trembling as he inhaled. "Okay. What was I doing? A lawyer. Yeah, that's it." He lifted the phone book onto his lap and ran a finger down the listings. "You know a good lawyer? Or aren't you allowed to recommend any?"

Neal grimaced at the cloud of acrid smoke and pushed his chair back. Technically smoking wasn't allowed in here. The clerk whose pack he'd filched always stood outside on her breaks. Tonight the cause seemed worth breathing in some secondhand smoke, disgusting though it was. But how any nonsmoker lived with this, he couldn't imagine. The idea of kissing a woman who smoked was singularly unappealing.

Damnation. The doubt hit him with the breath-stealing force of a revelation.

It took superhuman effort to wipe the intensity he felt from his voice. "I don't remember seeing you smoke before. You been trying to quit?"

Gardner knocked some ash off into the cup. "I'm careful not to smoke where the boys might see me. Here I am lecturing them all day about fitness and diet, and I'm killing myself with these things! I keep thinking, one of these days—" He broke off and his mouth twisted, as though he'd remembered that nicotine addiction was the least of his problems right now.

A growing sense of urgency brought Neal to his feet. Very carefully, so there could be no mistake, he said, "You haven't tried to quit this fall? Not even for a few weeks?"

"No. Not even for a few days. What's the big deal?"

"Nothing. DeSalsa!" Neal bellowed.

The officer appeared in the doorway. "Yeah?"

"Keep an eye on him." Neal grabbed his notebook and took himself to the nearest phone that was out of earshot. Too restless and filled with tension to sit, he flipped through the notebook until he found the right page, then dialed Kathleen Madsen's number. Busy.

Hell. He slammed the receiver down, swearing under his breath as he flipped pages until he found Lisa Pyne's number and stabbed the buttons. It rang again and again. Neal paced within the limits of the cord, muttering, "Answer me. Answer me. Damn it, answer!"

"Hello?" The voice was both sleepy and wary.

"Chief Rowland," Neal said with no preamble. "Miss Pyne, would you have noticed if the rapist was a smoker?"

"Noticed...?" A moment of silence evidently let her wake up. "I don't think so. I smoke myself."

"Sorry to bother you so late." Neal abruptly disconnected.

He dialed Kathleen Madsen's number again. Still busy. "Damn!" he muttered. Pacing, he wondered whether he'd get a straight answer out of Chelsea Cahill. Or had she so firmly made up her mind she wouldn't want to think about anything that might clear the football coach?

Less and less did he like knowing that Karen was home alone. Why the hell had he jumped the gun and pulled DeSalsa out of her house? He'd call her and satisfy himself that she was okay.

Her phone, too, was busy. He told himself she was probably talking to her hysterical friend, who'd needed a few calming words. For all her combativeness, it would be like Karen to provide them. But, damn, he wished she'd get off the phone.

Toni Santos had gotten out of the hospital that morning and flown home to California to stay with her mother. He had the number here somewhere. Was her jaw still wired shut? Neal couldn't remember the timetable.

He'd try the Madsen woman one more time. When the phone actually rang, the wave of relief he felt highlighted his growing tension. It was the son who answered. When Neal asked for his mother, the boy bellowed, "Mom!"

A moment later, she came on. Her voice, too, was wary. "Hello?"

Neal identified himself. "Ms. Madsen, would you have noticed if your assailant was a smoker?"

No pause this time. "Yes, I'm sure I would have," she said firmly. "I don't smoke, and you know how the odor always hovers around a smoker. What I remember is that odd sweet smell. I mentioned it, didn't I? But even that was just a whiff, not strong enough to disguise tobacco. No, I'm sure he didn't smoke."

Fear curled in Neal's stomach. "Thank you."

"What is it?" She sounded brittle. "Did you find him?"

He should have lied, but Neal was too damned scared to think up an evasion. Bluntly he said, "I think we just arrested the wrong man."

Through the open door of his office, he could see Joe Gardner, gratefully exhaling an acrid blue cloud. Neal tried to think clearly, not let himself rush off half-cocked. *He* hadn't noticed the odor of tobacco smoke clinging to Gardner. But then, until tonight he hadn't gotten any closer to him than five feet, either. And during the arrest, there'd been too many distractions.

If Kathleen Madsen was right, Joe Gardner couldn't be the perp. And if he wasn't...

God, if he wasn't, one of the other men there tonight was. And anybody watching would have seen the police chief taking Gardner into custody, would have known Karen was home alone.

Swearing, Neal snatched up the phone again, dialed—and got a busy signal.

A minute later, Joe locked in a cell, Neal gunned a squad car out of the parking lot, lights flashing and siren screaming.

OH GOD, oh God, oh God. It was a litany and a prayer. It was terror put into words.

The kitchen was a dead end. She'd never thought of it that way, but it was.

Frantically Karen swung around, to find Frank Morris already blocking the entrance. To escape through the side door, she had to get past him.

He looked so ordinary, so much as usual. She actually opened her mouth to bluff, to say something casual about how much she liked Mary Chapin Carpenter, to act as though the idea of him as a rapist hadn't entered her mind.

And then she saw the knife.

He held it so casually, a hunting knife, she thought, with a wicked blade, gleaming-new or lovingly polished.

"Frank..." she said, and retreated a step.

He advanced, silent, a man so bland she couldn't have conjured up a picture of his face if he hadn't been standing in front of her.

"Frank, you can't mean this." Another step back. Where was she going? Oh, God, she was out of reach of the silverware drawer with its butcher knives. She didn't want to get close enough to him to use one, anyway.

Okay. Battling panic, she tried to think logically. What could she use to defend herself? Karen eased backward, feeling her way, one hand sliding along the edge of the counter.

He held the knife in front of him, where the light skipped along the blade. His eyes glittered like the cold steel, and Karen heard Lisa, or was it Chelsea? *I'll never forget his eyes.*

But he was letting Karen see his face. Which meant he couldn't afford to let her go.

"Frank." Despite the strain in her voice, she sounded almost reasonable. "Don't do this. I like you. If you put down the knife, I'll do my best to see to it you get help."

Her groping hand touched the tall cupboard door. She kicked it open and grabbed the broom. Half-hysterically, she thought, *I never was very domestic, and now my life depends on a broom!*

Still he advanced, and she'd come up against the wall. She tried again, "Mark Griggs scared me tonight. I was so glad to see you. You were a lifesaver. I'll tell the police that. It'll weigh in your favor."

He sounded reasonable, too, calm. "You were with *me* tonight. And you went off with Gardner. Women always do."

Past the knot in her throat, she said, "I'd rather have danced with you. But you didn't ask me." She sidled along the wall until she hit the corner.

He wasn't four feet from her now. "Well, you can dance for me now," he said, sounding eerily like the man who worried about whether her daughter grasped math concepts. "You can make up for getting the whole town so upset."

I could dance, she thought. Stall for time. If Neal somehow guessed, if he was on his way...

Oh, God, how she'd have liked to believe that! But he wasn't. She had only herself to depend on. Stalling for time was useless.

"No," Karen said almost regretfully. "I can't dance for you. You should have asked me tonight at the high school. I would have then."

He lunged so suddenly that Karen's only response was reflexive. She swept up with the broom handle and struck him in the throat. Gagging, he staggered back. She sidestepped, crablike, circling toward the kitchen door.

Snarling, Frank thrust at her. As hard as she could, Karen chopped down on his arm with the broom handle, then retreated a few more steps. Half crouching, he stalked her like a cat with a mouse, the knife his wicked claw. Never taking her eyes from him, Karen backed through the doorway.

Okay, left, she thought. *If I can just reach the door...*

Then what? Terror spurted anew. There was no way to buy the time to open it. She had bolted and chained the side door when she'd come in. That care doomed her now. Frank would be on her long before she could get it open.

"I'll hurt you if you don't dance," he said.

What could she do but retreat toward the living room, where Mary Chapin Carpenter's voice swelled from the speakers? Terror was nearly despair now, numbing her. All Karen could think of was Neal. Neal, who thought he'd failed his wife. Who'd be certain he'd failed her when he found her.

No. She wouldn't give up. *Break a window. Scream.*

Would anyone hear through the thick shrubbery around the house?

Hysteria was closer now. Thrust, parry. Frank meant to kill her, she saw it in his eyes. Now he was slashing for her throat and chest.

She bumped against the coffee table, circled it. *Abby,* she thought with terrible pain and love. *Neal.* Oh, God, what a coward she'd been. And she'd believed herself so brave, always ready to take a risk when others weren't. But she had only fought when she was certain to win, she saw now.

Her temper sparked. What, was she going to lie down and die just because he waved a knife at her? By God, she wouldn't give him the satisfaction of scaring her so easily!

Her legs came up against an end table. She dropped the broom and in the same movement snatched up a tall ebony statue of an African woman with a basket on her head. Karen swung like Babe Ruth, releasing her makeshift weapon to whistle through the air toward his head. Frank ducked, barely in time. It crashed into the wall.

"It'll be a cold day in hell before I'd dance for you!" she snapped. Karen grabbed the lamp, yanking the cord from the wall, flinging the whole thing one-handed. It grazed the side of his head and shattered on the floor in front of him.

"You bitch!" he bellowed, and lowered his head to plow at her.

Karen made it behind the couch. There she grabbed the broom again and swung it at him. The blade of the knife half-severed it, but before he could make his next move, she snatched books from the shelf and threw them.

He was screaming profanities now, and she was yelling right back at him, kicking furniture in his way, hurling everything from pillow cushions to the vase from the top of the piano.

During one of his rushes, she fell, tripping over a cushion. Frank grasped the knife in both hands and plunged it at her belly, but she rolled at the last minute and kicked at his legs. By the time he regained his balance, she was back on her feet, shoving the ottoman at him.

"You goddamn bitch!" he roared, and charged her again.

She skirted the piano. Her breath whistled in and out, and her vision began to blur. Still the music played, Mary singing about running from the arms of lovers. He was tiring, too, Karen saw. His hands shook and his rushes were blinder, more frantic. But, oh, God, he would get her on one of them. Each time he came closer. One of her hands was slick with blood when she shoved the piano bench in his way and looked desperately for something else to throw. She didn't even remember being cut.

If only the music would stop. Why had she bought a tape deck that automatically reversed direction? She grabbed it from the shelf and flung it, too. The music cut off in midword.

Or was it still playing? Confused, she took a second to realize the wail she heard was a siren.

"Neal!" she screamed, just as Frank's face twisted with demonical hatred and he flung himself at her, knife slicing for her throat.

She felt a sting across her neck and fell beneath him. Dimly, far away, Karen thought, *Shouldn't it hurt worse than this?* Somehow she heard herself still calling Neal's name, which mixed with the siren and the obscenities and the crash as something—someone—hurtled through the window.

Frank half rose off her, and the tip of the blade pricked the skin on her exposed throat. It trembled as his hands shook.

"I'll kill her!" he swore. "I'll kill her! I mean it!"

Karen held her breath so that she didn't move at all. She rolled her eyes to one side. Amidst the chaos of her living room, not three feet away, Neal stood with his feet braced apart, gun in both hands. Pointed at Frank's head.

"Hurt her and you're dead!" Neal snapped. "Don't screw up! Right now, I'd like to pull the trigger. Drop the goddamn knife! Drop it. Now!"

"I'll kill her!"

"Then you'll go, too," Neal vowed. Not once did he look at her; teeth set, he had death in his eyes.

She would've blacked out if she hadn't released a breath and rasped in air. For just an instant, the knife probed deeper and she closed her eyes and prayed. If she just had another chance, for Abby's sake and Neal's . . .

In the next second, the tip was no longer against her neck. The knife clattered to the floor and Frank rose to his feet beside her.

"Don't shoot!" He held up his hands. "I wouldn't have hurt her, even though she's a bitch. She was supposed to dance for me."

Neal stepped across Karen and slammed Frank Morris up against a wall, wrestling his hands behind him and cuffing them.

"That's all I wanted. For her to dance."

"You have the right to remain silent . . ." Neal began.

Karen tuned the rest out. She couldn't seem to make herself try to stand up, even though she knew she should. Another siren wailed, and another. It seemed only moments before a second police officer appeared in the window.

The cop uttered a startled profanity, and she realized how completely her living room had been destroyed. The next instant, he'd swung himself inside. At a word from Neal, he grabbed Frank by the collar and shoved him toward the door.

Neal dropped to his knees beside her. His voice was thick, uneven. "Tell me you're all right. Tell me you're just resting."

"I'm just resting," she said obediently.

"Damn it!" His hands were moving roughly over her. "Don't quit fighting now!"

"Who said I'm quitting?" Her neck stung and fire licked at one forearm, but otherwise she was catching a second wind. "If you'll get out of my way, I'll sit up."

With amazing gentleness, he helped her. She scooted back and leaned against the piano. Her house seemed to be filled with police officers, and a medic, ignoring Neal, gently wiped her arm and began wrapping it in gauze.

"Don't look around," Neal said gruffly. "The son of a bitch tore your place apart."

"Actually," Karen said with a certain amount of satisfaction, "I did it myself. I didn't feel like dancing. I told him to go to hell. I'll bet he has a few bruises at least."

"God almighty." Neal pulled her into his arms. She felt the shudders tear through him. He held her so tightly it hurt, but she couldn't think of anyplace on earth she'd rather be. His voice was raw. "I was afraid I'd lost you."

Against his shoulder, she whispered, "I thought about you. The whole time. It made me mad, to think you'd never know..."

"Know what?" He held her away, in his eyes enough fear and gratitude to make it easy to say what she had to.

"That even if you are old-fashioned and sexist and bullheaded, I love you."

Neal almost smiled, though his eyes were still dark with terror. "I guess it takes pigheaded to know bullheaded," he suggested with a gravelly undertone. "Maybe we're made for each other. You want to go ten or twelve rounds? Maybe give ourselves forty or fifty years?"

She was peripherally aware that a couple of the cops were grinning, and the medic winked at her before he stood and backed up a few steps. But all she cared about was the man crouched in front of her. He might as well have squeezed her heart in his hand. She could barely say, "If that's a proposal, my answer is yes."

His smile faded, leaving so much vulnerability, so much hunger showing on his face, she thought she'd never get to the bottom of it. She never wanted to.

Then his lips found hers, and gratitude and tenderness and triumph rose in her, hot and sweet. She had her chance now. *They* had their chance. She wound her arms around his neck and kissed him back just as fervently.

Their audience applauded.

EPILOGUE

NEAL LEANED BACK in his chair and enjoyed the sight of his intended trying to beguile people she'd previously specialized in ticking off. The occasion was a Rotary Club dinner two days before the election.

Wearing the red silk dress that brought back some fond memories for him, Karen gripped the wooden podium and leaned forward. Her intensity held her audience in thrall.

"The number-one issue has to be communication," she told them. "Our school board represents the public. How can it if the members don't know what the community wants?

"This is a two-way street, of course. It's not fair to blame the board when we don't like a decision if we haven't been to meetings, if we haven't called to express opinions, if we haven't even bothered to find out what issues face our school district.

"But I believe we can widen at least one side of that street. I think our school administration and board can work harder to encourage community participation in major decisions."

Her gaze roved over the businessmen and women sitting along each side of the long table. "Many of you know me well. I'll bet there isn't one of you who could deny that I'm an expert on communication. You may not always like what I say, but I say it, anyway, popular or not. How else can we start a dialogue? Sometimes the only way is for somebody to open his or her big mouth and get everybody fired up.'' She flashed a quick grin. ''That's my favorite role.''

Amidst the applause as she stepped back from the podium was laughter. They knew her, sure enough, and there were undoubtedly a few people here who didn't like her. But she was right; if they didn't want the administration's decisions rubber-stamped, if they wanted somebody to probe and question and get voters involved, she was their candidate. And considering a few of the administration's decisions lately, Neal's money was on her.

He stood and stretched, watching as first her friends and, more slowly, others went up to chat and thank her for the talk. He could tell she was still giving mini-speeches, her hands waving to punctuate her points, but her smiles were a little softer than they'd been two months ago, and she was a little more willing to listen to other opinions. Either that, or she was doing a damned good job of pretending.

His mouth twitched at the idea. Wouldn't surprise him if her tenure on the school board was followed by a term as mayor. Could the state legislature be far behind?

''Well, Chief Rowland,'' a hearty voice asked, ''are you endorsing either candidate?''

Neal turned to see Pete Eksted, editor of the *Pilchuck Times*.

''Darn right I am,'' he said. ''I like a lady with real guts. Of course, I just might be prejudiced, since I'm marrying her.''

"Damn!" Pete said, shaking his head, but a grin playing at the corners of his mouth. "Dottie and I had a bet on that one."

"I take it you're the realist and she's the romantic?"

"Yep." The editor slapped Neal on the back. "I don't mind being proved wrong, though."

"Better pay up now," Neal advised him. Pete raised his eyebrows. "Before you take that nice long vacation after your endorsement comes out tomorrow."

"Won't be a surprise to anybody." Pete ran a hand over his balding head. "Karen has my vote."

"She'll be glad to hear that," Neal said.

Someone else slapped him on the back. "Congratulations! Karen tells me you're engaged." Several other men turned to add their congratulations.

"You here as our police chief, or her fiancé?" The speaker was Darrell Holm, who owned the town's one furniture store. The jocularity didn't quite cover his essential hostility.

Neal glanced around the group, trying to decide whether they all felt as Holm did or whether most were more sympathetic. Karen had come up behind Holm, unnoticed by the others. Neal's gaze touched hers briefly, but it was long enough to warm him.

"I'll tell you what," he said, meeting Holm's eyes. "I fell in love with Karen Lindberg because of all the same qualities that will make her a dynamite school-board member—her commitment, her idealism, her intelligence and caring. Since I met her in the line of duty, I can't separate my opinions into one category or the other. Does that bother you?"

Holm actually flushed. "Did I say it did?" he asked. He turned and found himself face-to-face with

Karen. She smiled sweetly and came immediately to Neal's side. Holm beat a retreat. After a sidelong glance, Eksted pulled the others into a discussion about a proposed solid-waste-transfer station.

Karen slipped her arm through Neal's, drew him a few steps away and murmured, "I'm blushing."

Against her ear he said softly, "You don't know how."

"Well, my heart's going pitty pat, anyway." She grinned and plunged back into the electioneering.

Only on their way out to the car a while later did she ask, in an oddly serious tone, "Did you mean all of that?"

He held open the car door for her. "What?"

Karen made no move to get in. "The idealism and commitment and...what else?"

November had brought the first snap of winter, and he felt her shiver when he cupped her chin. Even though it was dark, a full moon and lighted windows behind them let him see her elfin face, grave and...waiting.

"Caring and intelligence," he said. "Do you doubt I mean it?"

Once she would have gotten prickly. Now her lashes fluttered and then she smiled wryly.

"Somewhat to my surprise," Ms. Flowerwoman admitted, "no, I don't."

He bent his head to kiss her, but paused with his mouth only inches from hers. "I left one quality off my list."

"Really." Her fingers were playing a rhythm on his chest. "And what was that?"

"Passion," he said huskily, and sampled it.

HARLEQUIN SUPERROMANCE®

WOMEN WHO DARE
They take chances, make changes
and follow their hearts!

Dangerous to Love
by Carol Duncan Perry

Vicki Winslow refuses to do the sensible thing—enter the
witness protection program. She's done nothing wrong and
she isn't going to cut herself off from her family. So now she's
hiding out, protected only by secrecy and her own wits—if
you don't count her eighty-seven-year-old great-aunt, her
poetry-quoting cousin, two large dogs, one rifle and a pet
skunk named Sweetpea.

Caine Alexander aims to change this situation. Not that
Caine's any knight in shining armor. *Hell, no.* A man could get
killed playing hero. Still, he's promised to protect Vicki, and if
any man can make good on such a promise, Caine's the man.
Too bad Vicki doesn't want his protection.... Because she's
stuck with it.

**Watch for *Dangerous to Love*
by Carol Duncan Perry.**

**Available in July 1995 wherever
Harlequin books are sold.**

THREE BESTSELLING AUTHORS

HEATHER GRAHAM POZZESSERE
THERESA MICHAELS
MERLINE LOVELACE

bring you

THREE HEROES THAT DREAMS ARE MADE OF!

The Highwayman—He knew the honorable thing was to send his captive home, but how could he let the beautiful Lady Kate return to the arms of another man?

The Warrior—Raised to protect his tribe, the fierce Apache warrior had little room in his heart until the gentle Angie showed him the power and strength of love.

The Knight—His years as a mercenary had taught him many skills, but would winning the hand of a spirited young widow prove to be his greatest challenge?

Don't miss these **UNFORGETTABLE RENEGADES!**

Available in August wherever Harlequin books are sold.

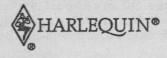

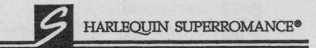

HARLEQUIN SUPERROMANCE®

presents

Big Luke, Little Luke
by Dawn Stewardson

This July, meet the third of our Four Strong Men:

Mike Alexander was the best friend Navy pilot Luke Dakota
ever had. So when Luke received a letter from Mike's wife,
Caitlyn, he wasn't too concerned—until he opened it. In the
letter, Caitlyn told him about Mike's death and the birth of
their son, Luke. His namesake.

Drawn by a sense of responsibility to Mike, Luke arranged for
a leave of absence and set off for Arizona.

Once there, his life was sent into a tailspin. He learned that
Caitlyn's business was in the red, military intelligence
wouldn't leave her alone and, worst of all, she was convinced
that Mike's death was the result of foul play. Luke became
determined to help Caitlyn fight her unseen enemies. But
he soon found himself up against an enemy he couldn't
conquer—himself. Because Luke Dakota was falling in love
with his best friend's wife....

**Look for *Big Luke, Little Luke* in July 1995
wherever Harlequin books are sold.**

HARLEQUIN SUPERROMANCE®

A KISS TOO LATE
by
Ellen James

It *must* be a bad dream—but it isn't. There actually *is* a naked man sleeping in Jen Hillard's bed. Worse, it's her ex-husband. Sexy, handsome, exciting—Adam Prescott's always been able to sweep her into bed. He's just never cared enough to sweep her into his heart.

But now Jen's finally found the nerve to make a new life for herself, so how could she have let this happen? Silly question. Well, okay, so what if she's done the one thing she'd sworn she'd never do—let Adam Prescott back into her bed? She'll be damned if she'll let him back into her life. And her heart? Well, that's another matter. He's always been there.

REUNITED!
First Love...Last Love

Available in July wherever Harlequin books are sold.

This June, for the first time in paperback

NEW YORK TIMES BESTSELLING AUTHORS:

SUE GRAFTON
TONY HILLERMAN

and many more...

Bring you

2ND CULPRIT

Newcomers, international names and old favorites offer up a varied itinerary for the adventurous traveler in crime! Join *New York Times* bestselling authors TONY HILLERMAN and SUE GRAFTON, plus an additional cast of 24 of the mystery genre's most popular authors, for 2ND CULPRIT, a choice collection of short stories.

Available in June wherever
Worldwide Mystery books are sold.

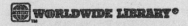 **WORLDWIDE LIBRARY**®

2CUL

ANNOUNCING THE

PRIZE SURPRISE SWEEPSTAKES!

This month's prize:

L-A-R-G-E—SCREEN PANASONIC TV!

This month, as a special surprise, we're giving away a fabulous FREE TV!

Imagine how delighted you and your family will be to own this brand-new 31" Panasonic** television! It comes with all the latest high-tech features, like a SuperFlat picture tube for a clear, crisp picture...unified remote control...closed-caption decoder...clock and sleep timer, and much more!

The facing page contains two Entry Coupons (as does every book you received this shipment). Complete and return *all* the entry coupons; **the more times you enter, the better your chances of winning the TV!**

Then keep your fingers crossed, because you'll find out by July 15, 1995 if you're the winner!

Remember: The more times you enter, the better your chances of winning!*

PRIZE SURPRISE
SWEEPSTAKES
OFFICIAL ENTRY COUPON

This entry must be received by: JUNE 30, 1995
This month's winner will be notified by: JULY 15, 1995

YES, I want to win the Panasonic 31" TV! Please enter me in the drawing and let me know if I've won!

Name_____

Address _____ Apt. _____

City   State/Prov.   Zip/Postal Code

Account #_____

Return entry with invoice in reply envelope.

© 1995 HARLEQUIN ENTERPRISES LTD.   CTV KAL

PRIZE SURPRISE
SWEEPSTAKES
OFFICIAL ENTRY COUPON

This entry must be received by: JUNE 30, 1995
This month's winner will be notified by: JULY 15, 1995

YES, I want to win the Panasonic 31" TV! Please enter me in the drawing and let me know if I've won!

Name_____

Address _____ Apt. _____

City   State/Prov.   Zip/Postal Code

Account #_____

Return entry with invoice in reply envelope.

© 1995 HARLEQUIN ENTERPRISES LTD.   CTV KAL

OFFICIAL RULES
PRIZE SURPRISE SWEEPSTAKES 3448
NO PURCHASE OR OBLIGATION NECESSARY

Three Harlequin Reader Service 1995 shipments will contain respectively, coupons for entry into three different prize drawings, one for a Panasonic 31" wide-screen TV, another for a 5-piece Wedgwood china service for eight and the third for a Sharp ViewCam camcorder. To enter any drawing using an Entry Coupon, simply complete and mail according to directions.

There is no obligation to continue using the Reader Service to enter and be eligible for any prize drawing. You may also enter any drawing by hand printing the words "Prize Surprise," your name and address on a 3"x5" card and the name of the prize you wish that entry to be considered for (i.e., Panasonic wide-screen TV, Wedgwood china or Sharp ViewCam). Send your 3"x5" entries via first-class mail (limit: one per envelope) to: Prize Surprise Sweepstakes 3448, c/o the prize you wish that entry to be considered for, P.O. Box 1315, Buffalo, NY 14269-1315, USA or P.O. Box 610, Fort Erie, Ontario L2A 5X3, Canada.

To be eligible for the Panasonic wide-screen TV, entries must be received by 6/30/95; for the Wedgwood china, 8/30/95; and for the Sharp ViewCam, 10/30/95.

Winners will be determined in random drawings conducted under the supervision of D.L. Blair, Inc., an independent judging organization whose decisions are final, from among all eligible entries received for that drawing. Approximate prize values are as follows: Panasonic wide-screen TV ($1,800); Wedgwood china ($840) and Sharp ViewCam ($2,000). Sweepstakes open to residents of the U.S. (except Puerto Rico) and Canada, 18 years of age or older. Employees and immediate family members of Harlequin Enterprises, Ltd., D.L. Blair, Inc., their affiliates, subsidiaries and all other agencies, entities and persons connected with the use, marketing or conduct of this sweepstakes are not eligible. Odds of winning a prize are dependent upon the number of eligible entries received for that drawing. Prize drawing and winner notification for each drawing will occur no later than 15 days after deadline for entry eligibility for that drawing. Limit: one prize to an individual, family or organization. All applicable laws and regulations apply. Sweepstakes offer void wherever prohibited by law. Any litigation within the province of Quebec respecting the conduct and awarding of the prizes in this sweepstakes must be submitted to the Regies des loteries et Courses du Quebec. In order to win a prize, residents of Canada will be required to correctly answer a time-limited arithmetical skill-testing question. Value of prizes are in U.S. currency.

Winners will be obligated to sign and return an Affidavit of Eligibility within 30 days of notification. In the event of noncompliance within this time period, prize may not be awarded. If any prize or prize notification is returned as undeliverable, that prize will not be awarded. By acceptance of a prize, winner consents to use of his/her name, photograph or other likeness for purposes of advertising, trade and promotion on behalf of Harlequin Enterprises, Ltd., without further compensation, unless prohibited by law.

For the names of prizewinners (available after 12/31/95), send a self-addressed, stamped envelope to: Prize Surprise Sweepstakes 3448 Winners, P.O. Box 4200, Blair, NE 68009.

RPZ KAL